Jennifer McMahon grew up in suburban Connecticut. She has worked as a house painter, farm worker, paste-up artist, pizza delivery person, homeless shelter staff member, and has assisted mentally ill adults and children. She lives in Vermont with her partner and their daughter.

PROMISE NOT TO TELL

Kate Cypher returns home to Vermont, concerned about her mother's failing health. On the night she arrives, a young girl is murdered, a horrific crime that eerily mirrors another from Kate's childhood. Three decades earlier, her misfit friend Del, derided by her classmates as 'the potato girl', was brutally slain. The killer was never found, and Del achieved immortality in local legends and ghost stories. Now Kate is drawn irresistibly into the new murder investigation. Her past and present collide in terrifying ways. Nothing is quite what it seems. And the grim spectres of her childhood are far from forgotten . . .

JENNIFER McMAHON

PROMISE NOT
TO TELL

Complete and Unabridged

ULVERSCROFT
Leicester

First published in Great Britain in 2008 by
Orion
an imprint of the Orion Publishing Group Ltd.
London

First Large Print Edition
published 2009
by arrangement with Orion Publishing Group Ltd.
An Hachette Livre UK company
London

British Library CIP Data

McMahon, Jennifer
  Promise not to tell.—Large print ed.—
  Ulverscroft large print series: suspense
  1. Murder—Vermont—Fiction 2. Psychological fiction
  3. Large type books
  I. Title
  813.6 [F]

  ISBN 978–1–84782–594–0

Published by
F. A. Thorpe (Publishing)
Anstey, Leicestershire
Set by Words & Graphics Ltd.
Anstey, Leicestershire
Printed and bound in Great Britain by
T. J. International Ltd., Padstow, Cornwall

This book is printed on acid-free paper

For my mother, who taught me
to believe in ghosts
And my father, ever skeptical

PROLOGUE

NOVEMBER 7, 2002
9:30 P.M.

'When the Potato Girl was murdered, the killer cut out her heart. He buried it, but the next day, she rose again — from that *exact same spot*.' Ryan poked the campfire with a stick for emphasis, sending a shower of sparks up into the night.

Opal inched closer to Ryan. He was fifteen, kind of cute in that farm-boy way. Tori said Ryan had a huge crush on Opal. Tori was the one who'd set the whole thing up, said it would be fun to go into the woods and make out with the older boys. Opal was twelve and had never kissed a boy before but it wasn't like she was going to admit that to anyone, even her best friend.

'What, like a zombie?' Tori asked. Opal was quiet — she hated the Potato Girl stories.

'Yeah, back from the dead like a zombie. It's like a potato: you cut it up into pieces, bury any one of those pieces — even a little bit of peel if it has eyes — and another plant

1

grows.' Ryan snapped a stick as if he were breaking a bone and tossed it into the fire.

Opal shivered. She thought of the visit she'd had just that afternoon. But no, she mustn't think of these things. And she knew better than to tell the others. They'd think she was lying or crazy or maybe a little of both.

'And she roams these woods now,' added Sam. 'You know how you can tell when she's coming? By the smell. That rotten potato reek. You can smell her a hundred feet off.'

'Oh, puh-leeaase!' Tori rolled her eyes. Sam was her sort-of boyfriend.

'Let me get this straight — you don't believe the Potato Girl is real?' Ryan was incredulous.

'I believe she existed once. I know she did. My mom went to school with her. She was just some poor kid who was murdered. All this ghost shit? It's . . . whaddaya call it. An urban legend.'

'Jesus, Tori, are you forgetting that Dan and Chris saw her right here just last week?' Opal said. 'And what about Becky Sheridan's little sister, Janey? She says the Potato Girl met her down in the Griswolds' old field and locked her in the root cellar.'

And what about me? Opal thought.

'God, would you guys grow up? Dan and Chris were wasted, as usual. Janey was just

2

screwing around and got stuck.' Tori spread her hands in a tah-dah gesture.

'Right,' said Opal. 'The door was latched from the outside, brainiac. How do you figure she pulled that one off?'

'All I'm saying is, shit can be explained.'

'And all I'm saying is, there's some shit that can't,' Opal said.

Opal knew Tori was still mad at her about the jacket. Earlier that afternoon, before meeting the boys, Tori had found out about Opal's borrowing her cross-country jacket — without asking. That was bad enough, but Opal happened to wear it while fixing the chain on her bike, and Tori was furious about the grease stain on the left sleeve. Opal had to promise to have it dry-cleaned, paying for it with her own money. And in the meantime, Tori could borrow her jacket. Only it wasn't exactly her jacket. It was her mother's oldest and most favorite jacket, which Opal had borrowed on many occasions without asking and now was forbidden to so much as touch. It was fawn-colored suede with fringe on the sleeves and front. A cowgirl, rock-star jacket that Opal had to admit looked better on Tori, who was a little older and actually had a figure. The two girls had the same haircut (both done by Shirley at Hair Today on the edge of town) and both were blond, but the resemblances stopped there. Opal knew Tori was the pretty one, the one the boys looked at; the truth was, most days she couldn't care less. She had bigger things to worry about than boys.

Opal knew her borrowing annoyed people, and that one day she might get in real trouble for it, but she couldn't seem to make herself stop. Half the time, she wasn't even aware she was doing it. Like the night she took Tori's cross-country jacket, she was most of the way home before she even realized she was wearing it. Some people smoked. Some chewed their nails. Opal borrowed. It wasn't stealing exactly. She took things only from people she knew, people she liked and felt close to. And she did her best to return the things unharmed before anyone even noticed they were missing. It gave her a thrill. A sense that she was so much more than her twelve-year-old self when she carried pieces of other people around with her. They were like good luck charms — talismans — imbued somehow with little bits of other people's souls.

★ ★ ★

It was a cold night. The four friends sat close to the fire, while the boys swapped more

4

Potato Girl stories. Tori mostly kept silent, smoking the Camel Lights she'd pilfered from her dad, occasionally fluffing her hair, snorting and shaking her head at the most outlandish tales. There were plenty of stories to go around without her input. Every kid in New Canaan had grown up hearing about how the Potato Girl walked the woods where she was killed, searching for her murderer, taking her vengeance on anyone who crossed her path.

'I bet the reason she hasn't left is that the killer's still here. She knows who it is and won't rest until he's dead,' Ryan said.

'But it's not just him she's pissed at — it's the whole fucking town. She's cursed the *whole town*,' Sam said.

'Curse or no curse, I have to pee. I'll be right back.' Tori rose, pulling the suede jacket tight around her.

'Take the flashlight,' said Sam.

'Moon's out. I'll find my way,' replied Tori as she headed off, out of the circle of firelight.

'Be careful! I smell rotten potatoes!' shouted Sam after her.

'Asshole!' she called back.

They listened to her footsteps, crunching over dead leaves and twigs, moving farther away, then disappearing altogether. They heard her curse quietly once — probably got

5

her foot tangled in the undergrowth. The fire crackled. They told more stories.

After five minutes, Opal said Sam should go look for her. The guys brushed it off, said girls took forever pissing, had a good laugh about just what it was girls did that could take so long.

When ten minutes had gone by, they called to her, but there was no response. The guys said Tori must be fucking with them. Trying to give them a good scare.

'Fine,' Opal said finally. 'You two macho men stay here. I'm gonna go find her.' She snatched the flashlight from Ryan and marched out into the darkness.

⋆　⋆　⋆

Ryan and Sam stayed by the fire laughing at how hysterical girls could be. Wasn't that what they were doing there to begin with? Hadn't they come to the haunted woods, as countless other boys had done, hoping the girls would get a little scared, need a little comforting? Wasn't all the ghost-watching shit just an excuse to get out in the woods and fool around? Weren't the woods behind the Griswolds' old place littered with bottles and condoms, specters of couples who had come before, with not one sign of some tormented little girl ghost?

Opal's scream interrupted them. They ran away from the warm glow of the fire, toward the shrill cry in the dark and tangled woods. They saw the flashlight bobbing in the trees and heard Opal sob as they drew near.

Ryan got there a second ahead of Sam — he stopped short, backed up a step.

'What the fuck?' he breathed.

Under a big gnarled maple lay Tori, naked, a cord wrapped around her neck and a square of skin neatly removed from her left breast. Her clothes had been carefully placed in a folded pile beside her. Opal stood over her, one hand clapped to the side of her face, making a horrible mewing sound. The beam from the flashlight danced over Tori's pale skin.

'It's a joke,' Sam cried, laughing a harsh, crazy-sounding laugh. 'Fucking sick joke. C'mon.' He nudged Tori's body with his foot, pushing her face into the beam of the flashlight. Her tongue protruded slightly from blue lips. Her eyes were bulging in their sockets, wide and glassy like a doll's. Sam, too, began to scream.

It was Ryan who broke the spell, took the flashlight from Opal, said they had to go get help. The boys took off running, and didn't notice when Opal, who had been right behind them, turned back.

She made her way to the clearing, choking back sobs, willing herself not to look at her dead friend, and went straight to the pile of clothes. The suede jacket was at the bottom, folded neatly. She removed the other clothes, noticed the white lace panties on top, folded and glowing like a large moth in the moonlight.

Then she slipped on the jacket — it still held Tori's heat and this made bile rise in her throat. She glanced one more time at the body. The other girl looked like a plastic mannequin, splayed out on the forest floor. It wasn't possible that this was the same girl who had just bitched her out hours ago for wrecking the cross-country jacket. The girl who refused to believe in ghosts.

Opal felt as if she were being watched, not by the blank staring eyes of her dead friend, but by someone else — *something* else. Slowly, reluctantly, she turned.

And then she caught a glimpse of it: a small pale figure in a long dress behind a tree not twenty feet away. Opal watched as it backed away from her, zigzagging through the maples, floating off into the dark heart of the woods before disappearing altogether.

Opal ran as fast as she could until she caught up with the boys, heart hammering, biting her tongue to keep from screaming. She prayed they wouldn't notice she had on the jacket Tori had been wearing all evening. They didn't. And she sure wasn't about to tell them what she'd seen when she'd gone back to get it.

Only hours later, back at home, once the questioning was over and the coroner had come to take Tori's body away, did Opal realize what a mistake it had been. She hadn't wanted to explain why her dead best friend had been wearing her mother's jacket, the jacket Opal had been forbidden to touch. But really, who would've given a shit? And what was wrong with her that she was even *thinking* about a stupid jacket? Now she'd tampered with a crime scene, which, she was pretty sure, made her a criminal. The best thing to do was hang the jacket back in the closet and never mention it to anyone. And that's just what she was doing when she noticed what was missing.

The star. The tarnished metal sheriff's star she'd pinned on it just that afternoon was gone.

'Shit!' she said, fingering the two small pinpricks in the suede where she'd pushed the pin through.

It must have fallen off in the woods somewhere. The only thing to do was go back

9

and find it. She had to return it before it was discovered missing.

And for the millionth time, she told herself, 'This is it. No more borrowing,' and she believed she really meant it.

NOVEMBER 17, 2002
10:20 P.M.

My name is Kate Cypher and I am forty-one years old. I killed someone tonight.

I have always believed myself to be a person incapable of murder. Suicide has crossed my mind once or twice, but murder? Never. Not this white-winged dove. I've marched for peace and give money on a regular basis to Amnesty International. I'm a school nurse who draws happy faces on Band-Aids, for Christ's sake.

But none of this changes the fact that it was little old me who pulled the trigger and, with near-perfect aim, put a hole in another human being's heart.

And in order to truly explain it, I'd have to tell the whole story. I'd have to go back, not just to Tori Miller's murder in the woods ten days ago, but to one that happened more than thirty years ago. My story would have to start back when I was in the fifth grade with a girl named Del Griswold. It's not a name many folks around here even remember. There isn't a soul in town who hasn't heard of the Potato Girl, though. She is, by all accounts, the most famous resident of New Canaan — which is funny because, back when she was alive, she was just a skinny kid with scabby knees who, you could tell just by looking, would never amount to much.

How wrong we all were.

PART I

Now and Then

SPRING, 1971
NOVEMBER 7–16, 2002

One potato, two potato, three potato, four
She used to live here long ago,
she doesn't anymore

1

LATE APRIL, 1971

'Touch it,' she said.

'No way. Gross.'

'I dare you.'

'No way. God, what happened to its eyes?'

'Pecked out, I guess. Or just dried up and fell out.'

'Sick.' I shivered. Partly from the cold breeze, partly from the idea of those eyes. It was early spring. The ground below us was thick mud, still half frozen. The week before we'd had the last snowstorm of the season and there were still patches of it clinging to the ground, melting in pools and rivers across the lumpy field.

'Come on, Kate, you gotta do what I say. When you're at my house, I make the rules. You were the one caught trespassing. I could have you arrested. Or get my daddy to come out here with his shotgun. Now touch it!'

'I will if you will.'

Del's pale face contorted into a smile. She reached out and stroked the dead bird, starting at its head and moving her fingers with their dirty nails all the way back to its tail feathers. Her touch seemed almost loving — like the bird was her pet parakeet, a creature she'd named and fed. A bird whose song she knew by heart. Some Tweety Bird, Polly-Want-a-Cracker kind of pet.

The putrid crow swung heavy on its wire. She gave it a shove, making it fly toward me. It was as if Del and I were playing some sick game of tetherball. I jumped back. She laughed, throwing back her head with its stringy blond hair. She opened her mouth wide and I noticed that her right front tooth was chipped. Just a little corner was missing, not something you'd notice unless you were looking.

The crow swung, its left foot wrapped and tied with white plastic-covered wire — tougher than string, Del explained. It dangled about three feet from the top of a tall wooden stake driven into the center of the small field where uneven rows of green peas were just coming up. Smaller wooden stakes lined the rows, and rusty wire mesh was stapled to the stakes, forming a trellis for the peas to climb.

Del said her brother Nicky had shot the crow two weeks before. He caught it pecking the pea seeds up out of the dirt before they'd even had a chance to sprout and got it with his BB gun. Then he and his daddy hung the crow up just like they did each year, a warning to other crows to stay away.

I reached out and touched the greasy black feathers of its ragged wing. Bugs crawled there, working their way under the feathers and into the flesh. Metallic green flies buzzed in the air. Although dead, the bird pulsed with life. It stank like old hamburger left in the sun. Like the raccoon my mother once found under our porch back in Massachusetts, way back under the floorboards where no one could reach it. It just had to rot there. My mother sprinkled quicklime through the cracks in the porch floor, letting it fall down onto the bloated corpse like Christmas snow. For weeks the smell permeated the porch, worked its way into windows and open doors, hung on our clothes, skin, and hair. There's nothing like the smell of death. There's no mistaking it.

I had been crossing the Griswolds' fields on my way home from school every day for nearly a month on the afternoon Del caught me and took me to see the crow. I had been hoping to run into her. Hoping, actually, to catch a glimpse of her — to spy without being seen. Maybe then I could learn if the rumors were true — that her daddy was really her brother; that she had chickens sleeping in her bed; that she ate only raw potatoes. And the best rumor of all: that she had a pony who limped and who some kids claimed they'd seen her riding naked in the fields behind her house.

I knew better than to make friends with a girl like Delores Griswold. I'd lived in New Canaan only six months or so, but it was long enough to know the rules. Rule number one for surviving the fifth grade was that you didn't make friends with the Potato Girl. Not if you wanted any other kids to like you. Del was a pariah. The kid all the others loved to hate. She was too skinny, and came to school in worn, dirty clothes that were often hand-me-downs from her brothers. She was two years older than most of the other fifth graders, having stayed back in kindergarten and then again in fourth grade.

She had dirt so thick on her neck that it looked like maybe she really was dug up from the ground like one of the potatoes they grew on her family's farm. She was pale enough to be from underground. And if you got close enough to her, you got a whiff of moist earth.

Maybe, just maybe, if I'd had any other friends back then, if I'd sworn allegiance to anyone else, I wouldn't have started cutting across those frozen fields hoping to catch a glimpse of her naked on a pony. Maybe then I wouldn't have met her at all. She wouldn't have shown me her secret in the root cellar or made me touch the dead crow.

But I had no friends, and I, like Del, was an outsider. A kid from New Hope who came to school with a lunch box full of steamed vegetables, thick slabs of grainy homemade bread, and dried fruit for dessert. How I longed to be a white-bread-and-bologna girl then. Or even, like Del, to have the worn brass tokens the poor kids used in the cafeteria to buy a hot lunch each day. Something to link me to some group, some ring of kids, instead of sticking out like the sore thumb I was, eating my hippie lunch alone, smiling stupidly at anyone who walked by my table.

The Griswolds' farm was at the bottom of Bullrush Hill. At the top of the hill was the 120 acres owned by New Hope, the intentional community my mother had dropped everything to join the fall before. She'd met a man who called himself Lazy Elk back in Worcester, where my mother worked as a secretary and I had real friends — friends I'd known my whole life and thought I'd go on knowing, never needing to make new ones. Lazy Elk — whose real name was Mark Lubofski — swept her off her feet and talked her into going back with him to New Canaan,

19

Vermont, where he had been living on and off for almost a year. He said a man named Gabriel was starting something big, something revolutionary there: a Utopian community.

The truth is, I was as enamored of Lazy Elk and his stories as she was. He had a kind face with deep, craggy lines around his eyes and mouth. Self-conscious about his receding hairline, he wore a wide-brimmed leather hat with a brown-and-white-striped turkey feather in the band. He took the hat off only when he went to sleep, and even then, it often lay at the foot of the bed where some other couple's cat might sleep. He told me that the feather, which he'd found in the woods behind New Hope, was a talisman — a magic power object that helped keep his spirit free.

So away we went, free-spirited, in his orange VW bus, expecting to find paradise. What we found instead was a few run-down buildings, a well that drew water with a rusty hand pump, a herd of goats hell-bent on destruction, and a large canvas tepee that would serve as our home for years to come. Lazy Elk had carefully left all of these details out of his descriptions of New Hope, and while my mother and I couldn't hide our initial disappointment, we still believed that we could make a new and better life for ourselves there as we'd been promised. So it was with hope and determination that my mother filled the tepee with colorful woven rugs and clean sheets. She scrubbed the filthy glass globes of the oil lamps and trained Lazy Elk to take his muddy boots off before coming in. Our little circular home, though far from paradise, was at least bright and clean.

At the bottom of Bullrush Hill, on the corner where our dirt road intersected with Railroad Street, which was paved, even back then, was the Griswolds' farm. It was an old dairy farm, but they'd sold the cows off some years before. You could still smell the cow shit when it rained, though. That, like the smell of death, was not an odor that faded easily.

The Griswold place was a leaning white farmhouse badly in need of a new paint job. The roof had bald patches where shingles had fallen off. Swallows nested in the eaves. The faded red barn with its old tin roof had fallen in on itself long ago, and the collapsed remains seemed to be the home of about a hundred feral cats and several dogs with various handicaps (one had three legs, one was missing an eye, and another bulged with large growths). In the front yard, which was more packed dirt than grass, beside the big black mailbox that bore their name, hung a white sign, hand-painted in red letters:

EGGS
HAY
PIGS
POTATOS

Beyond the sign, set back about ten feet from the road, was a little three-sided wooden shed with a rusted tin roof. There, on any given day, were three or four dozen eggs in cardboard cartons and some bushel baskets of potatoes, beans, corn, and whatever other crops happened to be in. The prices were written on scraps of paper thumbtacked to the back wall, and there was a metal box to put your money in.

MAKE YOUR OWN CHANGE. BE HONEST! THANK YOU read the sign taped to the top of the banged-up gray metal box. A dented scale hung from the ceiling, but the one time my mother tried to use it, the needle refused to move, the spring inside broken.

Another sign told you to ask at the house about hay, pork, piglets, and free kittens.

Before New Hope got chickens, my mother and I would walk down to buy eggs from the Griswolds' stand. We rarely ran into Mr Griswold, but sometimes we'd see him on his tractor off in the distance. His wife, we heard, had died of cancer years before, leaving him to care for his brood alone. Often we'd see one of the kids doing chores in the yard, or banging around under the hood of some rusted-out car on cinder blocks. There were so many kids — eight, including Del. All boys but her.

* * *

'You live up with the hippies, don't you?' Del asked me that day as we stood looking at each other in the field of peas reaching up with tiny, pale tendrils, the dead crow between us.

'Yeah.'

'You a hippie?'

'No.'

'Hippies are stupid,' she said.

I didn't respond, just kicked at the clumps of cold mud.

'Hippies are stupid, I said!' Her pale gray-blue eyes gleamed with anger.

'Sure.' I took a small step away from her, afraid she might haul off and hit me.

'Sure what?'

'Sure, I guess hippies are stupid.'

Del smiled, showing her broken tooth. 'I have something to show you. A secret thing. Want to see?'

'I guess,' I said, somewhat concerned that just a few minutes before she'd asked me the same question, then led me to the decaying crow.

I followed Del through the trellised rows of young peas, then across garden beds full of spinach, carrots, and beets. I recognized the plants from the gardens at New Hope. Our soil was darker, less clumpy, than the Griswolds'. And although our gardens were smaller, they seemed healthier and better organized, with special walking paths covered with wood chips between the planting beds. The Griswolds' fields were full of stones, rusted plow blades, and forgotten rolls of barbed wire, and we tramped right through the crooked rows of seedlings. Watching over this landscape, as if daring any living thing to grow, was the upside-down crow, hanging from a wire.

Del and I passed a small fenced-in pasture where a large gray mare was chomping hay. A spotted pony stood beside her. He started when he saw us, running off behind the stall, and I could see that he had a slight limp.

'Is that your pony?'

'Yeah. His name's Spitfire. He bites.'

Just past the horse pasture was the pigpen, where five enormous pigs were lounging in thick grayish mud along with maybe a dozen piglets. A plywood hut, like a large doghouse, stood in the back right corner of the pen. Along the front fence was a big metal trough full of water and another full of slimy food scraps.

I stopped and leaned against the top of the fence, my feet on the bottom rail, trying to get a good look at the piglets. The ammonia stench of pig excrement made my nostrils twitch. I was staring into the tiny eyes of a large sow with swollen teats, thinking that I'd heard somewhere that pigs were smart, smarter than dogs even, when Del snuck up behind me and gave me a shove. It was a hard push, no playful little messing around kind of tap on the back. My stomach slammed against the top rail, my head and shoulders falling forward. I nearly toppled headfirst over the fence into the mud.

'Careful,' Del teased. 'Pigs'll eat ya. You fell in there, they'd pick you clean.'

I jumped off the fence and swung around to face Del, thinking I'd clock her one, but she quickly distracted me and the urge passed.

'See that mama pig right there,' Del said, pointing to the sow I'd just been watching. 'She ate three of her babies just last week. Pigs're savages.'

I unclenched my fists, let myself breathe.

Del led me toward the back of their white house, at the crest of a small hill, as she described the scene of the mama pig gobbling up those babies.

'Teeth like razors,' she said. 'When she was

done, there wasn't nothing left but three little tails.'

About fifty feet from the house, we came to a wooden door tilted into the hillside. It reminded me of the metal cellar door that led to the basement of our old rented house in Massachusetts. Del leaned down and unlatched the heavy door, pulling it open. Rough wooden steps led down into a dark pit that could have been a dungeon or a bomb shelter.

'Go on. You first. I gotta close the door behind us.'

I began making my way down the steps, and saw that it was a root cellar: a small room, probably eight by eight feet, with cinder-block walls and sagging wooden shelves that went from floor to ceiling. On the shelves were rows and rows of canned goods and bushel baskets full of spongy, sprouted potatoes, bruised apples, and limp carrots. Del closed the door and everything went black. I wondered if she'd stayed outside and locked me in, leaving me to die in that damp place. Maybe it was a dungeon after all, some kind of torture chamber. I took a nervous breath. The air smelled of moist earth, forgotten vegetables. It was Del's smell.

'Del?'

'Hang on, I'll light a match.' I felt her brush by me, heard her feel around along the shelves, shake a box of matches, open it, and strike one. The small room glowed orange. Del pulled an old jelly jar with a candle in it from off a shelf and lit it. She blew out the match, then held the stubby candle in the jar up to my face like she was studying me, unsure of who I might turn out to be.

'Okay, if I show you my secret, you gotta promise not to tell. You gotta swear.' Her pale eyes seemed to look right through my own eyes, reaching all the way to the back of my skull.

'Okay.'

'Swear on your life?'

'Yes,' I muttered. She pulled the candle back from my face and set it on a shelf next to a row of dust-covered canned tomatoes.

'Cross your heart and hope to die?'

'Cross my heart and hope to die,' I said.

'I've got a tattoo,' she told me. Then she started to unbutton her dirty yellow shirt, which was embroidered with colorful little lassos, hats, and horses.

I wanted to tell her to stop, to say that I believed and didn't need to see, but it was too late. The shirt was off. To my relief, she wore a soiled white cotton undershirt with a tiny pink-petaled flower stitched at the center of the neckline. But then she peeled this off quickly, without hesitation, and I looked down, embarrassed, thinking that maybe the stories I had heard were true — and yet there I was, in the cellar with the Potato Girl. What was I thinking? If this ever came out at school . . . I shuddered. I struggled to think of an excuse to make a quick escape. The dirt smell intensified.

'Well, are you gonna look or what?' she asked.

I slowly shifted my gaze from the packed earth floor to Del's naked torso.

Del was a skinny kid — I could practically count her ribs. She looked like a person who'd had all the color washed out of her — even her nipples seemed pale. And there, over her bony cage of ribs, just where I believed her heart might be, was the letter *M*. I moved closer for a better look, trying to make myself forget that this was some strange girl's skin I was studying — not just skin, but the place that would one day be a breast. I could already see the beginnings of them, slight swellings that looked out of place on her skinny frame. But what my eyes were drawn to was not Del's developing breasts, and how different they were from my own flat chest, but the tattoo.

It was a cursive capital *M*, delicate and swirling. It had been etched into her skin in black ink, and done recently enough to still be red and puffy. It looked slightly infected and terribly painful. I backed away.

The only tattoo I had ever seen in my life had been a faded anchor on the forearm of one of my mother's boyfriends who'd been in the navy. There was him, and there was Popeye, but cartoons hardly counted, and meant nothing in the situation I now found myself in.

I tried to look unimpressed. But a tattoo? On a fifth grader? Del was more alien to me than ever.

'What's the *M* for?' I asked.

'Can't tell you that.' She smiled at the power of her secret.

'Who gave it to you?'

'Someone special.'

'Didn't it hurt?'

'Not really.'

'It looks like it hurts now.'

'It's a good kind of hurt.'

I didn't ask what a bad kind of hurt might be. I didn't get a chance to ask any more about it before the wooden door swung open and the root cellar filled with light. I looked up and saw the silhouette of a lanky boy standing at the top of the steps.

'Del, what the hell you doin'? And who's this with you? Christ, you two making out down here or somethin'?' His voice was scratchy, as if he had a sore throat and it hurt to talk too loud.

Del turned away quickly and threw on her undershirt.

'Scram, Nicky!' Del shouted with her back to him, and I realized I was looking up at the crow killer. I squinted against the light behind him to make out his features. I could see raggedy pale blond hair and strangely long arms that seemed to hang awkwardly. Orangutan arms. As my eyes adjusted, I saw that this boy was as tan as Del was pale. A dark-skinned ape boy in torn jeans and a white T-shirt, heavy work boots on his huge feet.

'Yeah, I'll scram all right,' said his raspy voice. 'I'll scram right back into the house and tell Daddy what I just saw.'

'You shit!' Del spat up at him.

'Who's your friend?' he asked with a sly, thin smile.

'None of your beeswax,' Del answered.

The boy laughed, white teeth flashing against the background of his bronze face, then backed away from the door.

'Man oh man, I'd hate to be in your shoes. Daddy's gonna give you one hell of a licking.' And then he took off toward the house, leaving the root cellar door open.

'You better go,' Del ordered. 'But come

back tomorrow. Meet me in the field after school. By the crow. Okay?'

'Okay,' I said.

She raced up the steps out of the root cellar, then stopped at the top and called back down to me, 'See you later, alligator!' before chasing her brother back toward the house.

I blew out the candle and crept up the wooden steps slowly, peering right, then left when I got to the door. I saw no one coming, so I bolted straight ahead, not daring to turn and look back toward the house, toward Del and Nicky. I ran past the pigs with their razor teeth; past the horse pasture with its limping pony; through the spinach, carrots, and beets; and back to the field of baby peas where the dead crow hung still on its wire like some broken marionette.

At the edge of the back field, the woods began and I found the path that would lead me all the way to the top of Bullrush Hill, all the way back to New Hope. It was only a fifteen-minute walk home, but after being with Del, it felt light years away. In just an hour, Del had shown me a whole distant universe with its own set of dangers and rules. I couldn't wait to return.

2

'I know who you are.'

They were the first words my mother spoke to me when I came home, her hello, as I hugged her on her doorstep. Her body was limp, unresponsive. Her arms dangled loosely at her sides, both hands wrapped in thick white bandages. Mummy hands. I had come three thousand miles to see her and she wasn't even going to hug me back. I pulled away from her with awkward, mechanical movements. The Mummy meets Robot Girl. Now all we needed was Lon Chaney or Bela Lugosi and we'd have ourselves a movie.

'It's good to see you, Ma.' I forced a smile.

She repeated the words. 'I know who you are.'

She stood before me, disheveled in a worn flannel nightgown. Her hair — long, straight, and white as paper birch — was tangled and greasy. She wore running shoes on her feet, the laces hanging loose, untied. She had what looked like dried egg yolk on her chin. I resisted the urge to say, *Yeah, you may know me, but just who the hell are you?*

I had just spent an hour in a somber meeting with Raven and Gabriel — two of the only three remaining members of New Hope, not counting my mother. The third was Raven's twelve-year-old daughter, Opal, who popped in halfway through our meeting holding a bicycle chain.

'Have you guys seen that big crescent wrench?' she asked as she hurried into the room, knocking over an empty chair, the grease-covered chain swinging from her filthy hand. She had a baseball cap on backwards and a blue and white varsity jacket with some other girl's name on it.

Opal had changed just enough in the two years since I'd seen her to give me pause. She was taller and thinner, and in spite of the bull-in-a-china-shop way she'd barged into the room, she seemed more graceful than the little girl I remembered so well.

She turned, her eyes fell on me, and her face cracked into a huge smile. She dropped the chain and gave me a big, greasy-pawed hug. 'I thought you were getting in tonight,' she said. 'God, I have like a million and one things to do right now — I've gotta get my bike back on the road and then go meet some friends — but I'll come find you later.

Tomorrow! Okay? Tomorrow. I've got so many new tricks to show you. I've totally mastered the jump from the barn. I can even do a somersault on the way down! And I just got this cool book on barnstormers with great pictures. You've gotta see it!'

Opal was a skinny, freckled girl who had been saying, since she was seven, that she wanted to be a stuntwoman when she grew up. She had broken her arm quite badly during my last visit, throwing herself from the old hay loft in the big barn.

Raven was running an errand down in Rutland and I had been the one to take Opal to the emergency room and sit with her. She seemed severely shaken, not just by the fall, but by whatever had happened in the barn just before the jump. She claimed someone had been up in the loft with her, but when Gabriel went up to check, all he found were a couple of rusted pitchforks leaning against the wall and a few clumps of long-rotted hay.

'Who did you see up there?' I had asked, but she'd never answered.

To distract her during the endless waiting between examinations, X-rays, and getting a cast, I asked her to tell me about her favorite stunts. She told me she'd been reading about the days of barnstorming and the wing walkers.

'Charles Lindbergh got his start that way,' she said. Then she went on to tell me about the women, her voice bubbling with admiration and excitement.

'This one lady, Gladys Ingle her name was, practiced archery on the top wing of her Curtiss Jenny.'

'Her who?' I asked.

'Curtiss Jenny. It's a biplane. I've got a model of one in the tepee. Anyway, Gladys Ingle was also famous for jumping from one plane to another, midair. How cool is that?'

'Pretty cool,' I agreed.

'Then there's Bessie Coleman. I did a report on her for school. She was the first African American woman pilot. She was a wing walker, too. Oh, and Lillian Boyer — 'Empress of the Air' — she quit her job as a waitress to learn to wing walk.'

'That's quite a career change.'

'And you've heard of Buffalo Bill? I bet you didn't know about his niece, Mabel Cody. She was the first woman to transfer from a speeding boat to a plane.'

By the time Opal described how the days of wing walking ended in 1936 when the government outlawed getting out of the cockpit below 1,500 feet, the mysterious visitor in the loft was forgotten. And by the end of our three hours in the emergency room, I was ten-year-old Opal's new best friend and she was right by my side every remaining minute of that visit, showing me pictures in books of wing walkers and models of early planes she had made. The Curtiss Jenny was hanging on fishing line from a pole high at the top of the tepee. Opal had glued a small plastic woman to the top wing, complete with a tiny bow she'd made from a stick and string and toothpick arrows. There was a bull's-eye target set up on the other end of the wing.

Opal, at least to my outsider's eyes, seemed to love life in the tepee, and it was never more apparent than when she showed me her curtained-off bedroom that afternoon and sent that plane flying in circles over our heads with a push from her fingertips. I looked around with a strange sense of déjà vu, and had to remind myself that it was not the original tepee, the one my mother and I had lived in, but the third or fourth incarnation. But now it, too, was going to have to be replaced, and my mother was to blame.

* * *

After Opal left to repair her bike, Gabriel, Raven, and I returned to the topic of my mother. We sat at the long wooden table in the big barn that had once served as the community kitchen and gathering place. The barn seemed cavernous and empty, our voices lost in all that space.

New Hope had gradually petered out over the years. Gabriel's vision of Utopia had somehow been lost along the way, falling to ruin along with the buildings and gardens. My childhood home was little more than a ghost town, a ruined shell of what it once had been, and although I was disappointed, I wasn't all that surprised. Call me a skeptic, but I've always thought that it takes more than organic vegetables and talking circles to make an ideal society.

Raven was ten years younger than me and had been the only other child at New Hope when I was there. She was born my third night at New Hope. I slept little that night, listening to her mother's screams coming from the big barn, which had been turned into a 'birthing center,' complete with a sacred ring of candles and a young hippie named Zack alternately playing 'Happy Birthday' and *The Lone Ranger* theme song on his guitar. I lay awake wondering what hell my mother had brought me to where babies weren't even born in hospitals.

When Raven was small, I changed her diapers and, later, taught her to tie her shoes.

This was my only legacy to her — accidental pinpricks and a story about making the limp shoestring into a bunny, then sending the bunny through a hole — things I doubted she even remembered.

Raven had grown into a striking woman — nearly six feet tall, with long dark hair and high cheekbones. She worked part-time at the town clerk's office and was taking night classes toward a degree in psychology. When I went away to college and never came home, Raven quickly became my mother's surrogate daughter, a fact that tugged at my heart a little, gave me pangs of jealousy and guilt whenever my mother mentioned her name over the years. Raven, not even my mother's flesh and blood, was the good daughter. The present daughter, who promised never to abandon home and who was able to give my mother the grandchild she never got from me. And me, I was the skinny kid in the photos my mother kept around the tepee — freckles fading in each consecutive picture as if to show that one day my whole self would disappear forever. The invisible woman who called once a week to say how tough college was, then nursing school, married life, one all-consuming job after another — always some excuse for not coming home. But that hardly mattered because Raven was there, standing beside my mother in her neatly tied shoes.

Raven's own mother, Doe, had died of pancreatic cancer — one of those horror stories where you go into the hospital for stomach pain, and three weeks later, it's all over. Raven's father, well, no one really knew whatever became of him. His disappearance, the reasons behind it at least, had been my fault, although I was the only one who knew it. It was yet another in a long list of New Canaan secrets I carried with me throughout my life — heavy and loathsome baggage.

Raven got pregnant with Opal when she was eighteen, just a few months after Doe's untimely death. I was in Seattle by then, and experienced the whole pregnancy through my weekly phone conversations with my mother — the morning sickness successfully treated with raw almonds and ginger tea; the hour's drive to special prenatal yoga classes in Burlington; the search for a midwife who would attend the birth in a tepee with no running water. The subject of who Opal's father might be was never addressed directly, though I always assumed he was just some hippie passing through New Hope. If anybody, including Opal, was the least bit concerned about her being 'fatherless,' I never heard about it.

Gabriel, at eighty-two years old, was still in excellent shape, both physically and mentally. With his round glasses, white beard, and red suspenders, he looked like a lean, off-season Santa. He had been the patriarch of New Hope, the founding father. His common-law wife, Mimi, had died the year before, leaving him to shuffle around the big barn alone, no doubt recalling more glorious times. Days when there had been many mouths to feed, quiet revolutions to plan.

At New Hope's beginning, in 1965, there were only four members: Gabriel and Mimi and another couple, Bryan and Lizzy. Over time, the numbers grew. When my mother and I moved to New Hope in the fall of 1970, there were eleven of us living there full time (the largest number there would ever be), not counting the college kids who stayed for the summer, drifters who came and went. There were Gabriel and Mimi, Bryan and Lizzy, Shawn and Doe, baby Raven, Lazy Elk and my mother, me, and nineteen-year-old Zack, the only single adult New Hope resident and unofficial community balladeer. However many people called New Hope home at any given time, it was clear they were all looking to Gabriel to give the place its bearings, to define Utopia.

I listened patiently, sipping one of Gabriel's herbal infusions, which tasted like licorice and mud, while he and Raven filled me in on my mother's condition as best they could. They warned me that she might not know who I was. She had had a bad week. There was the fire five days before, which was the last straw — the reason they finally called me and said I needed to come back and make some decisions about long-term care. They described how she had fought Gabriel when he was pulling her out, biting his arm viciously enough that he needed stitches. (His wound, I noted, was covered with a neat, sterile bandage, not a compress of rank-smelling weeds as it would've been in Mimi's day.)

Try as I might, I couldn't reconcile my mild-mannered, peace-loving mother with the maniac they were describing. I tried to picture her foaming at the mouth, shooting fire from her fingertips.

'Since the fire,' Gabriel explained, 'she's been on a downward spiral, lashing out at everyone around her.'

Ho-Ho-Ho.

When they were through describing the latest details of my mother's steadily declining condition, I told them my plans. I had taken a three-week emergency leave from Lakeview Elementary in Seattle, where I worked as a school nurse. Speaking to them as if addressing the school board, I explained how, in the next weeks, I would, with their assistance, assess my mother's situation and come up with a plan for long-term care, which meant, more than likely, getting her placed in a nursing home (and possibly fitting her with a muzzle — a suggestion I didn't mention). I'll admit that I sounded like a social worker, not like a daughter, but in a way, that's how I felt. This was my responsibility, and I intended to fulfill it — but I hadn't really been a daughter since I left home at seventeen.

Gabriel and Raven nodded at me, satisfied with my plan, with my level-headedness. They were pleased, although perhaps slightly puzzled, with how very well I seemed to be taking things. But wasn't that my job? Wasn't that what they'd called me in for? To do what they knew needed to be done, but hesitated to do themselves. It would be me who made the final decision to lock up my mother, to take away all her freedoms for what I would tell her was her own good. Neither of them wanted that on their conscience. And who could blame them? They set me up to be the bad guy, the villainous prodigal daughter, and

I fell right into it, as if it were a role I was born to play.

★ ★ ★

'I told you, Doe, I don't want her here.' My mother's five-foot-two, ninety-pound frame occupied her doorway, rocking back on her heels, then rolling forward to stand on her tiptoes. Back and forth she moved like some hypnotic snake, trying to make herself look bigger. I stepped back, giving my mother some distance, half expecting her to let out a hiss.

Raven sighed, putting a hand to her forehead. 'I'm Raven, Jean. Doe's daughter. And this is your daughter, Kate.'

'I know who she is!' my mother spat, shifting her gaze from Raven to me. 'I know who you are!' She was leaning forward when she said it. Spittle sprayed my face. Her hands hung at her sides like oversized white paws, odd and useless. Raven and Gabriel were right. I was in no way prepared for this. There was a fire in my mother's eyes I'd never seen. I took another step back.

'Well, Kate's staying. She's going to stay with you in your house.'

'This is not my house.'

Raven tried another tack.

43

'Jean, where's Magpie?' She opened her shoulder bag and retrieved a can of StarKist tuna. The muscles in my mother's face loosened and she gave a half smile.

'Inside. She must be inside. Under the closet. Inside the bed. Magpie! Here, Miss Magpie! Breakfast!' My mother turned and walked inside, calling to the cat. Raven nodded at me, and we followed my mother into the cabin.

I had seen my mother's tiny house for the first time during my last brief visit two years before. She was just adding the finishing touches, the trim and moldings, after building the whole thing herself. There had been a few more residents at New Hope then, and they helped raise the framed walls and roof. Opal and some friends dug the pit for the outhouse. But other than that, it was my mother's project. The four-room cabin was built by her own seventy-year-old hands almost entirely from donated and salvaged materials. It seemed to me then, as she took me on my first tour of the place, to be more a work of art than a home. She proudly showed me the built-in shelves, the flooring from an old silo that Raven had helped her nail down, the flat slabs of granite rescued from the reject pile behind a polishing shed in Barre that now served as her kitchen countertops.

My mother, after years of living in the tepee and then in the loft of the big community barn, had made a home that was truly hers. It was to be her house to grow old in, tucked about three hundred feet behind the big barn, bordered on the back side by the sloping woods that led back down the hill, away from New Hope, right into the farmland once owned by the Griswolds.

★ ★ ★

Looking back on my last visit to New Hope, I found there were signs of my mother's sickness even then. There had been little clues all along, but nothing that set off any alarms, rang any bells that would toll loud and clear with the weight of the words *dementia, Alzheimer's*. She had seemed a bit more absentminded, more scattered. She repeated herself, forgot things I'd told her. She seemed preoccupied, a little on edge. I figured the strain of building the house was taking its toll. She was a seventy-year-old woman, after all.

During that visit two years ago, I learned that she'd wrecked her car and had decided not to get another one. When I asked what had happened, she said she was out for a drive and fell asleep behind the wheel. The car went off the road and into a drainage ditch. Luckily, she escaped with only minor bruising. It happened near Lancaster, New Hampshire.

'But what were you doing in Lancaster in the middle of the night?' I had asked. And she shrugged off the question. Later, Raven told me she'd been getting lost from time to time, finding herself farther and farther from home. Usually, she'd run out of gas and call Gabriel or Raven to come rescue her. She kept the New Hope numbers pinned to the Pontiac's visor. My mother had known those numbers by heart for years. Her needing to pin them to her visor should have set off alarms, but it didn't. Her body was strong and healthy enough to build a house. But her mind was going, and she must have felt it slipping away, memory by memory, beginning, perhaps, with something as simple as those phone numbers.

As I followed Raven through the front door into the living room, I saw that the inside of the house looked the way I remembered: the same overstuffed plum-colored couch, wooden rocking chair, and braided rug. To the left of the door was a bench to sit on while taking your shoes off and there was a row of coat pegs along the wall. Hung on it were a yellow rain slicker, a down parka, and a blaze-orange vest for walking in the woods during hunting season. No doubt about it — I was back in Vermont.

Walking forward and turning left into the kitchen, I saw the white enamel wood-burning cookstove and the round wooden table that had been with my mother since the tepee days. The door to my mother's bedroom at the far end of the house was closed. Beside it, the door to her painting studio was ajar, and I caught a glimpse of the colorful canvases and the cot and dresser pushed against the far wall. The house smelled of wood smoke, oil paints, and the lavender lotion my mother used. Familiar smells that I couldn't help but find comfort in.

What was different about the house were the notes tacked up everywhere — signs on white paper written in bright markers. On the inside of the front door: KATE, YOUR DAUGHTER, WILL BE HERE THIS AFTER-NOON. And below it, someone had taped up a snapshot of me taken during my last visit. In the picture, I'm staring straight ahead, eyes heavy and sullen — a regular *Wanted: Dead or Alive* mug shot. I could picture the description now: *crime of abandonment, reward offered.*

There were several signs in red marker

taped to the stove: STOP! DO NOT LIGHT! There were signs on all the cupboards saying what was in each one: DISHES, GLASSES, CEREAL. The phone on the wall had a list of names and numbers next to it. There was also a sign saying, Do NOT DIAL 911 UNLESS IT IS AN EMERGENCY! (I learned later from Raven that my mother had been calling 911 several times a day, asking whose house she was in, wanting to know if there was more yogurt anywhere.)

Magpie had been just a kitten when I last visited, a gift from Raven and Opal. Now she came trotting out of my mother's studio and wound herself around my mother's legs, doing little figure eights, loop de loops, a sleek little black-and-white thing. My mother picked up the cat, cooed at her and carried her over to the Servel gas fridge.

'What's for lunch?'

'You had your lunch, Jean,' Raven told her.

'What'd I have?'

'Grilled cheese.'

'What's for supper?'

'You just had supper. Gabriel brought you stew.'

'I'm hungry,' my mother said, her voice whiny as a child's. She unceremoniously dumped Magpie back onto the pine floor. 'What's for lunch?'

Raven ignored her. She opened the StarKist and plopped it into Magpie's bowl on the kitchen counter. The cat danced around her feet now, saying 'Murl?' again and again in a plaintive voice. My mother leaned in quickly and stuck her face into the cat's bowl. She gulped at the tuna, getting a good bite before Raven yanked it away.

'I'll fix you a sandwich, Jean. Now go sit down.' There was an edge to Raven's voice I hadn't expected — a touch of hostility. She gripped the edge of the counter and blew out a long breath.

My mother turned toward me. 'They're starving me,' she said. I just stared. Flakes of tuna were stuck to her face.

'I know you,' she said, smiling.

My stomach ached. I fought back the urge to run from the cabin, legs pinwheeling like a cartoon character's, jump in the rental car, and hop on the next plane back to Seattle. I hadn't been close to my mother in years, but I knew her to be a bright, resourceful, dignified woman. This person who had replaced her was a complete stranger. My mother, it seemed, had vanished completely without my even noticing she was taking her leave. Ah, I realized, she'd pulled the same trick on me that I'd pulled on her. Touché.

Later, after making my mother a sandwich, Raven and I put her to bed, then settled down on the living room couch. I longed for a stiff drink but knew there was nothing in the house. My mother had always frowned on alcohol — *'Katydid, I will never understand why on earth you would want to dull your senses, the wits God gave you, with that stuff.'*

Raven pulled a pack of matches from her pocketbook and lit the oil lamps in the living room. Just as it had been in the tepee, light came from candles and oil lamps, heat from the woodstove, and whatever water she needed was hauled from the well by the big barn in gallon jugs and buckets. When she needed to bathe, there was a tub in the big barn, too. It was a self-reliant lifestyle chosen by my mother when she *had* been self-reliant. It was a life I remembered all too well even after all those years. And I was sure it was the reason for my love of gadgets — my house in Seattle was full of them: blender, food processor, microwave, coffee grinder, espresso machine, electric can opener, Crock-Pot, electric toothbrush, and bright halogen track lighting angled carefully so that every corner blazed.

Raven dug around in the leather shoulder bag again like a magician searching for her next trick and handed me a large metal ring of keys. She showed me how they kept my mother in her bedroom at night with a brass padlock.

'Jesus,' I said. 'What is she, one of America's Most Wanted?'

Raven said if we didn't do this, my confused mother would wander and get lost. Nighttime was worse. My mother was more clear during the day. Raven promised I'd see a change in the morning.

Another key went to the lockbox on top of the fridge that contained the array of medications that Dr Crawford had prescribed over the past several months: lorazepam, haloperidol, Ambien, and a tube of burn ointment. Raven explained that they didn't like to use the pills, they just seemed to dope her up. I tried not to roll my eyes — what did she think the drugs were for? Inner peace? She said that before now, they medicated her only during really bad spells, but since the fire they'd had to increase the dosages. Most days, they had managed to get by giving her only the tinctures Gabriel made. There was a memory tincture with ginkgo that she got in tea twice a day. And at night, a sleeping tonic with valerian root. My mouth went bitter at the thought of it and I made a silent promise not to subject my mother to such botanical torture.

'For now, we'll stick with the heavy med regime Dr Crawford prescribed. I'd rather see her doped up than hurt again,' Raven said and I nodded in agreement, making a mental note that we needed a consult with a gerontologist as soon as possible. It wasn't that I didn't trust the town doctor, but my mother was on some heavy-duty medication, and I questioned how well it was being monitored.

There was a key to a padlocked kitchen drawer that contained knives, scissors, a nail file, nail clippers, and matches.

'Never, ever, ever give her matches,' Raven instructed, as if the bandages on my mother's hands weren't enough warning.

'Right,' I said, picturing again my rabid, foaming mother shooting fire from her fingertips. I shook the nightmarish image from my head.

Raven went on to explain the routine: getting my mother up, cleaned, and dressed; emptying her chamber pot; changing the bandages; serving her breakfast; going for a walk; making her lunch; having her take a nap; and making sure she gets each of her pills. I must have looked a little overwhelmed.

'I know it's a lot. And I know it must be a bad shock for you to see her like this. But I can't tell you how glad I am that you're here.

How glad Gabriel is, too. We just couldn't do it anymore. Not like this. Not with winter coming now. She can't be alone. Not here.' She looked around the cabin, gesturing helplessly at the woodstove, the oil lamps hung from the ceiling, well out of reach. 'See what you think once you've been here a few days. God, I'm so glad you came.' Then she hugged me — this woman whom I felt I barely knew, who had been only in second grade when I left home for good — put her arms around me and held tight. I was her life raft. I was the one who was going to come in and make everything okay, even if it meant packing my mother off to a nursing home. I let all my breath out as she squeezed. *Great,* I thought, *a life raft without air.*

The first thing I did when Raven left was undo the padlock on my mother's door. I was not going to be her jailer — at least not yet. I jingled the large ring of keys, feeling like a deputy in an old Western: *You're free to roam the open range, partner. Just get out of town before sunset.*

I peeked in and saw that my mother was sound asleep on her brass bed. The wind-up clock ticked loudly on the nightstand beside her. Its hands glowed. Only eight o'clock. It was just five back in Seattle. Jamie would be getting home from work soon. Tina or Ann or whoever his latest was might be there now, in his place waiting, dinner in the oven, white wine chilling. I wondered how he kept track of his girl of the month, sometimes girl of the week. He must have to mark his calendar, keep notes. With bitter amusement, I remembered his index card habit. He kept stacks of them in the office, the glove compartment of the car, next to the bed. He had them stuffed in the pockets of shirts and jackets and was always writing little notes to himself on them. Notes that he would promptly shove in some other pocket or between the pages of a magazine, his reminder to pick up stamps or check out a book he'd heard about on the radio, lost forever. Perhaps he now used the cards to keep a girl file: *Sasha — redhead w! appendectomy scar. Likes martinis, dislikes dogs.* I chuckled to myself as I imagined the card one day tumbling from the pocket of his blazer when some other girl dropped off the dry cleaning.

I carried the lamp into the room that had been my mother's painting studio, where there was a cot set up in the corner, piled high with blankets, wheeling my black suitcase, Magpie at my heels. The cat watched with her head cocked as I unpacked socks, underwear, and T-shirts and put them in the battered wooden dresser, no doubt a remnant from a long-gone New Hope resident. I came across my Swiss Army knife in my toiletry bag, among the tea tree oil shampoo and avocado body scrub — I had stuck it in there at the last minute when I realized I wouldn't be allowed to carry it on the plane. About the only things I ever used it for were opening wine and slicing cheese at impromptu picnics, but I am a woman who likes to be prepared. I considered locking it up in the sharps drawer in the kitchen, but finally tossed it into my purse.

Suddenly, I was exhausted. Not by the unpacking but by the whole afternoon. By being home. More than anything else, it was the guilt I felt seeing how much my mother had changed, slowly slipped away, while I held on to my careful little life back in Seattle — my life of electric appliances and halogen spotlights — oblivious, thinking she couldn't be that bad, thinking the phone calls from Raven were exaggerated.

I set the oil lamp on the bedside table and lay down on the cot to rest for a few minutes. Magpie joined me, purring like a lawnmower. My mind was racing and my body thought it was barely suppertime, much less bedtime — I could easily foresee the sleepless night before me, soon to be followed by a blurry-eyed day. What I needed was a drink, preferably something hot, with spiced rum. Then I remembered the locked box of drugs in the kitchen and made my way to it, keys jingling. Now, I am not a person to indulge in the casual use of pharmaceuticals, but one little Ambien never hurt anybody. To be on the safe side, I took two.

While I waited for the drugs to take effect, I studied the shadows of my mother's paintings as they glowed in the lamplight. They were still lifes mostly, the one on the easel half finished: a bowl of fruit in somber shades of gray. It was an underpainting, a scene stripped of its color, only a shadow of what it promised to become.

3

LATE APRIL, 1971

Ron Mackenzie was our bus driver back in
the fifth grade. He was a bulldog of a man
with a thick neck and beady, watchful eyes.
He always wore a black knit cap and worked
his jaw as he drove as if he were chewing on
his own tongue. Looking at him, you would
have thought he had always been driving
school buses, but the truth was that once he'd
worked for NASA. He'd tell the new kids on
his route this, letting them think he must have
been an astronaut or something, and only
when they pressed him did he admit that he
had driven trucks and forklifts, not lunar
landers. He had moved rocket parts around.
Ron Mackenzie had gotten to touch metal
that blasted off into space. He moved from
Cape Canaveral back home to Vermont
because his wife's mother got sick, and that's
when he started driving buses and working
down at the town garage.

On good days, Ron called us his chicka-
dees. When he was angry, when one of the

kids had disappointed him in some way, we were monkeys, and you could tell from his tone that monkeys were, in Ron's mind, a pretty low-life thing to be.

'I've had just about enough from you monkeys today!' he'd say through clenched teeth when the noise on the bus got too loud or when kids switched seats while we were moving.

Del and I caught Ron's bus each morning at the bottom of the hill by her mailbox. Three of her brothers rode the earlier bus that took them to the Brook School, where grades six through twelve went. Nicky, the crow assassin, was fourteen. Her twin brothers, Stevie and Joe, were seventeen, seniors in high school. Mort was nineteen. He had never graduated and was still living at home, helping out with the farm. Her other brothers, Roger, Myron, and Earl, all had places of their own in or near New Canaan. Earl, the oldest, was married with two kids not much younger than Del.

Stevie and Joe kept to themselves and showed no interest in Del. When they weren't doing chores, they were working on a GTO that they planned to race at Thunder Road. They had girlfriends — pimply, overweight girls who loved to ride in that red GTO, fixing their hair and blowing cigarette smoke through their noses while greasy wrenches and car parts rattled at their feet. They'd drive through town too fast, gunning the engine and squealing the tires at each intersection. Sometimes I would see the four of them riding or back in Del's yard — the ugly girls sprawled out and smoking on the brown lawn while Stevie and Joe banged around under the hood.

★　★　★

Del rode to school in the morning on Ron's bus, but took the afternoon kindergarten bus home right after lunch along with the three other kids in the Special Ed room. I guess the school figured half a day was about all these kids could handle.

The other three Special Ed kids were boys. Tony LaPearl had Down's syndrome. Artie Paris was twelve like Del — they'd both stayed back twice. He was a big hulking kid already growing a scraggly mustache. Mike Shane was twelve also, and the tallest, skinniest boy in our school. He could not speak. No one really knew why, but there were lots of rumors. The most believable was that he'd had some kind of illness as a baby that badly scarred his vocal cords. Mike went around with a pad of paper tied with a string around his neck, communicating by notes.

The morning after our first meeting in the field, while we stood waiting for the bus, I noticed that Del wore the same soiled cowgirl shirt. She had on a clean pair of tan corduroy bellbottoms that hung loose and were cinched above her narrow hips with a thick brown leather belt. The pants looked like hand-me-downs from one of her brothers. Pinned to her shirt was a silver metal sheriff's star.

Neither of us spoke. I waited and watched, leaving it up to her to make the rules. We scuffed the dirt with our shoes and stared down at the patterns we made. I thought of the crow, the letter *M* on Del's chest, covered, now, not only by the shirt, but by the silver star. Just before the bus arrived, I looked up and caught Del smiling at me and knew I had not imagined our meeting. I also knew, as I caught a glimpse of that broken edge of tooth, that I would return to the crow after school to see what might happen next.

When Ron stopped the bus, I got on before Del, just like always, and took the first empty seat in front. I half thought she might take the seat beside me and guiltily prayed she wouldn't. I said thank you to God when she passed me and went to the back to take a seat alone.

'I smell rotten potatoes,' whispered one boy to another when she passed.

'Potato Girl, Potato Girl, smells so rotten it makes your nose curl,' sang the other boy.

Ron Mackenzie, strict as he was about behavior on the bus, never once stopped the kids from teasing Del. He just gripped the wheel tighter, working his jaw extra hard, like he was embarrassed or something.

'Hey Del, how do spell *potatoes?*' asked the first boy, looking out at the misspelled sign in her yard.

'Retards can't spell. Retards just smell,' said the other.

Del just stared out the window, grinning widely, like the joke was really on them.

★　★　★

I saw Del only twice that day at school, at the same two times I saw her every day: morning recess and lunch. During morning recess I was on the monkey bars when I saw Del go to the maple tree at the edge of the playground. She was alone, as usual. She said something to herself, something out loud that must have been funny, because then she laughed. I watched with curiosity as she picked a twig off one of the lower branches and pretended to smoke it like a cigarette. Artie, the big

Special Ed kid, approached her with two of his fifth grade friends.

'What ya got there, Del?' asked Artie. 'Wacky tobbaccy?'

Del just kept smoking, pretending not to hear. She tilted her head back and stared up into the branches with their freshly unfurled leaves. I climbed to the top of the monkey bars to get a better view. Two other girls played below me — Samantha Lancaster and Ellie Bushey. They whispered and giggled to each other when I smiled down at them. They were best friends who wore their hair in identical braids, and each had a matching pink windbreaker. They were popular girls, surrounded by a glow of normalcy and self-confidence, the first two to be picked for teams, shoe boxes overflowing with cards on Valentine's Day. I went back to watching Del, doing my best to ignore Ellie and Samantha.

Over by the trees, Artie was still talking to Del, swaying a little as he spoke, as if he needed extra momentum to get the words out.

'Cat got your tongue, girl? You a mute like Mike now? Mute Mike and the Potato Girl. What a couple. I seen him passin' you notes in the classroom. Little love notes prob'ly. Maybe you two should get married. Have little dirty mute babies. Raise 'em on raw potatoes. Ain't that what you cut your teeth on, Del?'

Del said nothing, just sucked hard on her stick and blew invisible smoke rings, still staring up at the highest branches. When she leaned back like that, her sheriff's badge caught the sun and gleamed like a real star might. I remembered what Lazy Elk had told me about talismans and thought that maybe that silver star was Del's.

'Where is that Mute Mike, anyway?' Artie wondered out loud. He made a visor out of his hand and scanned the playground like a general surveying the battlefield. He spotted Mike.

'Get him over here, Tommy,' Artie ordered, and off lumbered Tommy Ducette, the fattest kid in fifth grade, to drag poor Mike over. By the time Tommy forced Mike back to the maple tree, a circle of curious kids had formed, including the two girls who'd been under the monkey bars. I climbed down and walked over to get a closer look. Samantha whispered something to Ellie, who then turned to look at me and blushed a little.

'There's that mute!' Artie grinned. 'There's your sweetheart now, Del.' And there stood Mike Shane, toothpick thin but taller than the other boys by a head. His wrists and ankles stuck out beyond his cuffs. The spiral pad hung around his neck on red yarn. Mike kept his head down, studying the worn rubber toes of his Keds.

I had watched Mike Shane before. He was, like Del, like myself, a kid who stuck to himself for the most part. I'd seen him playing checkers at recess with Tony LaPearl, the boy with Down syndrome, and from what I saw, Mike let Tony win each time. I had also noticed, as Artie had, that he passed notes to Del from time to time and, occasionally, she would lean close and whisper something in his ear that made him smile and look away, embarrassed.

'Now you two are gonna be married,' Artie announced. 'Stand together now.' Tommy gave Mike a shove so that the quivering string bean of a boy stood nearly touching Del, who continued to play-smoke like some glamour girl movie star.

'Do you, Del the Potato Girl, take Mute Mike to be your husband, for better or worse, in sickness and health, till death do you part?'

Del blew smoke in his face.

'That was a yes. Sure, sure you do. Now do you, Mute Mike, take this here smokin' Potato Girl to be your smelly old wife? A nod will do, Shane. You don't need to write it in your freakin' book.'

Mike Shane nodded, still staring at the

64

ground, jittery as a cornered hare.

'I hereby pronounce you man and wife. Now kiss your bride,' Artie ordered.

Mike looked up at this, his brown eyes wide and truly terrified. Del just smiled. Mike tried to bolt, but Artie and Tommy stopped him and pulled him over to Del. He made howling sounds like an animal trying to speak. Spit ran down his chin. The two bigger boys pushed him up against Del, who just stood her ground. She dropped the twig she was smoking and ground it out with her foot, then leaned forward and kissed Mike Shane on the lips. It was a long, soap opera kind of kiss, and when Del pulled away, Mike's face was no longer pale but a vivid, burning red. The kids gathered around squealed, laughed, said *gross*.

'Ew! Potato Girl germs,' Ellie said.

'Worse than cooties,' Samantha added.

'Poor Mute Mike,' one boy said.

'They deserve each other,' sang back another.

Then the party was broken up by Miss Johnstone, who demanded to know what was going on.

'Playing cowboys,' said Del. 'I'm sheriff,' she added, smiling, pointing to her shimmering badge.

'Why'd you let them do that today?' I asked later, when I met Del back by the dead crow.

'What?'

'The way they teased you and Mike. Why'd you kiss him? You didn't have to.'

'What was I gonna do?' she snorted.

'Go get Miss Johnstone. Holler out. Anything.'

'Yeah, right,' she said.

'You could have tried.'

'It wasn't so bad.'

'What was it like?'

'What?'

'Kissing Mike Shane.'

'Like kissing any boy, I guess.'

'Have you kissed lots of boys?'

She shrugged casually and pulled back the sleeves of her shirt. Her left forearm was covered in purple bruises that I was sure hadn't been there the day before.

'Enough.'

With that, Del tore off toward the pasture where her pony was penned, pointing her fingers like the barrels of guns, shooting everything in her path.

'I'm Wyatt Earp!' she hollered. 'Gonna get me a bad guy. Come on, Deputy. Catch me if you can!'

So I chased Del through the garden, past the horse fence, both of us shooting from pointed fingers, her yelling, *Catch me if you can*, the whole way. I chased her past the pigpen, keeping my distance from the fence, not slowing to try to get a look at their teeth. We ran to the root cellar, which Del announced was a bank being robbed. We drew our guns and threw the wooden door open, hoping to catch the robbers in the act.

'Shoot 'em dead!' Sheriff Del cried.

'Shoot who dead?' asked the raspy voice behind us.

We turned and saw Del's brother Nicky. He had a real rifle in his hands, a BB gun, probably the one he used to kill the unfortunate bird hanging in the field.

Suddenly Del wasn't Wyatt Earp anymore.

'Take us shooting, Nicky,' she whined, grabbing the fabric of his white T-shirt and twisting it into a ball as she pleaded.

'No way, Del.' The boy spoke to his sister, but studied me with his sly fox smile. He was long and tan. His arms hung low, looking impossibly dark as they poked out from the sleeves of his white T-shirt. He wore stained blue jeans and the same huge, worn work-boots as the day before. His face looked as if it were chiseled from some dark, exotic wood.

'Take us, or I'll tell Daddy about you know what,' threatened Del, still tugging at the shirt.

'Bullshit. I'll tell Daddy you've got a friend who comes over.'

'Take us, or I'll tell him, Nicky. I swear.'

'No way.' Nicky jerked his shirt out of Del's grip and took off running toward the back field.

'The bank robber's getting away!' shouted Del. 'Stop him! I think it's Billy the Kid!'

We took off after Nicky, chasing him through the garden, the field of peas, and into the woods, up the path that I took home. It looked like he was going to lead us straight to New Hope, but he jogged down an overgrown path I'd never noticed off to the left. The path went on a ways, the vegetation thick and jungle-like, before it opened into a clearing. In the center of this grassy area stood a tiny, leaning cabin, like something from a fairy tale. A witch's house, a gathering place for trolls.

Nicky was stooped over, his hands on his knees, gasping for breath, the gun in the weeds by his feet.

'Surrender, Billy!' sang Del as she tore into the clearing, pointing her loaded fingers at her brother. Her hair was plastered to her forehead and her words sounded wheezy.

He put his huge hands in the air and

smiled. His T-shirt was soaked with sweat and clung to his narrow chest.

'What is this place?' I asked once I caught my breath.

'Used to be a deer camp,' Nicky said. 'Daddy let it fall to shit. Our grandpa built it.'

It was a small building, about twelve by fifteen feet, more like a toy house than an actual place where men once slept. The cabin was leaning precariously to the left, looking like it might come crashing down at any minute. It was sided with rough slabs of wood, bits of bark still clinging to them. The wood-shingled roof looked spongy and was green and black with moss.

'Want to see inside?' Nicky asked, looking at me.

'Is it safe?' I asked.

Del snorted and ran inside.

'Sure it is,' Nicky answered. He picked up his gun and strode through the doorway, which lacked a door. I followed him in.

The cabin smelled like rotten wood, mildew, and mice — the scent of all things forgotten. There was a cast iron pot-bellied stove, a torn blue couch, a coffee table, and four cots, one pushed against each wall of the room. A ladder at the far end, near the stove, led to a loft. Nicky tucked his gun under his arm and climbed the ladder. Once up, he

69

leaned over the rail and grinned down.

'Coming?' he asked.

I started up the ladder while Del banged around with the cast iron stove.

A mattress took up most of the loft's planked floor. There were candle stubs, a smudgy oil lamp, a book of matches, cigarettes, and a stack of porn magazines. On top of the magazines was a small knife with a fake bone handle in a leather sheath. Nicky sat down on the ratty mattress and lit a cigarette. He shouted down to Del.

'Quit messing with that damn stove! It's eighty degrees in here!'

Del clambered up the ladder and made a sour face at Nicky.

'Give me one of them,' she ordered and Nicky handed her a cigarette. He offered one to me, but I shook my head. Del lit the cigarette and smoked it like it was the most natural thing in the world, something she did all the time. She even blew smoke rings, like the invisible ones I'd seen her play at making earlier that day. She blew them right into my face, smiling.

'So you gonna tell me your name yet, or do I have to guess?' Nicky asked me.

'She's my deputy. She swears allegiance only to me,' Del said.

'Does your deputy have a name?' asked

Nicky, taking a drag from his cigarette.

Del's eyes went from her brother to me, then back again.

'Her name's Rose. Desert Rose.'

'Like hell it is. That's the name of the stupid color you wanted Daddy to paint your room.'

Del's pale face grew red. 'IF I SAY IT'S HER NAME, THEN IT IS!'

Nicky's face crinkled, looked like it might fall in, then cracked into a big smile.

'All right then. Pleased to meet you, Desert Rose.' He extended his hand. His long dark fingers wrapped gently around mine. My own palm was sticky with sweat. His was dry as powder.

When the cigarettes were stubbed out in a tuna can, we went outside and Nicky showed us how to work the BB gun. We shot beer cans off stumps. Nicky stood behind me, his arms around my shoulders as he showed me how to hold the gun and aim. I'd never fired a gun before, but I hit each can dead center. Nicky said I was a natural. He smelled like sawdust, hay, and cigarettes. His body felt warm against mine. Del got impatient for her turn and practiced taking aim at the cans with rocks, knocking them down before we got a chance to shoot.

Afterward, we went back into the cabin and

I smoked my first cigarette. I coughed and wheezed, sure I was going to die, while Nicky and Del laughed at me, making fun of me until I learned not to draw the smoke in so deep, to just hold it in my mouth awhile, then let it seep out. Del tried to teach me to blow rings — I imitated her as she worked her mouth in perfect circles like a gasping fish, but my rings were sad blobs, amorphous shapes. Nicky practiced throwing the little plastic-handled knife into a dart board nailed to the wall. He never got near the center.

★ ★ ★

After a while, Nicky said he had chores to finish and left us alone.

'What happened to your arm?' I asked Del, eyeing the ring of purple bruises.

'Nothing,' she said, pulling the sleeve of her yellow shirt back down and picking up the knife.

'I got an idea,' Del said as she threw the knife into the dartboard, hitting it dead center, right in the bull's-eye.

I felt a little thrill of peril. It was being in the leaning cabin that did it. It was in the way the springs popped dangerously out of that mattress, the *thunk* of the knife's blade each time it entered the wall, the way the rings of smoke from Del's mouth drifted up, then disappeared, leaving behind only the stale ghost of a smell.

'Gimme your hand,' Del instructed.

I did. She held my hand, studied it like it was some strange wounded animal. In her other hand, she gripped the knife.

'Close your eyes,' she said.

'Are you going to cut me?'

'Trust me,' she said. 'C'mon, close your eyes,' she dared, and I did, not wanting to seem afraid.

She cut quickly, without hesitation. My eyes flew open and I tried to jerk my hand away, but she held tight.

'Ow! What the hell?'

She let go of my hand. The cut on my pointer finger was short, but deep. Blood dripped onto the mattress.

I watched as Del used the knife to cut her own finger with the same swiftness and confidence. Then she took my hand and pressed our two fingers together.

'We're blood sisters now,' she explained. 'You got my blood. I got yours. Forever.'

My finger burned against hers. Del was a part of me then, and I knew that whatever path our friendship might take, there would be no going back. Not ever. Try as I might later to separate myself, Del and I were bound.

4

NOVEMBER 8, 2002

'Katydid!'

My mother's voice brought me struggling out of a deep, unsettled, drug-induced sleep. My mouth tasted metallic. I fumbled for my watch on the milk crate next to my bed — it was seven in the morning, but it felt like the middle of the night. I had been dreaming that Del and I were in her root cellar and she was giving me a tattoo, using the rusty point of her sheriff's star to write *Desert Rose* across my chest. There was someone else down there with us, too — a man — watching. He stood in the corner and I couldn't see his face. Suddenly, as I lay there on the cot, I had this absurd feeling that if I turned around fast enough, I'd see him. That he'd been there, in the room with me, all night. But that was only a dream, right? So why was I so scared to turn around?

Magpie was curled up on my stomach, nose tucked under her white-tipped tail, and I was reluctant to disturb her soft, warm

74

weight. I counted to three and made myself look at the back corner. Nothing. Just specks of dust dancing in the sunlight.

'No more sleeping pills for you,' I whispered to myself.

My mother called me again, using the nickname I hadn't heard from her since I'd moved away. I rolled out of bed and shuffled into the kitchen barefoot, Magpie right behind me.

Every cabinet door and drawer in my mother's kitchen hung open. The fridge door was ajar. The counter was cluttered with mixing bowls, bags of flour and sugar, jars of honey and molasses.

Hurricane Jean had made landfall.

A bottle of olive oil lay open and draining onto the floor. Magpie dashed over to it and began to daintily lap it up, walking in circles, leaving a ring of oily paw prints on the burnished wood floor.

I remembered how impressed I had been with the neat efficiency of my mother's compact kitchen when I'd first seen it two years ago. If the woman who had painstakingly designed that space could see this mess now, she would weep.

'What are you doing, Ma?' I was stunned, both by the mess and by the fact that she'd remembered my old nickname.

'Making pancakes! Strawberry pancakes!'

They had once been my favorite — she had made them for me Saturday mornings in the tepee, cooking over an old Coleman camp stove. My mother's memory, it seemed, had not been completely erased.

I peered down into the bowl of batter she was about to attack with the wooden spoon held clumsily in her bandaged hands — the gauze filthy and beginning to unravel. In the bowl were about half a dozen eggs (complete with crushed shells), a pile of flour, a square of strawberries still frozen solid, all topped with what appeared to be maple syrup. Julia Child, move over.

'Ran out of eggs,' she said as she began flailing at her mixture. 'We'll have to run down the street to the Griswolds'.'

'Ma, the Griswolds don't live there anymore.'

'They don't?'

'No, Ma, they haven't for a long time.'

Mr Griswold died of heart failure twelve or thirteen years ago. The boys had all scattered to the wind.

'We're out of eggs,' my mother said.

'I've got an idea. Why don't we get cleaned up and I'll drive us to town for eggs? Then we'll come back and cook pancakes.'

'Have to go down to the Griswolds',' she

said again, reluctant to leave her bowl of batter.

I looked down at the mess on the table and, to my horror, saw that among the spilled flour and strawberries lay a small, black-handled paring knife.

'Where did this come from, Ma?'

My mother smiled as I held up the sticky knife, dripping red juice down my wrist.

'Needed to slice the berries,' she said.

I rinsed the knife in the sink, then found my key and locked it in the sharps drawer, all the while wondering what other surprises my mother had stashed around the house — more knives, matches even?

I helped my mother change out of her oil-and-flour-covered nightgown and into slacks and a sweater, then I set things up to change her bandages at the kitchen table. I soon discovered that it wasn't only the mess from the kitchen that had dirtied my mother: her nightgown and socks were smeared with what looked like mud. And the gauze that was left on her hands was covered in dirt and bits of leaf debris. And was that dried blood under the fresh strawberry juice stains?

I gave her a cursory exam, and began unwrapping the dirty bandages.

'Ma? Did you go out last night? Did you hurt yourself somehow?'

'We need eggs, Katydid.'

I resolved that I would begin locking her door at night, as Raven had instructed me to. I counted myself lucky that my mother had found her way home and appeared, from my quick exam, to be unharmed. What a sight she must have been, wandering through the woods, white nightgown trailing, like the Ghost of New Hope Past, while I lay snoring in some drug-induced, nightmare-infested coma. I prayed Raven, Opal, and Gabriel hadn't seen her. I wasn't off to the best start as my mother's keeper.

I studied her unwrapped hands, gently turning them in my own. Her palms were bright red and badly blistered. Some of the pustules were open and weeping clear liquid. I cleaned them, applied fresh ointment, and began to rewrap her hands.

'You're a good doctor,' she said.

'I'm not a doctor,' I told her. 'Just a nurse. A school nurse. About the only doctoring I do is passing out Ritalin.'

'You went to medical school.'

'I dropped out.'

'Why would you do that?'

'To marry Jamie.'

'Oh . . . Jamie. Such a nice boy. Where is Jamie?'

'Back in Seattle.'

'Why didn't he come?'

'We're divorced, Ma. Remember? We've been divorced for years.'

I suddenly wished I were the one with the Swiss cheese memory. It would be nice if you could have some control over it, deciding which memories would stay, which would be banished to the netherworld. *Poof.* Just like that.

My mother stared at me, smiled.

'I know you,' she said. I began taping the gauze in place.

'Tell me, Ma, how did you burn your hands?'

She thought for a minute. 'In a fire?'

'That's right. Tell me about the fire. The fire in the tepee.'

'It was the fire that gave me the stroke. Now I have a problem with my memory.'

'You didn't have a stroke, Ma.' *But it's quite possible that I might have one before all this is over.*

'Fire stroke.' She nodded vigorously.

'How did the fire start, Ma?'

'Stroke took away any memory.'

'Ma, you didn't have a stroke in the fire. You burned your hands.' I got up and began putting away the gauze and tape, locking the ointment back in the box.

'She was there,' my mother said while my

back was to her, the firm tone of her voice startling me.

'Who?' I turned and stared at my mother. She didn't respond. 'There was no one with you, Ma. Raven and Opal weren't home. Gabriel pulled you out. Remember?' *You bit him. Broke the skin with your teeth.*

My mother looked at me, then back down to her freshly bandaged hands. She smiled.

'She was there. She knows who you are.'

* * *

'Where are we going?' my mother asked as we walked out to the car.

'To town to get eggs.'

She seemed satisfied enough by this answer and got into the passenger side of my little blue rental.

'Seatbelt, Ma,' I said. She made no move to fasten it. I leaned across her, reached for the strap, and buckled her in.

'Where are we going?' she asked again. I repeated my answer.

'The Griswolds have eggs,' she said. 'Lazy Elk says they're no good because sometimes they've got a speck of blood in them, but that just means they're fertile.'

On the way to town, we passed the Griswolds' old place. I slowed when I saw two green state police cars in the driveway along with a Channel 3 news van. Behind the house, way back in the field, near the edge of the woods, I could see more cars and a white van. It was all eerily reminiscent of how things looked the day Del was killed. My mother stared straight ahead, a contented smile on her face, apparently oblivious to all the commotion.

I stopped at the corner where Bullrush Hill Road met Railroad Street. They'd put up a stop sign just before I went away to school.

I studied the front of the Griswolds' house, long abandoned, reminding myself that it was thirty-one years ago that Del was killed, not just yesterday.

So what the hell was going on?

I've never been a believer in the afterlife, but if I had to invent a hell for myself, it would look something like this: I'd be forced to relieve my worst moments again and again, powerless to change their outcome.

'The Griswolds have eggs,' my mother reminded me eagerly.

The house itself was listing to one side, and the last of the chipped white paint had finally peeled away. A piece of plywood with a NO TRESPASSING sign had replaced the front door.

The three-sided stand in the front yard had

81

collapsed, matching the barn behind it. The mailbox had been knocked over, by a snowplow maybe, or some kids out playing mailbox baseball with a Louisville Slugger. Beside the ruined mailbox, the old sign still swayed from its post on a rusted chain, the red letters faded: EGGS HAY PIGS POTATOS.

A state trooper came around the side of the house and looked over at our car, idling at the stop sign. I turned away, focusing my eyes on the road ahead, signaled left, and stepped on the gas a little too hard and fast. The tires gave a slight squeal as we drove off, down Railroad Street toward the center of town. An homage to Stevie, Joe, and their GTO.

I found a parking place right in front of Haskie's General Store. Next to the store was the old brick New Canaan depot from the days when the L&S Railroad carted timber and passengers between Wells River and Barre. The old station was now an antique shop that had a neatly hand-lettered sign on the door that said CLOSED FOR THE SEASON — SEE YOU IN THE SPRING! It had been owned, since I was a little girl, by the Miller family. They made their money on the summer people and the leaf peepers who came up each fall.

I undid my mother's seatbelt and walked with her into the store, which also served as the New Canaan post office. Jim Haskaway, the bearish man who owned the store, was town postmaster and chief of the volunteer fire department. It was an old-time general store with a few aisles of groceries, a case of guns and ammo, a good selection of hardware and camping supplies, and, of course, the obligatory displays of maple syrup and I LOVERMONT keychains. The wide-planked pine floor creaked, a coal stove burned in the corner, and Jim's fire and police scanner sounded out chimes, with staticky voices reporting the latest disasters.

'Why are we here?' my mother asked. She looked around suspiciously.

'To get eggs, Ma, remember?'

'The Griswolds have eggs. Lazy Elk says they're no good because they've got a speck of blood in them — oh, look! It's Jim Haskaway!' She said this in the tone of delight and surprise she'd use if we'd run into him by chance at the San Diego Zoo, not in the store down the road from her home, the store he'd owned and operated for a good thirty years.

'Morning, Jean! How are we doing today? And Miss Kate, back in town, huh? Grown up to be just as pretty as her mom.' Jim gave us a wink. He stood resting his elbows on the counter. There were two other men talking with him in low voices. All of them wore plaid. They continued their conversation as I guided my mother to the cooler.

'Said the body was the same as that other girl. Same cuts. Naked,' one of the men reported.

'They've had dogs in those woods all morning,' another said. 'Brought in the forensics van. I heard the FBI is up there now.'

'The troopers picked up Nicky first thing this morning,' Jim said.

'Won't keep him long,' replied the shorter, fat man. 'He was drinking at Flo's 'til closing. Made some trouble with a guy from outta state who come up to huntin' camp. Yeah, you bet everyone at Flo's will remember Nicky being there. It wasn't him who hurt that girl.'

I grabbed a dozen eggs from the cooler, then fixed myself a large coffee, trying not to be too obvious about eavesdropping. So Nicky was still in town, picking fights at Flo's. Old outlaw Billy the Kid. I had to smile.

My mother followed me around docilely, humming quietly. At the counter, I picked up the morning paper and saw the headline: 'Murder in New Canaan.' There was a school photo of a pretty girl with shoulder-length blond hair, a smattering of freckles, and a slight gap between her two front teeth. Jim nodded at the front page as he rang me up.

'Happened right in those same woods. Right behind your mother's little shack. Kids say it's a haunted place up there. I say it's a hell of a place to go fooling around in. Now this. Poor kid. Just thirteen. She wasn't gone from the others fifteen minutes. They didn't hear a peep. You all didn't hear anything strange last night, did you?' The other two men studied me, waiting to gauge my response. Sherlock Holmes and Dr. Watson in plaid.

I shook my head, feeling inexplicably like I was about to lie. I thought of my mother's dirty nightgown and socks, wondering when she'd gone out, where she might have wandered to, what she might have seen. Surely nothing. She'd probably just strolled around in the yard. Ghost of New Hope Past.

'Not a thing. We didn't hear a thing. We just noticed the police cars on our way here. There's a news truck there now, too. Channel Three.'

'Opal must be a mess,' Jim went on.

'Opal? Raven's daughter?' I said.

Jim gave me a look of pity — which Opal did I *think* he was referring to?

'Lord, Kate, she was there in the woods. It was her best friend who got killed.'

'Jesus,' I said, shivering.

'Damn terrible thing,' said Jim. 'They're saying she was killed the same way as that Griswold girl all those years ago. You remember that whole mess, I'm sure. You went to school with her, didn't you?'

I nodded, felt the old sting of accusation. 'We were in the same grade, but we weren't really friends. I hardly knew her.' The old lie came easily, despite how many years it had been since I'd had to tell it.

'Yeah,' Jim continued, nodding, 'what a mess that was. I remember how quick they were to point the finger at poor Nicky Griswold. But then they arrested one of the guys from up at New Hope, didn't they? What was his name . . . I can't think of it now. Oh well, it doesn't matter. They had the wrong guy. Never did get the right one. Never did. Well, let's see, that'll be three eighty-nine,' Jim said, looking down at the cash register, turning back to business.

I found my mother studying the rack of magazines. She had a copy of *Deer Hunter* in her hands and was staring at the dead doe on the cover. A man in blaze orange was propping the gutted animal up like a tired dance partner about to do the last waltz.

'Come on, Ma. Let's go home and make pancakes.'

'What's happened to that girl?' my mother

asked, and I realized she must have been listening.

'Nothing,' I lied. *It's just that we've been dropped into my own funny little idea of hell, but hey, what of it? We've got strawberry pancakes to make. My favorite. You remember.*

My mother dropped the magazine back into the rack upside down and walked up to the group of men talking at the counter.

'What's happened to that girl?' she demanded.

'Murdered,' the fat one said before Jim could get a chance to stop him.

'Poor thing,' my mother said and all three men nodded.

I took her arm and led her from the store.

I kept thinking about Opal, wondering how much of it she might have seen. I knew all too well how it felt to have your best friend brutally murdered. It was something you never got over.

'You knew her, didn't you?' she asked as we were going out the door.

'Who?'

'The dead girl. You used to wait for the bus with her. All those mornings. Wasn't she your friend?'

'No, Ma. Just a girl I knew. And that was a long time ago.'

'Poor thing.'

5

Del and I had been arguing for days about whether or not I really lived in a tepee. In the end, I gave in and agreed to take her up the hill so she could see for herself.

'Now you're not just a hippie but an Indian, is that it?' Del had asked during our argument.

'I'm not an Indian.'

'Your Ma an Indian?'

'Nope.'

'Your daddy?'

'I don't have a daddy. We live with Mark in the tepee. Mark's not an Indian, but he has an Indian name. Lazy Elk.'

'That's about the dumbest thing I ever heard. Hippies don't make no sense at all.'

It had crossed my mind over the previous weeks that I should invite Del home in some legitimate way — my mom would have been thrilled for me to bring someone home, even creepy, scrawny Del Griswold. My mother often asked how things were going at school,

88

if I was making friends.

'Sure,' I lied. 'Lots of friends.'

'What are their names?'

'Well,' I said, chewing my lip for inspiration, 'my two best friends are these girls Ellie and Sam.'

'What about that girl down the hill? The little Griswold girl?'

'Oh, we're not friends.'

'Why not?'

'She's kinda creepy. The kids all call her the Potato Girl.'

My mother made a *tsk-tsk* sound and shook her head.

'I hope you don't call her that.'

'No. Never.'

My mother smiled and ruffled my hair. I was her good girl, friends with the popular, bright-faced kids, knowing better than to make fun of outsiders.

Still, I wondered what it might be like to bring Del to New Hope. I tried to imagine her sitting down to communal dinner in the big barn, tried to picture how she might look as Gabriel served her a wooden bowl full of lentil soup. She would make faces, kick me under the table, think she'd gone to sleep then woke up on Mars.

But Del was my secret as much as I was hers and I never did invite her home. Instead, we agreed to view the tepee from a distance, to spy on my own home like a couple of Peeping Toms.

★ ★ ★

We had been walking through the woods for ten minutes when we passed the turnoff for the old cabin. I wondered if Nicky was there, smoking and looking at magazines, and I hoped we'd run into him on our way back to the Griswold place.

That's when Del said, 'I know someone who's got a crush on you.'

I had this eerie feeling she'd read my mind — but maybe she'd just caught me glancing down the tangled trail.

My face flushed.

'Who?' I asked, as if I didn't know.

'*Kate and Nicky, sitting in a tree, K-I-S-S-I-N-G,*' she sang. 'He's got it real bad for you. Ain't you the lucky one? But before you count your lucky stars, you should know a thing or two about my big brother. See, he's got his share of secrets. A few of 'em, bad. B-A-D spells bad.'

'Like what?'

'Like maybe I'll tell and maybe I won't. Maybe I'll let you find out on your own. I'm just saying things ain't always what they seem.' She fiddled with her sheriff's badge. She wore a stained pink T-shirt with the same corduroy pants she'd had on for days. Her hair was wet from a shower she'd taken just before I met her. She smelled like moist earth dusted with baby powder.

'Who says I want to know anyway? Who says I'm even interested in your big, ape-y brother?'

'You sure seem interested when you're with him, Desert Rose. You two are acting like little love birds already. It's enough to make a person wanna puke.'

It was true that I thought about Nicky a lot, felt a strange, live-wire sort of excitement when I was near him. But the idea that this was visible to Del embarrassed me.

'Is Desert Rose really the color you painted your room?' I asked, eager to change the subject.

'Nah. Daddy said I can't.' She paused for a beat, looked at the ground, frowned like she'd just remembered something. Then she was back. 'I've got the paint sample from Thurston's Hardware, though! I'll show it to you sometime. It's real pretty. I named you after a real pretty color.'

'I'd like to see your room sometime.' I had tried often to imagine what it might look like. If she really did have all the wonderful things she bragged about — the four-poster bed, a collection of more than one hundred plastic horses, the tails from those baby pigs in a canning jar full of rubbing alcohol.

'Can't. Daddy says we can't have friends over. Stevie and Joe can have their girlfriends sometimes, that's okay with Daddy, but they're almost grown up anyway. Daddy says family should be enough.'

As strange as things were at my house — if you could call a circle of canvas draped over poles a house — things seemed stranger still at Del's. I lived in a world of almost no rules — Gabriel believed kids would do a good job raising themselves if they weren't confined by adults and their hang-ups. Del, I knew, got slapped around when she didn't clean her plate at dinner.

As we walked, I told Del about my life at the top of the hill — camping out in the tepee, eating dinner in the big barn with the other New Hope members. I told her how Lazy Elk would turn on the little battery-operated radio in the tepee at night and pull my mother up to dance. Sometimes they'd get me to join them, too, all of us doing these crazy moves — pretending to be robots, snakes, birds. We'd swoop circles around the tepee, cawing like a family of ravens.

Lazy Elk was trying hard to be a dad, but I

couldn't take him seriously. He told me stories every night about Trickster Coyote and began calling me Katydid. Sometimes I helped him make his jewelry, piecing together necklaces from twigs, stones, and bits of glass and wire. I'd go with him on collecting missions where we'd come back with our pockets full of pretty stones, pop tops from beer cans, and old shotgun shells.

'Stuuupid!' exclaimed Del when I told her this. 'Who the hell wants to wear jewelry made from junk?'

I told her about the feather in his hat. How he called it a talisman.

'And I thought my daddy was crazy,' she said.

'He isn't my daddy. He's just Mark. He's okay. Just kinda goofy.'

The truth was, Lazy Elk was the closest thing to a father I'd ever had. I never knew my own dad, and none of my mother's other boyfriends had stuck around very long. All my life, I'd secretly hoped for someone to come along and fill that daddy void, and if that someone happened to wear a floppy hat, make jewelry out of junk, and dance like a bird, so be it.

'What is it he calls himself? Droopy Moose?'

I started to laugh. 'Lazy Elk,' I said. 'Come

on now, we have to be quiet, we're getting close.'

I could see the top of the tepee through the trees up ahead where the path ended and smell the smoke from the outdoor mud oven beside the big barn. I heard voices and struggled to make out who they belonged to as Del and I crept closer.

I knew the other residents of New Hope pretty well by that time and liked them all despite their various oddities. Gabriel was a smart man with a lot of patience. He was the one to go to for help with complicated homework or any sort of moral dilemma. His wife, Mimi, was a good ten years younger than he but her love for him was clear. It seemed to border on worship. He was her life and whatever visions he had for New Hope became hers by default.

Bryan and Lizzy were the only others who'd been there since the beginning. They were in their forties and made pottery, which they sold at craft fairs. They lived in a little shack next to the goat barn. The goats had been Lizzy's idea. She thought New Hope could make some money selling their milk, making cheese, maybe even goat's milk soap. Then, after the goats arrived, she discovered their milk dries up unless they keep getting pregnant — and the offspring are somehow disposed of. That seemed cruel to Lizzy, so the goats served little purpose except for the excitement they caused each time they found their way through the fence and into the garden or through some open doorway. Once, they'd eaten a hole through our tepee's canvas.

Shawn and Doe were a young couple who lived in a log hogan behind the greenhouse. Shawn was the resident mechanic and tinkerer. He kept the cars and tractor running. If something was broken, he was the guy who could fix it. Doe spent most of her time with Raven, a fussy baby who didn't like to be ignored.

Zack had been a freshman at Dartmouth when he read an article Gabriel had written for a socialist newspaper on the nature of community. Zack had hitchhiked to meet Gabriel and spend a weekend at New Hope — and just never left. When he wasn't reading battered paperback copies of *Siddhartha* and *The Communist Manifesto*, he was playing Bob Dylan songs on his beat-up six string. Zack was enamored of Gabriel and would spend hours in quiet but animated discussions with him about what a truly democratic society would look like.

★ ★ ★

As the trees thinned out to scrubby pine saplings and the ground leveled off, I recognized the voices of Doe and Mimi coming from the clearing. Del and I hid behind a huge boulder beside the entrance to the path. The tepee was just to our left, so close we could smell the damp canvas. To our right was the big barn. Between the two structures was the dome-shaped mud oven where we baked all our bread. Beyond the smoking, clay-covered mound, we could make out one end of the vegetable garden and the stuffed scarecrow my mother and I had made.

Doe and Mimi were standing at the long wooden table in front of the oven, kneading bread dough with their backs to us. Both women had long hair down past their shoulder blades — Doe's was black and curly, Mimi's was chestnut brown and straight. Raven was snoozing on a blanket in the shade under the work table.

'Told you I lived in a tepee,' I whispered. Del only nodded in response, her eyes wide, taking everything in. We strained to hear Doe and Mimi.

'I'm just saying it isn't right the way he treats you,' said Mimi. 'Refusing to even acknowledge the baby is his. I mean, who does he think he's kidding?'

Weird. Were they talking about Shawn? He doted on Raven — and Doe, for that matter.

'He knows,' Doe said back. 'Of course he knows. I think the problem is that he doesn't want other people to know and that's cool with me. I mean, Raven's mine. She's still gonna be mine whoever I say the father is.' She crouched down and stroked the baby's forehead.

'Well, I think it's disrespectful,' Mimi continued. 'It's like he's lying, that's all. Lying to everyone here — to her most of all. I think it's lousy. I think he can be so goddamn lousy. Gabriel thinks so, too.'

'Is it really Gabriel's place to pass judgment? I mean, let he who is without sin cast the first stone and all that.' Doe stood up from Raven and grabbed a tray of bread, which she carried over to the oven and pushed in using the large wooden paddle that hung beside the oven door. She stretched, reaching her arms up to the sky and leaning left, then right. Then she turned around to face Mimi, and Del and me, too.

'I shouldn't have said that,' Doe said. 'I didn't mean to insult Gabriel. That was kind of low. He's not the one I'm angry with.'

'So you admit you're angry with him?' Mimi asked.

'No. Not really. Sometimes it's just hard.

To keep a secret like that.'

'So don't keep it. Tell. I think you should tell everyone the truth.'

'Let's go,' I whispered to Del, but she didn't respond. Curious as I was, I didn't want to hear any more. New Hope wasn't the kind of place where people kept secrets and I found a certain easy comfort in that. Everyone shared everything during the circle meetings — all the women even shared when they had their periods (although they referred to it as their 'moon time').

I got up from my crouched position slowly and gently tugged at Del's arm. She stayed put.

'Look at her titties,' Del hissed. 'They hang down to her belly! Don't hippies know about bras?'

'I'm going with or without you. I don't want to get caught,' I whispered, feeling strangely like a trespasser outside my own home. Del just stared at Doe and Mimi as if they were some kind of exotic circus animals — peacocks or dancing bears. I turned and started to make my way back down the path, careful not to make too much noise stepping on sticks and dry leaves. I picked my feet up high and watched where I stepped.

In a minute, I heard footsteps behind me, as Del galloped up and grabbed my shoulders.

'Boo,' she whispered. 'You're walkin' like

98

you got a load in your pants.'

We both started to laugh and took off running so we wouldn't be heard. When we were sure we were out of earshot, Del began asking all about New Hope. She wanted to know everything all at once.

'So whose baby did that girl have? Ain't they married? Do hippies even get married? And who is this Gabriel guy? And who is it that's supposed to be so lousy?'

'Doe, that's the girl with the baby . . . '

'Doe like a deer? Like a goddamn she-deer?' Del asked.

'I think it's short for Dorothy or Doreen or something,' I explained. 'Anyway, she's with this guy Shawn, but I don't think they're married, and he's not lousy at all. He can fix pretty much anything and he's real good with the baby.'

'He's the daddy?'

'I guess so.' The truth was, I wasn't so sure anymore. But I made up my mind to try to forget everything I'd heard, to not let it weigh on me. There were not supposed to be any secrets at New Hope. I was the only one with a double life, the friendship no one knew about.

'Whaddaya mean, you guess so? Goddamn, hippies are worse than people say. You got a girl named after a she-deer who maybe is and maybe isn't married to the guy who maybe is and maybe isn't her baby's father, and a guy named after a droopy moose who makes jewelry out of sticks and stones. My best friend's living in a goddamned for-real Indian tepee, and people are baking bread inside a mound of dirt. What the hell, Kate? What the hell kinda place is that?' Del's eyes were wide with wonder and I felt truly elated. I saw for the first time that I was interesting to her — that it wasn't just the other way around. And she'd called me her best friend. After only a few weeks of really knowing each other, I had become best friends with the Potato Girl.

School would be letting out in another month or so, and already I was imagining a summer spent in the fields, root cellar, and leaning cabin. Del might let me ride her pony. Maybe I'd meet the person who gave her the tattoo. I'd keep her entertained by telling wild stories about New Hope. I'd take her spying. Maybe show her Doe breast-feeding Raven right on the porch of the big barn. Bring her pieces of Lazy Elk's jewelry and sing Zack's songs about revolution. She'd call me Desert Rose and teach me to blow smoke rings. I'd perfect my aim with Nicky's BB gun and learn to throw the knife with the plastic bone handle into the dart board on the wall. And maybe, just maybe, Nicky would ask me to be his girlfriend and tell me what his big secret was, and once I'd heard it, it wouldn't be so bad. It would just make me like him more.

'Race you to the pigs,' Del called out, pulling me out of my daydreams. She'd already started running. 'Catch me if you can!'

And I took off running, but as always, she got there first. I never could catch her.

6

Magpie disappeared my third day back. The cat had been the one constant in my mother's life — she never forgot Magpie's name and never failed to be soothed by her mere presence, even at her most agitated.

We looked all through the house, then walked around New Hope calling her name in high, pleading voices. We searched the big barn, where Gabriel joined us, pushing aside old furniture thick with dust and cobwebs.

'How's Opal doing?' I asked him.

'Holding her own I guess. Raven says she's not sleeping well. Nightmares. She's made an appointment with a child psychiatrist.'

I nodded. 'That sounds like the best thing. She went through a hell of shock.'

'Maybe you should talk to her,' Gabriel said. 'You went through a similar thing with the Griswold girl, didn't you?'

I shook my head. 'It wasn't the same. We weren't very close.'

He looked at me like he knew I was lying.

102

Good old Gabriel still had the ability to see right into your soul.

★ ★ ★

What I neglected to tell Gabriel was that I'd already tried to talk to Opal, the morning after the murder. I went over to the big barn with my mother after our pancakes and heard all the gory details about the murder from Raven. Opal staggered out of her room and joined us at the table.

'You should sleep, sweetie,' Raven said.

'I can't,' Opal said. Then she turned to me and asked, without missing a beat, 'Do you believe in the Potato Girl?'

Raven drew in a breath. My mother let out a soft chuckle.

'I don't believe in ghosts,' I told her. 'Del Griswold was a girl made of flesh and blood, the same as you and I.'

'So you don't believe people can come back? Once they're dead, I mean.'

'No, I don't.'

'What if I told you I've seen her?' Opal's eyes were desperate.

'Sweetie, I thought we were through with this,' Raven said.

Opal ignored her and kept staring at me, waiting for an answer.

'If you told me you'd seen her, I'd take you seriously,' I said, answering as carefully as I could.

Opal nodded at me, then got up from the table and went back to her room, shuffling her feet like a zombie.

'She thinks the ghost killed her friend,' Raven whispered, her hands trembling a little as she gripped her coffee cup tighter. 'Last night, she even said she believed the Potato Girl was after her. That it was *her* she meant to kill, not Tori.'

I nodded sympathetically.

'She's lost a lot, Kate. First, all of her things burned up in the fire. All her books and airplane models. Now this. I don't think . . . I'd appreciate it if you wouldn't say or do anything to encourage these ghost . . . fantasies.' Raven looked up at me coldly. 'Okay?'

I nodded again, feeling stupid. 'Of course not,' I said.

My mother abruptly barked out a laugh, which startled Raven, who spilled her coffee and hissed, 'Shit! Shit! Shit!' until she got up from the table and threw her empty cup in the sink. She stood with her back to us, crying but pretending not to.

★ ★ ★

104

Gabriel, my mother, and I walked past the mud oven, dissolved to a sad lump of clay and bricks, and over to the charred remains of the tepee, calling, 'Magpie!' in a chorus of desperate voices. I kicked at the cold black coals and realized it was a miracle my mother got out at all. I again found myself wondering how the fire started; if it was just a simple case of my mother trying to light a lamp, or if it was more sinister than that — if she set the match to the canvas deliberately.

Upon seeing the burned tepee, my mother began to sob.

'MAGPIE!' she cried, falling to her knees. It was as if she'd found the cat's small bones among the ruins. Gabriel led my mother back into the barn and fixed a pot of tea while I continued my search.

I walked through the gardens, overgrown with thick, dried weeds — thistle, witch grass, burdock. At the north edge of the gardens, brambles encroached: raspberry and blackberry canes formed an impenetrable fence between the garden and the small pasture and barn that once housed goats, chickens, and sheep. Behind this I saw the shack Bryan and Lizzy had called home before moving on to start a community of their own in Hawaii shortly after I left for college. The roof dipped deeply in the center, the rusted metal chimney leaning at a forty-five-degree angle against the edge of the crater. Another victim of the Big Bad Wolf of time.

On the west side of the gardens, the greenhouse lay in a flattened heap. *I'll huff and I'll puff, and I'll blow your greenhouse in.* I got down on my knees and called to the cat, trying to peer under the ruins. I pulled a splintered board out of the way to get a better look underneath and tore the sleeve of my shirt on a rusty nail. Upon further investigation, I saw I was bleeding, too.

'Shit,' I mumbled, trying to recall the date of my last tetanus shot. 'You owe me forty bucks, Magpie. And if I get lockjaw . . . '

I scrambled to my feet. Beyond the remains of the greenhouse stood the eight-sided log hogan Doe and Shawn had lived in. It seemed in good enough shape and I wondered why Raven had chosen to live in the tepee and not her childhood home built by her mother's hands. I guess we all sought independence in our own way.

There was no sign of Magpie anywhere. I was making my way toward the big barn when I saw the old path leading into the woods and down to the Griswolds'. Someone was coming up it. I blinked, not quite believing what I was seeing. It was a girl. A girl carrying a long stick that she was using to poke through the dry grass. She was bent over, peering at the ground intently, parting the dead weeds one way and then the other. She was a skinny girl with untidy hair and rumpled clothes. And for a second, just a second, I held my breath and thought, *It can't be . . .*

And no, it wasn't. I saw when she lifted up her head that it was only Opal. I walked over to meet her and she threw down the stick guiltily.

'Lose something?' I asked.

She looked flustered. I wondered if it was a good idea for her to be out roaming the woods where her friend was murdered.

'Just looking for Magpie,' she said.

It was a strange way to look for a lost cat — a lost hamster, maybe — but I didn't say so.

'So no sign of her, then?' I asked.

'Who?' she asked.

'Magpie. The cat?'

'No. No sign.'

'Well then, let's go back to the big barn and have some tea. I think Gabriel's got a pot on.' I touched her arm lightly to lead her back to the safety of the barn, but she didn't budge.

'Hey,' I said. 'Did you get the plane? Was it the right one?'

I'd gone to the hobby shop in Barre the day

before and bought a Curtiss Jenny biplane model to replace the one that had been burned in the fire. I figured a little model making might be therapeutic. The owner gave me an odd look when I asked if he had any tiny plastic women who might be the right size to walk on the wing, but he showed me a collection of people in the same scale and I picked a woman in jeans in a walking pose.

'God, yeah, I'm sorry,' Opal said. 'Thank you so much. I love the wing walker. It's all perfect. I started it last night.'

'The guy at the store picked out the paints and glue.'

'They're perfect. Really. It's gonna be way better than the one I had before. It was really sweet of you. Thanks.'

'You're welcome. It was my pleasure.'

'Kate, can I ask you something?'

Uh oh, I thought, knowing it wasn't going to be any airplane model advice. *Here we go.*

'Of course.'

'You knew Del Griswold, right?'

'A little.'

'Did she know my mom?'

'Your mother was a baby when Del died,' I told her.

She considered this, and then: 'Can you think why Del would want to hurt me?'

I took a deep breath. 'What makes you

think she would want to hurt you?'

'If I tell you a secret, do you promise not to tell?' Opal asked.

I thought I knew where this was going. Maybe I should've stopped it — after all, Raven had specifically asked me not to encourage this Potato Girl nonsense. Opal was fragile, damaged maybe, and I didn't want to make things worse. But she needed someone to confide in, someone who would let her tell her tale. She felt drawn to me because I had known Del, maybe even because I'd been the one to take care of Opal when she was hurt two years ago. I remembered running to her as she screamed, writhing on the ground beside the pile of mattresses, how small and frightened she'd seemed. *Someone's up there*, she moaned. And when I looked, didn't I think I saw something, too? Just the edge of a shadow, pulling away from the open door to the loft. When I held her there on the ground, wasn't it true that both our hearts were pounding?

Whatever Opal's reasons for wanting to share secrets with me now, I couldn't turn her away.

I thought back to my first meeting with Del.

Okay, if I show you my secret, you gotta promise not to tell. You gotta swear. Cross your heart and hope to die.

'I promise,' I said.

Opal squinted up at me. It occurred to me then that she was the exact same age Del was when I met her. She looked a little like her, too. More than a little. Or was it just my imagination?

Jesus, I thought, *just don't tell me you've got a tattoo.*

'The Potato Girl came for me that afternoon. Before I met Tori and the guys in the woods.'

'Came for you?'

'Yeah, I was in my room and I saw her. She was standing there, looking right at me. Then she opened her mouth to say something, but no sound came out. Just this cold, moist air. Like from a cave.'

I said nothing. I only nodded and tried not to look too much like a disbeliever.

'It wasn't the first time I've seen her. It's been awhile though — almost two years. I used to see her all the time when I was a little kid. Sometimes, I'd just catch little glimpses out of the corner of my eye, nothing I could be sure of. But once in a while, I'd be riding my bike or walking in the woods, and there she'd be, right out in the open, just watching me with this real creepy smile on her face. Like she knew something I didn't.

110

'The older I got, the less I saw her. I kind of thought she'd gone away completely until that day in the loft. Remember? When I broke my arm? And you helped me?'

'I remember,' I said, thinking, *I was only just recalling it, in fact.*

Opal leaned against the big boulder Del and I had hidden behind all those years ago. She looked over in the direction of the ruined bread oven, but I could tell she wasn't seeing a thing.

'That day? I was about to do my jump, like right on the edge, crouched over, ready — and then I saw her, right there, just a couple of feet away, totally . . . *real*, you know? Not like a ghost would look, but like a real girl. She reached for me, with both hands, quick, and I freaked out. Lost my balance. Totally missed my landing pad.' She shook her head ruefully, still mad about a failed stunt. If one of her much loved lady wing walkers had made such a mistake it would have meant much worse than a broken arm.

'Here's the thing, Kate: I think Del's out to get me. I'm pretty sure it was me she was after, not Tori. But what I don't get is *why*. I was hoping you could help me with that part. That maybe if you told me about her I'd be able to figure out what it is she wants with me.'

'Why do you think you were the target?' I asked, keeping my voice level, nonjudgmental.

'Here's the part you have to swear not to tell, okay? It was the jacket. Tori was wearing *my* jacket. One I borrowed from my mom. But no one knows — not the police or anybody.'

'How could they not know?'

'I kinda . . . took it back after she was killed. I didn't want to get in trouble.' She rolled her eyes. 'I know, how lame, huh? Worrying about a *jacket*. But I've been thinking about it a lot and I think maybe the jacket made her look like me, in the dark. I mean, I wear it all the time, and it's got all this fringe on it, and it's just very *noticeable*' — her voice was spiraling up toward hysteria — 'and both me and Tori are *blond* — ' I put my hand on her arm and she fell silent. I thought she would cry, but she didn't.

'And I saw something in the woods when I went back for the jacket.'

'What?'

'The Potato Girl. She was hiding behind a tree, watching. She was wearing this long white dress, and she just kind of floated away.'

'Opal, listen to me. What happened to Tori is horrible, unreal. Of course you want to understand it, explain it, maybe even blame yourself. That's normal. There's even a name for it: survivor's guilt. But you have to understand that you had nothing to do with what happened to Tori. And neither did Del.'

When Opal spoke again, she was whispering: 'I don't believe you. I know what I saw.'

I sighed deeply. So much for Psych 101.

'Let's just say that Del could come back — setting aside for the moment that she *can't*. There is no reason in the world that Del Griswold would want to hurt you. I'm sure there are plenty of other people she'd go after first.'

'Like who?'

'Like me. Like everyone we went to school with,' I said.

'Why?' she asked.

'Because we weren't very nice to her,' I said. *To put it mildly.*

'Hey, did you know you're bleeding?' Opal asked and I saw the cut on my arm had opened up and blood had soaked through my torn sleeve.

★ ★ ★

We made our way back to the big barn, where I washed the cut on my arm in the bathroom sink while Opal grilled me with questions about Del. Opal's face was flushed and she

113

seemed thrilled with any little tidbit I offered. She was looking less like Del now that we were inside and she had her color back, which was a great relief. I was beginning to wonder if I were the one seeing ghosts.

'What was she like?' Opal asked.

'She was strong-willed. Tough. Not afraid of much.'

'Was she mean?'

'I guess she could be. But mostly people were mean to her.'

'Why?'

'Because she was different, I guess. Don't you have some kid in your grade everyone picks on?'

'Sure, Johnny Lopez. He's got a lazy eye and wears pajama tops as shirts.'

'Well, Del was our Johnny Lopez.'

Raven appeared in the doorway, frowning a little to show she'd been there long enough to hear our topic of conversation. 'I thought I heard you two in here. Any sign of Magpie?'

'No,' I told her. 'I cut myself looking for her in the old greenhouse. Opal's giving me a little first aid.'

Opal helped me put some Band-Aids over the cut.

'Hey, you're better than me at this, and I do it for a living,' I told her. 'Any chance you'll give up on this stuntwoman thing and go into medicine?'

She laughed. 'No way!'

'It's less painful to set bones than break them,' I said.

'I'd rather break every bone in my body than be bored out of my mind putting *Band-Aids* on people all day!' Opal said.

'I think your mother's ready to go home,' Raven said and I took the hint, collected my mother, and gently led her back to her house, promising the cat would turn up. Cats went on adventures of their own all the time, I told her. They just pack up their little hobo bundles and set off to see the world and catch more exotic mice. It's their nature, I explained. Along the way, my mother moved from grief to suspicion to rage.

'You got rid of the cat!' she sobbed.

'I did not get rid of Magpie, Ma. She took off on her own. I'm sure she's fine. She'll come home when she's ready.'

'Why did you get rid of the cat? First you get rid of the cat, then you want to get rid of me. I'm not going to a home.' Her body shook as she cried, her wrinkled face slick with tears and mucus.

There, she'd said it. She didn't want to go. I'd brought up the idea of a nursing home with her the night before and she'd played catatonic, not seeming to absorb a word I'd said. Now here she was with her delayed response. Things were going to get mighty complicated if we were going to have conversations in twenty-four-hour cycles.

I moved to place a hand on her back and she pulled away as if I'd burned her. As if I were the one who could shoot fire from my fingertips.

'I didn't get rid of the cat, Ma. I promise. She probably ran off when the police were here. She got spooked, that's all. She'll be back.'

'Why were the police here?'

'To ask us if we heard anything strange that first night I was back.'

'What would we have heard?'

'Nothing. We didn't hear anything.'

And you didn't go out into the woods that night. I didn't find you sitting at the kitchen table with a knife the next morning.

'Why were they asking?'

'Because a girl got hurt in the woods.'

'I know. She's dead. The poor Griswolds. You rode the bus with her.'

'Yeah, Ma, I rode the bus with her.'

'But she wasn't your friend.'

'No, she wasn't my friend.'

'Where's my kitten? Magpie! Oh, Magpie!'

★ ★ ★

The truth was, the police had been by more than once and with each visit, their questioning took on a more accusatory tone. They'd come the day after the murder to question my mother and I, then Opal, Raven, and Gabriel. They returned the next day to talk to me alone, to ask me, all these years later, about my connection to Del.

'Jesus,' I said. 'That was more than thirty years ago. Don't you guys have enough to do with this new murder? That's ancient history.'

The detectives were stone-faced.

'Were you and Delores Griswold friendly, Miss Cypher?' one asked.

'I barely knew her,' I told them. 'She was a kid I rode the bus with. I think I tried to play with her a few times, but she was too . . . odd.'

'Odd in what way, Ms Cypher?' asked one of the detectives.

'She lied,' I told him. 'She was a compulsive liar.'

Ah, irony.

* ⋆ ⋆

When I was in nursing school, I worked nights as an aide at a state psychiatric hospital outside Olympia, Washington. My husband, Jamie, was finishing up his residency. We had agreed that once he finished school, I would go back full-time. I had originally planned to become a doctor, a pediatrician maybe, but a nursing degree would take less time, would put us less in the hole financially. And one doctor in the family was enough, and cardiologists did make more than pediatricians, after all . . . That's what we decided.

Or rather that's what he decided, and I was so gaga in love that I went along, telling myself it was for the best.

Am I bitter about giving up on my career? Only when I think about it too hard. Regret is overrated.

I met Jamie my first year in med school. He was in his last year. He was a blond from Long Beach in faded jeans and bright, gaudy Hawaiian shirts. What I was drawn to was the dichotomy: here was this gorgeous guy with the crazy shirts and surfer philosophy — laid back, waiting for the next wave — who just happened to be at the top of his class, the most dedicated student many of the instructors had ever seen. I fell head over heels the first time he looked me in the eye and drawled, 'Whatever.' I dropped out of school and we were married at city hall on Christmas Eve. We moved into a shabby little studio apartment and I enrolled part-time in a nursing program and took a job working the graveyard shift at the state hospital to pay the bills.

This is how I met a giant of a woman named Patsy Marinelli. The other women on the floor called her Tiny. Tiny was six foot three and weighed well over three hundred pounds. Tiny had shot first her husband, and then herself, in the head. He died instantly, but she survived, remarkably intact aside from some ugly scars and the total loss of her short-term memory. Everything that had happened right up to the moment she pulled the trigger was clear to her — childhood vacations with her big Italian family, crushes on movie stars, summer camp, high school graduation, first love, first drink, first betrayal. But no new memories could be made. Even though I saw her every night for two years, she would introduce herself repeatedly — sometimes several times a night. And nine times out of ten, after the introductions, she would ask me the same question.

'Tell me, what's the worst thing you've ever done?'

During the first year I worked there, I did not answer her. I shrugged my shoulders, made a joke maybe, then turned the question back around to her, as I had learned to do with the very depressed, delusional, and

119

psychotic. Inevitably, Tiny Marinelli would tell me about shooting her husband. She would cry and sob, all three hundred pounds shaking — not quivering like jelly, but erupting with the force of a volcano.

During my second year at the hospital, Jamie admitted to having an affair with another resident — the first in what would be a long series of infidelities. He claimed my emotional distance had driven him to it. We had been fighting constantly over money, household chores that weren't getting done, and whose job it was to pick up milk at the store. I felt stretched to the limit. The classes I was taking were more difficult, money was tighter than ever, work more stressful, and all I wanted to do was sleep, which Jamie took personally when I rebuffed his infrequent attempts to make love.

I didn't turn him down every time — obviously, because I got pregnant shortly after learning about the affair (which he promised was over — done — *finis* — and besides, it was purely physical). I was on the pill, but in my exhausted state, I must have skipped a morning or two. I was afraid to tell Jamie, sure he would blame me, accuse me of manipulating him, which maybe I was on some subconscious level. Jamie didn't believe in accidents. The truth was, neither did I. I also didn't believe that our shaky marriage could survive news of a pregnancy. And we had decided (yes, *we* this time) that we were going to try to make things work. I still loved him — loud shirts, roaming eye, and all. I'm kind of a sucker that way — once I love someone, I can't seem to turn it off.

I was the one who had made the mistake, so it only seemed right that I should be the one to fix it — on my own.

I had the abortion on a Friday afternoon and spent the weekend in bed, cramped up, swallowing Motrin. I told Jamie I had the flu.

That Monday night when I dragged myself into the hospital, Tiny introduced herself to me and asked me the question. We were alone in her room during bed check.

'Tell me, what's the worst thing you've ever done?'

All I could think about was the abortion; I ached to tell someone, to share the burden. Whatever I confessed to Tiny would be forgotten in five minutes.

But, of course, that was not the worst thing I had ever done.

'I betrayed my best friend and then she died.' I found myself saying the words without thinking them through. I just blurted it out.

'Did you kill her?' Tiny wanted to know.

'I wasn't the one who strangled her, no, but I'm partially to blame. If that day had gone differently, then, I don't know, maybe . . . '

'Do you think she blames you?'

'No.' I shook my head, remembered who I was talking to. 'She's dead, Patsy.'

'The dead can blame.'

I stared at this enormous woman. Her eyes, nose, and mouth were too small for her moon face.

'The dead can blame,' she repeated.

* * *

I began leaving an open can of tuna and a saucer of milk on the front porch to lure Magpie back. Each morning, the tuna and milk were gone, but there was no sign of Magpie. Little sneak. She was playing us for all we were worth.

'Why'd you get rid of the cat?' my mother continued to ask.

Because she kept asking the same questions over and over.

'First the cat, then me. I'm *not* going to a home!' Then she would begin to cry the cat's name in sick desperation.

I upped the dosage of her medication. Sometimes it seemed to work; sometimes it seemed to have no effect on her at all.

* ★ ★

One evening, three days after she'd disappeared, I was putting Magpie's treats out by the front door when a banged-up blue Chevy pickup arrived. Out stepped a man I recognized immediately, in spite of his ragged appearance.

Out of old habit, I felt that electric tingle, only this time it seemed a little more dangerous, like touching a downed power line to see if it was live.

'It's true then,' he said, grinning as he hopped down from the cab of the truck. 'Kate came home.'

'How're you doing, Nicky?'

He took a few steps forward and I could see how he was doing. He looked a little drunk. He'd put on some weight and was in bad need of a shave and a haircut. Twenty-some years older than he was when I last saw him, but he still had the same gravelly voice and loping walk. His hair was pale and his skin dark. He wore a grease-stained John Deere baseball cap, clean T-shirt, red-and-black-checked hunting jacket, and jeans. He smiled his sly fox smile and my chest warmed. Like I already said, once I love someone, it's for life. In spite of everything. Crazy, I know.

I hadn't been in a serious relationship since Jamie finally left me five years ago for a young surgeon. She was pregnant, he explained, and he wanted a family. Sick with the irony of the situation, I broke down and told him about the abortion.

'You could have had a family,' I spat. 'You could have an eleven-year-old child right now. There's your fucking family!'

I knew, once I said it, once I saw his face, that the fate of our marriage was sealed. He would never forgive me. I was the one who ruined things — me, the emotionally distant, secret-keeping, child-murdering monster.

She had the baby — a boy named Benjamin — but it was over between Jamie and the surgeon inside of a year. When I heard this bit of news, I expected to feel vindicated, but didn't. Although Jamie and I did not keep in touch, over the years, the news of his string of conquests filtered back to me. My ex-husband, the successful cardiologist, broke nearly as many hearts as he fixed.

Right after the divorce, I went out a few times, a series of one-night stands, fuck-and-run sort of dates, but they left me empty and disappointed and I eventually opted for the role of spinster, rebuffing the advances of even the most promising men. My co-workers at the elementary school all presume I'm a lesbian and I've said nothing to correct them.

Standing on the porch before my first crush, or the man my first crush had become, I couldn't help but do a bit of quick arithmetic in my head — a little over three years. Yep, three years since I'd slept with anyone. I knew it was crazy to be attracted to Nicky Griswold, but there it was.

'Nicky.' I wanted to hug him, but resisted. I sat down on the steps and patted the spot next to me.

'Desert Rose,' he said as he folded his long body down next to me. 'Want a smoke?' He pulled out a pack of Camels and I took one, although I hadn't smoked in years. 'How 'bout a drink?' He pulled a bottle of Wild Turkey from his jacket pocket and took a swallow.

'Gobble, gobble!' He offered me the bottle.

'I could sure use some of that.' I took the bottle and took a long sip, letting the bourbon warm me through and through. Manhattans were my drink of choice, but I was willing to forgo the vermouth and cherry.

'It's good to see you, Nicky.' I meant what I said. After being with my mother for nearly a week, I was desperate for a friendly, familiar face. Someone other than Raven and Gabriel, who always ended their visits by asking what I'd done about finding a place for my mother. The fact was, I'd done nothing at all. I told them I was still assessing the situation, but they easily saw through to the truth: I was stalling and we all knew it. My mother's pleading was getting to me.

'So, how are you?' I asked.

'I reckon I'm surviving. It's sure good to see you, too.'

'What are you up to these days?' I thought of what I'd overheard at the general store — that he'd been picked up for questioning regarding the latest murder, but had a bar fight as an alibi.

'A little of this, little of that. I work part-time at Chuck's as a mechanic, do some small engine repairs on the side. I mow a few lawns in the summer, plow in the winter. Whatever it takes to pay the bills. Got a place over near the Meadows — not much, just a trailer, but it's mine and it's home.' He gave a smile. 'What about you?'

'Not much to tell. Still living in Seattle. Working as a school nurse.'

'Heard you got married.'

'Divorced about five years now.'

He nodded. 'Kids?'

'No.' I looked away. 'No kids.'

He was silent a minute, then nodded toward the house. 'How's your mom doing?'

'Not great.'

'I heard she was going to a home.'

'I don't know yet. That's where she probably belongs, but I don't know if it's the right thing. She's really against it. It seems like her life is in my hands now and I have just a little over two weeks left to make the right decisions, then my leave is up at work and I've gotta go back to Seattle.'

'You'll do right by her.'

We were quiet another minute, smoking our cigarettes, passing the bottle, and listening as the few leaves left rattled on the trees, speaking papery whispers.

'You hear about that girl they found in the woods?'

I took another deep sip from the bottle of Wild Turkey and wiped my mouth with the back of my hand.

'Of course. Pretty unsettling, I'd say. I guess it happened just on the other side of the hill, near where the old deer camp used to be.'

'Camp's still there,' he said.

'No way.' The surprise in my voice seemed to please Nicky, who nodded and smiled. 'I thought for sure it would have fallen in years ago.'

'No, she's leanin', but she's still standing. Kinda like me, huh?' He gave a wink.

My face flushed and I looked away.

'I'll be damned.'

Maybe it was the bourbon, but I found myself remembering how, when things started to go bad with Jamie, I used to wonder what it would have been like to have married Nicky. Not that he ever asked. Not that we even knew each other as adults. But in my mind, he'd grown into this idealized man, no-nonsense, a bit rough around the edges, someone who'd never do me wrong.

Nicky was quiet a moment and took a good slug of Wild Turkey before he spoke again.

'Kate, do you know anything about that girl who was killed?'

'Not much. Just what I read in the paper: she was thirteen, her name was Victoria Miller, her friends called her Tori. Opal and the other kids she was out there with didn't hear a sound.'

'Her mother is Ellie Bushey — married one of the Millers. Ellie and her husband, Josh, kinda took over the antique store after Mr Miller had his stroke. It was too much for the old lady alone.'

'Ellie. That's someone I haven't thought of in a long time.' A knot formed in my throat, a thick, painful knot in the shape of an *E*, for little Ellie Bushey and all her popular-girl promises.

'Well, I remembered the name,' Nicky went on, lighting a second cigarette. 'I remembered that something went on with you girls and Del. Just like I remembered about Artie Paris.'

Jesus, there was another name I'd just as soon forget. Nicky was dragging all of the skeletons out of the closet.

'What about him?'

'That he used to be real mean to Del. That he was the one who everyone said had her down in the dirt that last day at school. He was the one teasing, singing those stupid one potato, two potato songs.'

No, I thought to myself. *We all sang*. The knot in my throat tightened.

'Yeah, he was quite the charmer,' I said out loud. 'I'm sure he still is.'

'That's just it, Kate. He's not. He's dead. Happened just a few months ago.'

I let this sink in a minute. It's always unsettling to hear someone you know has died, and when it's someone your age it seems even more personal, even if it's someone you never liked. I wondered what he'd died of — heart attack? Car accident? Cirrhosis of the liver? It didn't really matter though — however he died, as far as I was concerned, it was good riddance. God, being back home was turning me into a regular saint.

'Really?' I asked. 'Wish I could say I'm sorry.'

'Don't you want to know how he died?'

I shrugged my shoulders and he continued.

'Folks say Artie choked to death on a potato. A piece of raw potato.'

I tried, unsuccessfully, to suppress a laugh. This sounded suspiciously like the latest Potato Girl yarn. Town legend in the making.

'There's more to it than that, Kate. He was home alone. His wife was working the night shift at the shoe factory.'

'Uh-huh,' I said, rolling my eyes a little, unable to believe that Nicky had fallen for such a story.

'Just listen, will you?' He eyed me impatiently. Satisfied by my silence, he leaned forward and continued, his voice low and secretive.

'There were no potatoes in the house. Not a single one. Artie hated them. Wouldn't let his wife buy 'em. But when the coroner did the autopsy, he found a chunk of raw potato lodged in Artie's windpipe.'

I laughed again. 'And I suppose you saw the coroner's report? Or better yet, you talked to him yourself?'

Nicky's face reddened a little.

'Nicky, he probably had a heart attack. But that doesn't make for good storytelling, so little by little, the tale of his death got embellished. That's the way it is in this town. Even the craziest rumor becomes fact by the time it gets to the third set of ears.'

'No, it wasn't a heart attack,' Nicky affirmed. 'He choked to death. His wife even said so. They ruled it an accident, but a lot of folks know better. I know better. The son of a bitch was murdered.'

'Murdered by whom exactly?' I asked.

'Oh, come on, Kate. Do I have to spell it out? First Artie and the potato, now Ellie's daughter in the woods, killed the exact same way Del was. It's her, Kate. It's got to be her.'

I wasn't following. Or maybe I didn't want to follow. Not going down that road, no sir. Not me.

'What are you talking about, Nicky? Her who?'

'*Del.*'

I paused a moment before saying anything. I thought about the stories I'd grown up hearing, how they got more tangled every year. Through her murder, Del took on mythic status. Three decades of kids had grown up not being able to say when New Canaan had been incorporated, or the name of the tribe of Native Americans who called the whole valley home first, but they all knew the Potato Girl stories. The jump rope rhymes. The jokes. Kids at slumber parties would sit in front of a mirror in a darkened room, chanting *Potato Girl, Potato Girl* until she appeared, sending them screaming for the light of day.

Del would have loved it, of course. Relished her power to inspire fear. But to propose that these stories were real? That there really was a Potato Girl — Del back from the grave — who haunted the woods, seeking revenge, actually killing people. Did they believe in the Headless Horseman, too?

It was one thing for a twelve-year-old kid like Opal to entertain such ideas, but a grown man?

The Nicky I saw before me was no longer the tall beautiful boy of my childhood, but he seemed no less sincere. It struck me how heavily his grief and guilt weighed on him. It would almost be a comfort to believe that his little sister, so sly and brave, had outwitted even death. But not me. I wasn't going there. The only ghost I believed in was sweet little Casper, and I planned on keeping it that way.

'Nicky,' I began with my best ex-psych ward aide smile, placing my hand gently on his knee, 'I think that Wild Turkey is getting to you. Halloween was a week and a half ago.'

He shook his head, frustrated.

'I know it sounds crazy, but just think for a minute. Just ask yourself, what if I'm right? If it is Del then she might come after us, too. I mean, think about it. Remember how angry she was the day before she was killed? If she's going around picking off people she's pissed at, we're on the list.' He sloshed the liquor in his bottle, looked down at the splintery wood between his big work boots. 'You better believe we're on the list.'

The front door to the house opened behind us and we both turned our heads, startled. I jerked my hand away from his knee, guilty as a schoolgirl.

'Who are you?' my mother asked, leaning down to see Nicky's face in dim evening light. She looked at me with a touch of panic. 'Who is he?'

She was covered with bright smears of acrylic paint. She'd rubbed it on her clothes, her face. The bandages on her hands were like smeary rainbows. She'd told me earlier she was going to work on a painting, but I'd assumed she'd forget this idea before it went anywhere. Raven had said my mother hadn't painted in months. And with the amount of medication I'd pumped into her that day, I was amazed she was standing, much less working on her latest masterpiece.

'I'm Nicky Griswold, ma'am.'

'You live at the bottom of the hill.' She gestured with her bandaged hands.

'I used to.'

'I'm so sorry about your sister. Poor thing.

When's the funeral?'

Nicky looked from my mother to me. Now he was the one looking panicked.

'Uh, we had it, ma'am.'

'She's at peace then?'

'I suppose so,' Nicky mumbled.

'Good. The dead need to be at peace.'

'Yes, ma'am,' he agreed, rising to his feet. 'It was nice to see both you ladies. I'll drop by again some time soon.' We watched him get in his truck and pull away. He unrolled the window and called out, 'Think about what I said, Kate. Just think about it. That's all I'm asking.'

'Who was that?' my mother asked as we watched his tail-lights go.

'A friend, Ma. Now what have you been up to in your studio?' She gave me a blank look. 'Let's go see what you've been working on, okay? Is it another still life?' I stood up and together we walked into the studio where my cot was. On the easel was a large three-by-four-foot canvas covered in smears of color — mostly reds, yellows, and oranges. There were a few flecks of blue and purple.

'Pretty colors,' I said, realizing it was something a mother would tell a four-year-old. My mother's illness was giving us a serious case of role reversal.

'It's the fire,' she told me. 'The fire that

gave me the stroke.'

'You didn't have a stroke, Ma.' I let myself touch her bony shoulder, some gesture of comfort that seemed to go unnoticed. My mother stepped away from me and up to her painting.

'She's in it.'

Jesus. That again.

'Who is?' I, too, moved closer, standing directly behind my mother's small frame.

'Don't you see her?'

I studied the canvas, saw only thick slashes of acrylic paint.

'No, Ma, I don't. Come on, let's get you cleaned up. It's nearly time for dinner.'

'I'm not hungry,' she said.

'You've got to eat.'

'Where's Magpie?' She whipped her head around, abruptly desperate. 'What have you done with my Magpie?'

★   ★   ★

After we'd eaten dinner and I'd given my mother her nightly sedatives and put her to bed, Opal came by.

'I saw Nicky Griswold's truck here earlier,' she said.

'He stopped in to say hello,' I told her, my voice a little too defensive. Shit, there I was feeling like I had to explain myself to a twelve-year-old. How did that happen? And why was it that lately, whenever I saw Opal, she put me on edge? I guess it was all her questions about Del, the way they were bringing me back, making me remember a whole chapter of my life that I never wanted to open again. To say nothing of the fact that sometimes, when I looked at Opal, I was sure I was seeing Del. It was almost like, through her obsession, Opal was *becoming* the dead girl. Crazy, I know, but that's how it seemed.

'Hey, how's the biplane coming?' I asked.

'Great! I've finished the fuselage, which is the hardest part.'

She looked around the room a minute, then, rather pensively, brought up the real reason she'd stopped by.

'I've been wondering if maybe Del's after me because of something having to do with my grandparents. If maybe they could have been connected to her murder somehow,' she said.

I couldn't help but laugh. It was a nervous laugh, but a genuine one.

'Doe? She barely knew Del. And she was the biggest pacifist I ever knew. She cried when she hurt an earthworm with a spade in the garden. And your grandfather, well, you probably heard he was a suspect but was cleared.'

'Maybe they were wrong in clearing him,' she said.

'I don't think so. He did a lot of things wrong, but he would never hurt someone like that. He had a good heart. And the so-called evidence they had linking him to her was totally faulty. It was just a big misunderstanding.'

'But how do you know?' she asked.

Because I was the cause of the misunderstanding.

'I just do. Trust me on this one.'

Opal left, dissatisfied, after asking me some pretty graphic questions about Del's murder that I decided it was best not to answer. The kid was already having nightmares; no need to give them more fuel. She'd had enough of a horror finding her dead friend. And from her description, it sounded like exactly the same scene Nicky came upon the afternoon he found Del. But Opal didn't need to hear that.

After she'd gone, I lay in bed and thought things over. Like it or not, it bothered me that Tori had been wearing Opal's jacket. What if Opal was right? Not about the ghost part, but what if the killer, who I was sure was all too human, was really after her?

But who on earth would have any reason to want to hurt Opal?

Later that night, I woke up and heard my mother talking. My first thought was that the cat had come back and my mother was filling her in on all that she'd missed. The truth is, I never could manage to lock my mother in her room at night. Each evening I would try, standing before the door to her bedroom, my hand on the brass padlock, but I couldn't bring myself to do it. It felt wrong, and I realized I wasn't capable of being my mother's jailer. So I slept with the door to my room open, thinking I'd hear her if she got up. That I was a light enough sleeper to catch her before she got out of the house.

I padded out into the living room to find my mother talking on the telephone. The only light in the house came from the moon through the frosty windows. The fire had gone out and the cabin was cold.

'Who are you talking to, Ma?'

My mother was crying. She dropped the handset, letting it bounce on its curled wire, banging against the floor and wall. I reached down and picked it up. The plastic was warm.

'Hello?' I said, keeping an eye on my mother, who had dropped to the floor crying. 'Who is this?'

'Emergency services. What's your name, please?'

Jesus. What next?

'Oh God, I'm sorry. I'm Kate Cypher. That was my mother, she has Alzheimer's. I'm so sorry.'

'She says you killed her cat.'

So this was how it was going to be. I sighed, feeling six days' worth of frustration rising to the surface.

'I'm sorry. Like I said, she's sick.'

'She says you know a girl who was murdered.'

That did it. I'm a calm and patient person. I don't usually lose my cool, especially with authority figures, but my pleasant little facade had been developing hairline cracks since the day I'd arrived.

'Oh *did* she? Are you hearing me? She. Has. *Alzheimer's*! She's talking about something that happened when I was a little girl! She doesn't know what year it is, or how to make pancakes, or who's dead and who's living, okay? Just forget it! Why can't you people just let things go? Jesus!'

'Ma'am, I — '

I slammed the phone down on the quiet, sensible voice and got my mother back to bed.

7

'You friends with the Potato Girl?'

I studied the girl below me on the monkey bars — Ellie Bushey. She had a freckle-covered snub nose and smelled like strawberries.

I didn't say anything. Ellie had been following me from one spot to another all through recess, her nearly identical sidekick, Samantha, close behind. Samantha had lost patience finally and joined a game of hop-scotch at the edge of the playground.

'I'm just asking because Travis said he saw you two standing there talking when the bus picked you up this morning,' Ellie continued, squinting up at me. 'He's seen you talking to her a few times now.'

My face grew hot. If Ellie knew, word would spread fast, and by the end of the day everyone would know my secret. Soon I'd have my very own rhyme.

'Just 'cause I talk to someone doesn't mean we're friends. You're talking to me now, right? Does that mean you're my friend?' I asked,

140

looking down at Ellie, who scrunched up her pale, dotted face while she thought of an answer.

'You might be. I have lots of friends.' She studied me as she said this, like she was looking to see if I was potential friend material. Me, the freak hippie girl. I knew I didn't have a chance, but I let myself imagine it anyway. Me and Ellie playing on the monkey bars. Sharing a table at lunch. Passing notes in class.

'I already have a best friend — Samantha — so you couldn't be my best friend,' she continued. It was a tease. A game. She had me going for a minute, then the bottom dropped out. 'But I couldn't be friends with anyone who liked the Potato Girl. Not now, not ever.' She shook her head and turned away from me to emphasize her point.

'Maybe I don't really like her. Maybe I'm just pretending,' I suggested, scrambling, desperate to get her to turn around. I succeeded. She spun back and narrowed her eyes at me.

'Why would you want to do that?'

'To spy,' I told her, thinking fast on my feet. 'To gather information.'

'What kind of information?' Ellie asked, looking at me skeptically.

'Good stuff. Secret stuff. Things about the

Potato Girl that only I know.'

'Like what?'

'There's a lot.'

'Tell me one thing.'

'Okay,' I said. 'She has these pigs, right? And one of the pigs ate three of her babies, leaving just the tails. You know what happened to the tails? Del kept them. She's got them saved in a canning jar full of alcohol in her room. She looks at them each night before bed. They're the first thing she sees when she gets up in the morning.'

Ellie laughed. 'Oh my god! Sick! Why would she do that?'

I shrugged my shoulders. 'Who knows why she does the things she does? I'm not saying I get it, I'm just saying there're things I know about Del. Lots of things.'

'Sam's gotta hear this,' Ellie said. 'You have more stories like that?'

'Lots.'

'All gross?'

'Some are gross. Others are just weird.'

The bell rang, signaling that recess was over.

'Tell me more tomorrow,' she said and I smiled.

Just like that, I saw how Del's friendship might buy me the friendship of Ellie and Sam — who had their own large circle of friends that I imagined myself fitting into, like a missing link in the chain. And I told myself I wouldn't necessarily need to betray Del. I could make up whatever I told the others. I would throw a few pieces of truth in here and there, but mostly I would tell them what I thought they really wanted to hear: the very gross and very weird details of the Potato Girl's life.

* * *

When I met Del in her field that day after school, Nicky was with her, shouldering his rifle. He didn't make eye contact with me. The peas had grown and were working their way up the wire trellis, pale tendrils grabbing and clinging. The crow stank, its feathers greasy and ragged.

'Deputy Desert Rose,' Del greeted me, her face serious. 'Today we're going hunting.'

I fell in beside them and we began to follow the path up the hill, listening to the birds sing around us. The *dee-dee-dee* of chickadee flocks, the trill of a lone hermit thrush. It was a perfect late-spring day. The combination of the afternoon sun and brisk walk had us all sweating.

'What are we hunting for?' I asked, breaking the silence.

'Tigers, squirrels, whatever we find,' Nicky answered, smiling at me at last. Del caught him and he looked away.

'Traitors,' Del hissed, but she said it so quickly that it came out as a blur. *Traders*, she could have said. Trailers. Trainers. Trains. Maybe we were hunting train robbers.

Again, no one spoke. Our feet crunched in the leaf litter and sticks on the path. Nicky adjusted the gun, resting the butt against his shoulder, squinting down the barrel as he searched for a target. We turned toward the cabin. Nicky took aim at a chattering red squirrel in a tree. He pulled the trigger and missed. The squirrel jumped down and scampered off, scolding us.

'Pisser!' Nicky exclaimed, using the back of his hand to wipe the sweat from his eyes.

'Good try,' I told him, knowing even as I spoke that it was a stupid thing to say. I glanced sideways at Del just in time to catch her roll her eyes. Ahead of us, the little cabin was coming into view, a strange leaning island in a sea of ferns.

It was much cooler in the cabin but the musty mouse smell made my throat tighten. Del went up the ladder first, me next, Nicky and the BB gun right behind me. Del lit three cigarettes in her mouth at once, sucking hard to get them started, then passed Nicky and me ours. Nicky laid the gun down on the bed and picked up a dirty magazine. He leafed through it quickly, flipping pages like he was looking at some boring business journal or something. I was trying to look at the pictures without seeming like I was interested, just the way he was. I was so focused on the magazine, on Nicky, that I wasn't even noticing Del. She had Nicky's BB gun pointed right at my forehead before I'd even realized she'd moved. She pushed the gun forward so that the metal mouth of the barrel pressed against my skull. I held my breath. Didn't move a muscle.

'What the hell are you doing?' Nicky asked, his voice more irritated than scared as he looked up from the magazine.

'Interrogation time,' Del answered. 'Desert Rose, what were you doing talking to Ellie today at school?'

'Just talking.' I let myself exhale as I whispered the answer, then took a slow gulp of air.

'About what?'

'Nothing.' I kept my eyes on the worn mattress, afraid to look up.

'That's bull. No one talks about nothing.'

'It was nothing. Nothing important. I don't even remember. I guess she's trying to be my friend or something. Something dumb like that. No big deal.' The barrel of the gun was cold and hard against the middle of my forehead. I knew it was just a BB gun, that it wouldn't kill me, but it would hurt and leave a hell of a dent in my head. I believed Del would pull the trigger if I said the wrong thing.

'You're *my* deputy! My friend! You swear allegiance only to me!' Her voice was frenzied, so loud and shrill it made my teeth ache.

I stared up at her, gave a careful nod.

'Say it! Say you swear allegiance only to me!'

'I swear allegiance only to you.'

'And you'll do whatever I tell you!'

'Anything you tell me.'

''Cause I'm sheriff of this whole rotten town!'

'You're sheriff.'

'And I'm your best friend,' Del added, her voice calm now, quieter.

'You're my best friend.'

'Forever,' she said.

'Forever,' I promised.

'Okay, you two,' Nicky said, leaning over and guiding the barrel of the gun away from my head, pushing it down to the ground, 'now kiss and make up.'

'Girls don't kiss girls,' Del spat back at him.

'The ones in this book sure do,' Nicky

answered, gesturing to the magazine. 'Well then, shake on it at least.'

Del set down the gun and extended her hand to me. I took it and as we shook, her grimace turned into a satisfied smile. Then Del leaned forward and kissed the middle of my forehead, right where the indentation of the gun barrel must have been. Her lips were cool and clammy. Her breath smelled like hot wind through a damp cave.

'Now let's go hunting!' Nicky said, leaning over to pull the gun from off the floor and set it in his own lap while he stubbed out his cigarette in the dented tuna can.

*   *   *

We spent an hour or so roaming through the woods on the hill, hunting tigers, crocodiles, wildebeest. Every time we heard a sound, Del would say it was some new and improbable animal: hippopotamus, wild boar, python.

As we walked through the woods, scouting for prey, we talked about how stupid those girls at school were. Del said they deserved to be put in their place.

'Ellie and Sam think their shit don't stink,' she said.

'Maybe we can bring them down a peg,' I suggested.

'How?' Del asked.

'I dunno for sure yet. But I have an idea.' And I did. A plan that came together in my mind fast and hard. 'I could spy on them. You know, pretend to be their friend and get them to trust me. Then I could learn some bad secret about them. Something we could hang over their heads.'

'What kind of secret?' Nicky asked, interested in the downfall of these girls he didn't even know.

'I dunno. But everybody's got secrets, right?'

'You think even girls like them have secrets?' Del asked, her thin eyebrows raised, her right hand fluttering absently above her heart, playing with the fabric of her dirty blouse, protecting her own secret.

'One way to find out,' I said.

'Okay, Deputy. Your orders are to spy on the enemy camp. But you have to tell me everything you learn. I mean everything. And if you fail, you go on trial for treason.' She pointed her finger at me with this warning, turning her hand into a pistol. Then she fired right into my chest, laughing.

I agreed to Del's conditions, and silently congratulated myself for my skillful manipulation — now I had free rein to be friends with both Del and the other girls. The perfect plan.

After a lot of whining, Del convinced Nicky to give her back the gun. She said she felt lucky and he gave in at last not only because he was sick of her pestering, but because once again, she threatened to tell on him — to reveal his big secret to the world.

Del was about ten paces ahead of us, aiming the gun into tree-tops. Nicky was close beside me and reached out to take my hand. We walked like that for several minutes — Del concentrating on the hunt, Nicky holding my hand tight, like he might never let go.

Suddenly, Del fired at something in a fir tree and let out a shriek of delight. Nicky dropped my hand and we ran to see what she'd shot. Only when it hit the ground did I see what it was: a mourning dove. It was still alive, a sleek gray bird with a pointed tail, fluttering its wings as we approached, moving itself in frantic circles.

I can't say how long we stood in silence watching that poor dove struggle on the forest floor. I can say only that it felt like hours, and when the bird finally gave up, stopped moving, its wings resting at odd angles in the pine needles and maple leaves, Del dropped down on her knees to touch it. She stroked it tenderly and held it in her hands like it was ever so fragile. She turned the bird in her hand, and her fingers found the place on its chest where the BB had entered — a small, bloody hole in the putty-colored breast. She carried the dead bird the whole way home and even then did not let it go, hiding it in the soft folds of her shirt before turning to go inside with no good-bye, Nicky following solemnly behind her, no final words spoken.

8

That night, after Nicky tried to convince me
that Del's ghost was murdering people, after
I'd finally started locking up my own mother,
I dreamed of Patsy Marinelli. *The dead can
blame,* she kept saying. *Tell me, what's the
worst thing you've ever done?*

When I woke up, the sun was just starting
to rise and I had that feeling again that
someone had been watching me while I slept.
I counted to three and checked the back
corner — nothing. Then I looked over at my
mother's painting of the fire on the easel. It
was too dark to make out the details, but as I
studied the shapes of dark against light, I saw
that hidden in the high left corner of the
painting was what appeared to be a pair of
eyes looking back at me, watching. Then, in
my half asleep state, it seemed that they
moved. Gave a sidelong glance in my
direction.

I damn near fell out of bed. I lit the oil
lamp on the crate next to my cot with shaky

151

fingers, carried the light over to the painting, and saw that, of course, there were no eyes, no face. Just bold strokes of bright color — not much different from a child's finger painting. Nicky's ridiculous ghost story had gotten to me after all.

I pulled on my slippers and searched for my watch, sure I'd left it on the crate next to the cot. But it wasn't there. I thought maybe the cat had knocked it down, then remembered the cat was AWOL. I scrabbled around on the floor and couldn't find it.

'Shit,' I mumbled.

I'm sort of unnaturally attached to my watch. It's a fancy diving watch with a lighted digital readout, alarm, stopwatch, timer and all those other bells and whistles. It was Jamie's but I inherited it when he bought his first Rolex. I've never been diving but I like going into the shower and hot tub with it, knowing I *could* go diving any time I wanted and still be able to keep excellent track of the hours, minutes, and seconds as they passed. And, pathetic as it may be, I like knowing that it was Jamie's. My wedding band went long ago, but the watch remains.

After my futile search, I shuffled into the kitchen, the oil lamp swinging in my hand, my wrist feeling small and naked without the clunky old watch. It was a cold morning and I eagerly started a fire in the cookstove and filled the blue enameled coffee perker with water, measuring ground beans into the basket before setting it on a burner. I opened my mother's bedroom door and peered in to find her fast asleep. I gently closed the door and turned back towards the kitchen. That's when I heard it. A meow — soft, yet insistent — coming from outside.

'Magpie?'

I held the front door open and waited hopefully. No cat. Had I imagined it? Surely not.

There was only the surprise of fresh snow — the first of the year. I ducked back inside, pulled on a coat and boots over my pajamas, and stepped out into the white morning. There was a little less than an inch of soft, fluffy snow covering the steps and yard. The bowls of tuna and milk were empty, and I was sure my mother's cat was close by. An image rose tantalizingly in my mind: me gently settling the cat next to my mother's sleeping form, her pure delight when she awoke and found a somewhat bedraggled — but healthy and whole — Magpie in bed with her. Kate saves the day. But I saw no cat tracks leading up to the empty bowls. What I saw in the half-light of dawn looked an awful lot like human footprints. Small footprints. The impressions a child's boots might make.

My still-sleepy brain tried to make sense of what I was seeing. A feral child in the woods with a taste for tuna and milk?

The tracks led up to the bowls, then back down the steps, leaving the same way they'd come — across the driveway and into the woods. I took a deep breath of cold, snow-scented air and began to walk beside the tracks, letting them take me right to the path that led down the hill. It was the path I used to follow on my way to and from Del's every day that spring long ago. The path I'd caught Opal coming up the day before, poking at the grass with a long stick as if she were looking for snakes. I hadn't been down the trail since the day before Del's murder, and though I wished for a long stick, it sure as hell wasn't snakes I was afraid of.

The Volkswagen-size rock that Del and I hid behind once, listening to the voices of the women baking bread, was to the left of the path's entrance. *Disrespectful*, Mimi had said to Doe. And only later did I realize who they were talking about. Only later would Raven's true father be identified, shaking up all of New Hope.

I rested against the cold boulder, inhaling the scent of wood smoke from my mother's chimney and staring down the path at the two sets of small footprints, one coming, one going. I am, by nature, a curious person. I don't like unsolved mysteries. I pushed off from the rock and stepped into the woods, determined to find the child.

I could almost hear Del's footsteps coming after me, feel her hand on my shoulder. *Boo,* she said. *My best friend's living in a goddamned for-real Indian tepee.*

The old path to the Griswold place was overgrown but not impassable. Some of the saplings trying to grow in the middle of the trail had been recently trimmed, showing that someone had worked to keep the path clear. Opal was the only one I had seen using it, so maybe it was her handiwork. But these tracks looked too small to be Opal's — she was a tall girl, like her mother. My feet in their boots sank into the soft snow, just as the child's feet had. I continued on, my heartbeat quickening. I felt slightly dizzy. Disoriented. Part of me was ten again, hurrying down to Del.

Catch me if you can.

The tracks turned right onto the side path that led to the old leaning hunting camp, as I had somehow known they would. I stopped there at the fork, my heart thudding, and tried to convince myself to go home. Turn around. The coffee would be ready and in another hour or so the sun would melt the snow and the footprints would be gone. I could tell myself I dreamed it. It was just part of the dream I had that started with Tiny Marinelli's warning: *The dead can blame.*

The few details I knew from the latest murder popped into my mind. Where had Tori's body been found? Near the old cabin? Would I come across lines of police tape? Would there still be signs of what had happened just a week ago? And just what *had* happened? Was it really possible that whoever killed Del had killed again? That he had been in town this whole time, waiting, watching, living his life? And *was* Opal the intended target? Each question I asked seemed more absurd than the last.

I felt that old sense of danger that being in the cabin used to give me and pulled my coat tighter around me, wondering if I dared go on. I mean, there I was at seven in the morning in flannel pajamas. I wasn't ready to go traipsing into a crime scene or come face-to-face with a killer. I hadn't even had my coffee yet.

Despite my quickened breath and the cool dread that filled me, it was too late to turn back. There I stood, looking down the path that led to the old cabin Del's grandfather had built. To a place I hadn't been since the day before Del's murder, when Del stormed out on me and Nicky, furious. Nicky said the building was still standing and I decided I needed to see for myself. There was nothing to be afraid of. It was just a kid I was chasing. I worked in a public elementary school after all — I could handle kids. I continued toward the cabin, eyes on the child's tracks in the snow.

The old hunting camp was closer than I remembered. And smaller. Like a slightly over-sized playhouse. There was no bright yellow police tape, no sign any crime had occurred either last week or thirty years ago. The front door was still missing and snow had drifted in. The small tracks led right through the cockeyed doorway. I stopped where I was and studied the crooked building. A house of cards, I thought. Just waiting to fall.

Then I thought I heard laughter inside — the soft giggle of a child.

'Who's there?' I called. 'Is that you, Opal?'

Silence.

'Come on out now, I know you're in there!'

More silence.

'You're not in trouble. I'm not angry with you. I just want you to come out.' I tried to fill my voice with an adult authority I did not feel.

There was nothing. No sound or movement.

'I'm going to count to three and then I'm coming in there. I mean it. One,' I said, shifting from one foot to the other, hoping to see a small frightened face appear in the doorway.

'Two!' I didn't want to go in there. Not then. Not ever. Seeing the dark little cabin was enough for me. I was ready to head home, make myself a steaming cup of coffee, and forget all about the footprints. I was too old to be playing Nancy Drew.

'Three!' Okay. It was just a child. A child playing games. Nothing to fear.

I mustered up my courage and stepped through the doorway. There was the same musty, mousy smell. The old cots were still along the walls, the potbellied stove was more rusted, but had not been moved. Nothing appeared to have changed. There had been no vandalizing, no *Ted luvs Ann-Marie* graffiti spray-painted on the walls. If kids had been there, they'd treated the place with respect; treated it like a shrine.

I looked under the cots and into the dark corners of the room. There was no sign of anyone downstairs. Then I heard a rustle from the loft. A soft scuttling that, absurdly, reminded me of a giant crab.

'Who's there?' I called.

Just a child. A tuna- and milk-stealing child. No claws or pincers, no hideous exoskeleton.

'Hello?'

I half expected a familiar voice to come back to me: *It's Del. It's Nicky. Come have a smoke.*

But that was thirty years ago.

I approached the ladder and started up, gripping each rung tightly and stopping with each step to listen. The ladder felt steep and dangerous, a sure sign that I was not ten anymore. The rustling happened again, then stopped. I clung to the ladder, nearly halfway up, holding my breath, listening.

'Is anyone there?' I called, my voice high and soft, despite my best efforts. There was no response. No more sounds of movement above me. I continued my climb, the ladder creaking a little.

My head came level with the loft's floor, and I nervously peeked over the edge at the open space, surprised yet relieved to see that I was alone. *Mice,* I told myself. *Squirrels.* Some trespassing rodent had made the sounds I heard. But wasn't I the trespasser? And what about the footprints? A kid doesn't just disappear into thin air. I scanned the empty space, not quite believing I was alone.

There was no mattress. No magazines. No place for a child to hide. There was only an old box of wooden matches, which had been chewed through by mice. Blue-tipped matches lay scattered, but there was something odd

159

about the way they were spread out, something orderly. I hauled myself up into the loft for a closer look. There, where the mattress used to be, someone had used match-sticks to make letters that spelled out:

FIND ZACK
DEPUTY

My heart did a slow crawl into my throat and I could feel it pounding there, choking me. The command in matches stared up at me, daring me not to do as it said. My mind raced for an explanation, spinning its wheels in sand until finally, a plausible idea occurred to me, putting me back on solid ground. Back in the land of the living. Opal, it had to be Opal, desperate to make me believe. Then it occurred to me that only one person other than Del knew my old nickname.

'Nicky,' I mouthed the name, my throat still too full of fear to make a sound. I kicked the matches away, scattering them.

'Son of a bitch,' I gasped. 'He knew I'd come here. Son of a *bitch*.' I backed down the ladder slowly, feeling tentatively for each rung beneath me. Once my feet were on the wooden floorboards, I heard a rustling in the loft again, but instead of climbing back up, I tore out of the cabin as fast as I could, my lungs aching for the fresh air.

The sun was up over the tree line, bright and blinding. The snow was melting quickly, taking with it the foot-prints I had followed. As I hurried back toward home, I wondered how Nicky had managed the trick with the footprints — he must have paid some kid to do it. He had set up the matches the day before, and then dropped by for a visit and set *me* up, talking about the old cabin. I had walked right into it — pathetic, really. But why had he gone to the trouble — to what end? To make me believe in ghosts? To send me on some wild goose chase back into my past? *Find Zack, Deputy.* What the hell could Nicky have to gain by my finding Zack, a man I had all but forgotten? A man who, last I heard, was up in Canada somewhere.

Zack had left New Hope shortly after Del's murder. The police brought him in for questioning a few times (as they had done to several of the residents of New Hope) and once he was cleared of suspicion, he packed up his books and guitar and hitched a ride out of town.

★ ★ ★

I walked quickly, fueled by my anger, and it was not long before I reached the boulder and saw the smoke rising from my mother's chimney. A hot cup of strong coffee was just what I needed to clear the cobwebs and imaginary giggles from my head. A figure stepped out of the cabin's front door and onto the steps. She turned my way, waving madly. It was Raven.

'Kate!' she called. 'Where's your mother?'

Shit. So much for that cup of coffee.

I started jogging through the slush.

'In her room?' I called back hopefully.

'No. Her door's unlocked and she's not in the house. I thought maybe she was with you. Where were you?'

'I went for a quick walk. I was gone only twenty minutes, a half hour at the most.' She shot me an exasperated look and I knew she was right — my mother could do a lot of damage in half an hour.

But would she come back with a knife this time? Dried blood on her bandages?

'Come on, we've got to find her. I think she went out to the road.'

I jumped into Raven's Blazer, self-consciously pulling my long coat closed to cover my pajamas.

'I thought I heard Magpie,' I told her, deciding not to mention the footprints. 'Opal wasn't out in the woods this morning, was she?'

162

'Jesus, Kate. Of course not. She was up at six and at the bus stop by six forty-five.'

I tried to picture the size of Opal's feet and the more I thought about it, the more I convinced myself she couldn't have made those tracks. They would have had to start at the big barn. These tracks seemed to begin and end at the old cabin.

Just some kid Nicky slipped five bucks. Some kid who had a talent for levitation. Maybe she swung her way to the cabin and back on tree limbs, Tarzan-style.

Raven and I wheeled out of the driveway, following what could've been my mother's tracks through the slush. They headed out of New Hope and onto Bullrush Hill Road, where we lost them. Raven continued down the road, both of us desperately scanning the woods on either side.

'Kate, this is exactly why she can't be on her own. I brought you some numbers. People to call about long-term care. There's a facility in St Johnsbury that would be perfect.'

'She doesn't want to go to a home.'

'I know. I know she doesn't. But you're a nurse, for Christ's sake. You must understand the situation. She's not going to get any better. There's this woman who teaches at the college — Meg Hammerstein. She wrote a book on dementia and runs a memory clinic

163

for Alzheimer's patients. I put her name and number in there for you, too. You should look her up.'

Raven was driving too fast. I strained to look into the brushy landscape rushing by. A snowshoe hare zigzagged across the road and into the woods. White as a ghost. Were ghosts white? Casper was white. White and harmless. Besides, there was no such thing as ghosts. Only desperate men playing elaborate games to make you believe. Damn him.

'It's got so that your mother's a danger to herself and others,' Raven continued. 'That fire could have been a real disaster. As it was, we just lost the tepee. But what if there had been someone asleep in there? What if Opal or I had been in the tepee? It was the middle of the night. It was only dumb luck that Opal was sleeping at Tori's and I was at my boyfriend's.'

'My mother didn't see anyone on the way to the tepee that night, did she?' I asked.

Raven took her eyes off the road and flashed me a look of disbelief. She glanced from my face to my pajamas and shook her head.

'Kate, it was three in the morning. Gabriel saw the flames from his window. He thought I was in there. He came running over in his underwear and found only your mother. She struggled with him. She bit his arm when he pulled her out — like she didn't want to go.'

Now it was my turn to shake my head, not in disagreement, but just because something didn't quite fit.

'She keeps telling me there was someone in there with her.'

'Sure she does. She's got people with her all the time, Kate — dead people, people she hasn't seen in ten years, young people who are now old. It's part of her illness. She can't differentiate between now and then. She can't tell who's there and who isn't.'

Maybe it's catching, I thought, remembering my wild goose chase this morning.

Raven slammed on the brakes when we got to the stop sign at the bottom of the hill. The Blazer skidded in the snow. The Griswolds' farm was on our left. The EGGS HAY PIGS POTATOS sign swayed in the wind by the side of the road. I thought of the pigs, how badly I once feared their razor-sharp teeth.

'Damn it!' Raven pounded the steering wheel with her gloved hand. 'Where the hell is she?'

* * *

Raven and I looked all morning for my mother. My penance for losing her was running all over town in my pajamas, asking everyone we came across if they'd seen her. Raven parked the Blazer and she and I went door to door — you haven't by any chance noticed an old lady in a nightgown traipsing through your flowerbeds this morning? Gabriel searched the grounds at New Hope. Jim at the general store called the state police for us, and got some volunteer firefighters together to search through the woods between New Hope and town. Raven and I finally returned to my mother's house to wait for word, only to discover that the phones were down again. The lines on Bullrush Hill seemed to go dead every time the wind blew or a few flakes of snow or ice fell. Sometimes they'd be out for days for no apparent reason at all. It had been this way as long as I could remember.

I put on some clothes while Raven started a pot of soup — she said she had to keep busy or she'd go nuts. I stood on the front steps and opened the pack of cigarettes I'd picked up at Haskie's, knowing how absurd it was. I haven't smoked since college. I'm a nurse. I jog many miles a week through the rainy hills of Seattle, only occasionally treat myself to a non-fat frozen yogurt, always choose the baked potato over the fries. But I sure as hell wasn't going to be calmed down by slicing up a bunch of carrots and rutabagas.

Opal surprised us by coming home from school early.

'What's wrong?' Raven asked.

'Headache.'

'Again?'

'I'm fine, Mom. I just needed to come home.'

Raven filled her in on my mother's escape, placing the blame heavily on me, which I willingly accepted. Opal offered to help with the soup and pulled up the sleeves of her sweater before getting started.

'My watch!' I said.

Opal looked puzzled, then touched it, smiled self-consciously, and took it off, handing it to me without explanation — almost as if she hadn't realized it was there. Like it had suddenly materialized from the ether as soon as she entered the cabin.

'Uh, I think I'm gonna go to the big barn and lie down,' she said, more to Raven than to me. In fact, she was studiously avoiding eye contact with me.

Raven nodded and Opal slunk away, shoulders hunched, eyes on the floor.

'She borrows things,' Raven explained once Opal had gone. 'She only does it to people she likes, so count yourself lucky. She would have given the watch back eventually. She doesn't mean any harm. Most of the time, I don't even think she's aware she's doing it.'

Now it was my turn to nod. Kleptomania with a touch of amnesia thrown in for fun. Add death threats from ghosts to that and some psychiatrist was going to have a field day with this kid.

When had Opal taken my watch? Surely I would have noticed if she'd done it during our visit last night. Did she sneak back into the studio once I was asleep? Was she to blame for my feeling this morning that someone had been in the room, watching me sleep? And had she come to visit before? If so, what, if anything, had she taken?

'I know she's becoming quite attached to you,' Raven said. 'But I have to ask again that you please not encourage these ghost fantasies. I don't want Del Griswold talked about. Not in any context. Have I made myself clear?'

'As crystal,' I said, buckling my watch on tight.

★ ★ ★

Around noon, we heard a car pull up in the drive and rushed out to see Nicky Griswold helping my mother out of his truck.

Raven ran to her and gave her a suffocating hug.

'Jean, you gave us such a fright!'

'Had to get some eggs,' my mother said. She looked at me and winked. 'I know you,' she said.

Raven put her arm around my mother and led her into the house.

'Where'd you find her?' I asked Nicky.

'She was walking around in the woods out behind our old place.'

'And what were *you* doing there?' Grateful as I was that he'd delivered my mother safely home, I was unable to hide the accusing tone in my voice.

'Just poking around. I had this crazy dream last night that the old cabin burned down. Someone was playing with matches.'

This was too much.

'Yeah, I bet you did.' I couldn't hold back any longer. 'Someone was playing with matches all right. That was a pretty strange idea of a joke, Nicky.'

He looked bewildered.

'Look, I just went out there to see if the cabin was okay, and I came across Jean in her nightie and slippers. I brought her straight back here. I knew you'd be worried sick.'

'Yeah, and what about yesterday? Were you out there yesterday, too? Is that when you did it? Was it before or after you talked to me? And where'd you find the kid who left the tracks this morning?'

He shook his head slowly, held his big hands up in a let's-all-calm-down gesture. He was going to do his best to make me feel as if I were the one who'd gone off the deep end. I couldn't believe I'd felt so drawn to him the day before — I was ready to throttle him now.

'Kate, I don't know what you're talking about. Sounds like you're the one who's been bit by the Wild Turkey.'

'*Find Zack, Deputy!* That's what I'm talking about. The message you left for me in the cabin. Pretty twisted, Nicky. I don't like being played with.'

'I didn't leave any message in the cabin. I haven't been to the cabin in months. Find Zack? That's crazy. Zack's right here in town. He teaches up at the college. We go out for a beer now and then.'

Nicky was a convincing liar and it made me furious. I took a ragged breath.

'I appreciate your bringing my mother home, but I'd like you to leave now.'

He looked like a dog that had been kicked in the belly. I almost regretted being so harsh.

'Look,' he said, chewing on his lip before continuing. 'There's something else. Something I found in the woods before I ran into your mother.'

He walked around to the back of his truck

and reached down into the bed to pull out a bundle wrapped in red cloth. I moved in for a closer look, suspicious but curious. Raven opened the door, came down the steps to join us, and reported that my mother was in dry clothes eating lunch.

'What's that?' Raven asked as she stared at the wadded-up flannel shirt in Nicky's arms.

He lifted up a corner and we saw a tuft of fur. I reached out and pulled the shirt back the rest of the way, letting out a stifled cry.

'Jesus!'

It was Magpie. Her throat was slit clean through, the white fur on her chest soaked in blood. Her body was soft and limp, the blood still damp. She hadn't been dead long. I jerked my hand away and rubbed it clean on my jeans.

'Jesus,' I said again.

'Your mother's, isn't she?' Nicky asked.

I nodded, glancing at Raven. Her eyes were huge.

'You think it was a fisher? Or a coyote?' Raven asked.

'It wasn't any animal.' Nicky shook his head slowly. 'Not a four-legged one, anyway.'

He reached into his pocket and pulled out a wadded-up red bandanna. He opened it up and took out a Swiss Army knife. I recoiled. It looked an awful lot like *my* knife. But they were common things. Red knives with a large blade and small, bottle opener, screwdriver, corkscrew. And *my* knife was tucked safely in my pocketbook, wasn't it?

'That cut on her throat is clean and straight, and I found this next to the body. Far as I know, fisher cats don't need Swiss Army knives.'

Raven shivered. 'Where'd you find her?'

'Out in the woods, along the path that runs between our old place and here.'

'Wait a minute,' Raven said, 'isn't that where you went for your walk this morning, Kate?'

'Yeah, but I didn't see anything. I thought I heard the cat out there, so I went to look.' I sounded unconvincing, even to myself. I knew better than to throw in the minor details of the child-sized footprints and the giggle I imagined in the cabin.

Raven folded the old shirt back over Magpie and took the cat from Nicky's arms, carrying the wrapped bundle over to her Blazer, where she laid it down carefully in the backseat.

'I'll bury her,' she said. 'We shouldn't tell Jean. We can't let her see this. It would wreck her. And I want that knife, Nicky.'

Nicky handed her the Swiss Army knife, nodded at both of us — his wordless good-bye — got in his truck, and backed out of the driveway. Raven followed, saying she'd be back later to check on my mother.

'Don't leave her alone again,' she said, her words more a warning than a request.

I stood a minute, listening to the car sounds fade. As I turned to go back into the house, my mother appeared in the doorway, holding a torn piece of bread topped with sliced turkey and an egg-sized glob of mustard.

'Where'd he go?' My mother asked. 'I brought him a sandwich. Such a nice man. If you weren't already married, I'd say you should settle down with him.'

'Nicky's a turd, Ma.'

'Who?'

'Nicky Griswold. The man who brought you home. The man you made the sandwich for.'

My mother nodded serenely.

'Such a nice man. His sister was killed in the woods. Poor thing. They slit her throat, you know.'

No. Del was strangled. It's the cat with the slit throat.

She took a bite of the mangled sandwich and wandered back inside.

'Poor little thing,' she mumbled, her mouth full of turkey and bread.

9

It was the last day of school, June 16, that my great plan backfired, as the plans of unpopular fifth graders desperate to make friends are doomed to backfire. I remember the date clearly, even now, because it was later that evening that Del's body was found. These two events — my betrayal and her murder — have become so strongly linked in my mind that it is like one could not have existed without the other. Other than her killer, I was the last person to see Del alive. And when I last saw her, she was running from me. Running as fast as her scrawny legs with their scabby kneecaps would carry her.

In those last weeks before both my fifth grade year and Del Griswold's life ended, things at New Hope were coming to a head. Life in the tepee had been far from peaceful. Lazy Elk, it turned out, was the father of Doe's baby, Raven. Mimi was the one to tell my mother, who — instead of tearfully, yet with quiet dignity, thanking Mimi for her

174

honesty — immediately accused Mimi of being a meddler and rumormonger who couldn't stand to see anyone else happy. Mimi stalked out of the tepee, with my mother shouting after her, 'You don't know anything *about* it!' Soon after that unhappy scene, Lazy Elk slunk through the tepee's flap, sent, no doubt, by Mimi or even Gabriel himself. He admitted that, yes, there had been one, or perhaps three or four, indiscretions with Doe, some time ago, but they had just been having a good time, you know, maybe they'd smoked a little, and it didn't have anything to do with his feelings for his Jeanie-Bird. Jeanie-Bird wasn't having any of it. She pummeled his chest, sobbing, saying, *Liar!* over and over. Then she told him to get the hell out.

There was a heated community meeting in the big barn that evening that went on past midnight. Doe's boyfriend, Shawn, was not in attendance — apparently he had hopped into his battered El Dorado and set off for California that morning as soon as he had learned Raven wasn't his. I was sent out after the first hour, when things began to turn nasty. I listened from time to time outside the door to the raised voices, the pointed accusations. Doe and my mother went at each other — Lazy Elk attempted to intervene, but they both turned on him. Everyone, it seemed, had some choice words for Lazy Elk. The problem, announced Gabriel again and again, was one of deception. No one was judging Lazy Elk for sleeping with Doe — after all, they were consenting adults, and nobody at New Hope bought into the patriarchal trip of obligatory monogamy, of ownership of one person's body by another. The issue was that he had lied to everyone about it, and had insisted that Doe cooperate in the lie. It was the lying he was on trial for and, in the end, found guilty of. The decision that came near one in the morning was unanimous — Lazy Elk was no longer welcome at New Hope. So the next day, Mark Lubofski packed his clothes, his table, and his jewelry-making supplies into his VW bus and got an apartment in town. No one was sure why he hadn't gone farther. He wanted to be close to the baby, some speculated. He still loved my mother and hoped she would take him back, was what a few murmured to one another.

I subscribed to the latter theory. In the days following his banishment from the hill, I would ride my bike into town and circle around his apartment building. Once, I caught him watching me from an upstairs window. I signaled for him to come down, and he just gave an awkward wave, then closed the curtain.

Before Lazy Elk moved out of the tepee for good, I stole something from him. It was a necklace he'd made from bits of carved wood, beer can pop tops, and a shotgun shell. I kept it under my pillow, my own talisman for calling him back to us.

Just days after Lazy Elk left, my mother took New Hope's youngest member (not counting myself and baby Raven) — nine-teen-year-old Zack, the college dropout — as her lover. My mother was forty-one, the same age I am now.

It was his heartbreak song that did it. He came by the tepee with his guitar after Lazy Elk had moved out the last of his things and sang my mother a song (an original this time, not one of Dylan's) — 'I wrote it thinkin' about what happened to you, Jean' — about how being wronged was no reason to close down your heart for good. I stood behind him and made gagging motions, trying to catch my mother's glance and crossing my eyes. But my mother, with tears in her eyes, hugged him tightly for so long that I thought she might never let go. I couldn't believe it.

'It's just a dumb song,' I said as she clutched him.

She flashed me a look over his shoulder,

banishing me from the tepee as well. I stomped out. When I came back later, Zack's guitar was next to the closed curtain that surrounded her bed.

'Just a dumb song,' I mumbled as I got into bed and clung to the necklace.

Zack, unlike Lazy Elk, seemed to have no expectations of me. He did not try to treat me like a daughter or go out of his way to befriend me. He did not take me on walks through the woods or tell me bedtime stories about Trickster Coyote. Zack barely acknowledged me, coming and going from my mother's bed like a thief with a nervous little smile on his face. If I stared at him long enough, I could make his ears glow red.

But the thing I remember most about their brief affair was how he made my mother laugh. I don't know what he said or did, but night after night, I would hear my mother's laughter from behind the curtain enclosing her bed. She would laugh quietly at first, a little embarrassed maybe, then her laughter became louder — uncontrollable, hysterical, almost weeping. And beneath this, I would hear the sound of his whispers, the rustle of sheets.

It was also around this time that my mother began to sew. Needlework was my mother's first foray into the world of arts and crafts.

After this, she would try weaving, pottery, and, finally, painting, which would stick, but in the beginning, my mother sewed.

She set up a little sewing table in the area of the tepee where Lazy Elk had made his jewelry — as if she had to fill that space somehow, make it her own. Her first project was a pillow with cross-stitching: *A Happy Home Is a Home of Love*. It seemed a funny message considering all that had happened in her own home. And a funny picture: a carefully stitched, square white house with neat blue curtains and perfectly symmetrical trees in the yard. I tried to imagine the tiny family you might see if you could open the door or pull back the curtain. I knew they'd be a different family than we were. The kids would have a mother *and* a father. A dog maybe. Hot running water. Steak dinners. The tiny people who lived in that house had nothing to do with our lives, is what I thought back then, at ten years old, watching my mother sew.

Sewing seemed to keep my mother happy, to give her something to help fill her days. And at night, she had Zack. After dinner, he'd play his guitar while she sewed, then they'd give each other a conspiratorial look and rush off to bed.

Desperate, I rode my bike down and left a

note in Lazy Elk's mailbox, telling him about Zack and that he needed to come home and make things right before it was too late. He never came. I guess he figured it was already too late, Zack or no Zack.

When I filled Del in on the saga of Droopy Moose (deciding to leave out the part about Zack) she laughed and said he must not have been so droopy after all. Not the important parts at least. I pretended to get the joke. I also pretended that it didn't matter that he was gone. No skin off my butt. He was just a dumb hippie with a goofy name anyway.

★　★　★

The day before school let out, I went to the field looking for Del in the afternoon, carrying the necklace I'd taken from Lazy Elk to give to her. No longer believing it held the power to bring him back, I wanted it gone. I was hoping to use it as a sort of conciliatory gesture: Del had not been entirely satisfied with the job I'd done spying on Ellie and Sam.

My double agent scheme had been going as planned for weeks. I simply told both sides what they wanted to hear, sprinkling the made-up stories with bits of truth. To win and keep the friendships of Ellie and Samantha, I reported that yes, it was true that the Potato Girl rode her pony naked — I even told them he was called Spitfire. I told them her bedroom was really the root cellar and that she knew how to shoot a gun.

I told Del that Ellie wore a retainer at night, that Samantha had an older sister who was retarded (both true), and that they were both secretly in love with school bad boy Artie Paris (this, of course, was pure fiction, but Del ate it up).

In the last week of school, both sides were desperate for the ultimate dirt. They seemed unimpressed with whatever tidbits I brought them. I was afraid of losing my hold on Ellie and Sam, who demanded that I bring them something really good. And Del was unmoved when I told her that both Ellie and Sam had had lice, warts, pinworm. I had to pull out the big guns.

So I told Del that Ellie had invited Artie over to her house and they ended up kissing. Del didn't believe me — she rolled her eyes, shook her head, and said simply, *No way.* I worked hard to convince her, making up details as I went along: they were in Ellie's basement, Artie forced Ellie into it at first, then she realized it wasn't so bad and gave in. I even told Del that Ellie, who didn't know any better, worried that she'd gotten pregnant from the kissing and was always asking her friends if they thought she was starting to show.

'Stuupid!' Del exclaimed, and I wasn't sure if she meant my story or Ellie thinking she was pregnant.

And to Ellie and Sam, I told a half truth, simply because I'd run out of lies. I told them I knew Del had a tattoo.

'No way!' they squealed. 'What of?'

We were standing in our usual meeting place, under the monkey bars. Other kids walked by, and I felt warm all over, proud and glowing to be seen talking with Ellie and Sam day after day. Only when Del watched us did I feel the cool pangs of guilt and regret.

'I'm not sure,' I told them. 'I only saw the edge of it when she was changing once.'

'Are you sure?'

'Swear to God. It's right on her chest.'

'It's probably a potato!' Sam suggested.

'The part I saw was all black,' I told them.

'A *rotten* potato!' Ellie cackled.

What I didn't know, what never occurred to me, so secure had I become in my role as informer, was that a boy named Travis Greene, who had a crush on Ellie, would also be told about the tattoo, and that he in turn would tell most of his friends, including Tommy Ducette, the fat kid and number-one henchman of Artie Paris. Nor did I know that on the last day of school, Artie Paris had something planned — his good-bye gift to Number 5 Elementary School and its graduating class of fifth graders.

★ ★ ★

When I could not find Del in the fields or root cellar, I decided she must be up at the cabin. I began to make my way from the root cellar to the woods, Lazy Elk's necklace tucked into my pocket, but was stopped by the excitement in the pigpen. One pig, it seemed, had gone crazy.

It trotted in circles around the pen, squealing — screaming, really. When another got in its way, the crazy pig would lash out, butting against it, biting.

I stood, pressed against the fence, trying to get its attention.

'It's okay, Pig,' I said. 'Come on now, Pig.'

But the pig just ran harder, faster, looking like it would take flight, like it thought if it just could run fast enough, it might be able to escape.

'You get away from them pigs now!'

I jerked away from the fence and turned to see Del's father standing before me, a man I'd only glimpsed from a distance. Ralph

Griswold was a tall man in dirty bib overalls, with large square shoulders and a boxy jaw covered in dark stubble. His black hair peeked out from under his cap and was just long enough to cover his ears. He had Del's pale gray-blue eyes.

About the only thing on earth that Del was afraid of was her own daddy and there he was, three feet away from me.

'I was . . . just looking for Del.' As I spoke, I noticed the man's hands, big as boards. In his right hand, he carried a large pistol.

'Well she ain't in the pigpen is she? Now get! You're worrying my pigs!' He waved his hand at me, the one that did not hold the gun. I took off running and when I got to the path, I heard a single shot, but did not dare to turn around.

I was out of breath when I made it to the clearing. My legs felt like rubber bands. I heard voices from inside the cabin and called out as I approached.

'Del? Nicky?'

My shouting was followed by silence, then I watched as a familiar figure hurried through the leaning cabin's doorway. It was Zack — the boy who made my mother laugh herself to sleep each night. He wore a white T-shirt and blue jeans with holes at the knees. He was barefoot, just like always. Zack had not worn shoes since I met him, except for a pair of red rubber boots he slipped on to go out in snow. I imagined my mother's sheets must have been filthy from the dirt he carried in on his feet.

'Hey,' he said when he saw me. It was the greeting he always gave, whether he was sitting down opposite me at community dinner in the big barn or crawling out from behind my mother's curtain first thing in the morning.

'What are you doing here?' I asked, truly perplexed. I watched as his ears reddened. I felt unsettled, like my two worlds had somehow slipped together without my knowledge or consent. I would've been just as surprised to find Del shoveling a loaf of bread into the oven at New Hope.

'Nothin'.' He shrugged, looked around the clearing as though I bored him. 'Just out walking. See ya, Katydid.' And with this, he was headed back down the path with his usual tall man loping gait. First, Zack invaded my life in the tepee, now here he was at Del's. Who did he think he was?

I stepped inside the cabin and heard rustling from the loft.

'Del?' I called. My mind raced. Had Zack been there to meet Del? Could he be the mysterious boy who gave her the tattoo? It dawned on me abruptly that Zack's last name was Messier — was that what the *M* stood for? My stomach churned at the thought.

'Just me,' Nicky's voice drifted down. He peeked his head through the loft's rail and smiled down at me. 'Come on up, Desert Rose. Have a smoke with me.'

I climbed the ladder. Nicky was sitting on the mattress. Beside it sat a good-sized bag of pot. The air was sweet with its smoke. It was a smell I knew well from New Hope. It was Lazy Elk's smell.

'What's new?' he asked as he handed me a Camel. His eyes were red and glossy. He was playing with the plastic-handled hunting knife, sliding it in and out of its leather sheath.

I breathlessly told Nicky about what I'd just seen down by the pigs, about meeting his father with the gun and the shot I heard fired. Nicky only nodded.

'That sow's not right. Hasn't been the same since she had the piglets. Daddy's turning her into bacon. One shot, right in the middle of the head.' Nicky turned his hand into a gun. 'Bang,' he said, then blew on his fingertip.

I was quiet a minute. Nicky sat smiling stupidly at me, looking like some part of him was far away.

'You've been smoking dope,' I said.

'And?' he asked, eyebrows raised.

'And how do you know Zack?'

'I know lots of people.'

'Well what was he doing here?'

'Bringing me this,' Nicky answered, nodding at the pot.

'He gives it to you?'

'No, dummy, I buy it from him. It's some good stuff. Want to try a little?'

'Nope.'

'Wimp.'

'Am not. For your information, I could smoke that stuff anytime I wanted at home.'

He shook his head, grinning now.

'You're *such* a wimp.'

'Bullshit,' I said.

'Ouch, the little lady swears. You been hangin' out with my trash-mouthed sister too long. She's what you might call a bad influence.'

'Funny, she says the same about you.'

'Double ouch. And tell me, Desert Rose, just what has Del told you about me?'

'That you're really just fourteen, not sixteen like you say, that you're B-A-D spells bad, and that you've got some kind of secret or something.'

'My oh my, how the baby sister talks. And did she say what this big secret I'm supposed to have is?'

'Nope. Just that I might not want to know you if I found out.'

Nicky chewed on his thumbnail.

'You really think if I told you, you might not want to know me anymore?'

I shrugged my shoulders, looked at his moist eyes, and thought, *No way.*

'What, did you kill someone or something?' I laughed.

'Nah, it ain't nothin' like that. It's . . . well, it's complicated. That's all.'

'I know all about complicated,' I said, thinking of the mess at New Hope.

'It's not that I think you wouldn't get it, it's just that I don't know how to explain it right. But I will. I promise. I'll figure it out and I'll tell you the whole story.'

'When?'

'Soon, Desert Rose. I promise.' He reached out and took my hand, looked down at it, then smiled his sly fox smile. 'I got another secret, though. Want to hear it?'

'I guess,' I said, disappointed that I would have to settle for some second-rate confession.

'Long as you promise not to run away and think I'm B-A-D spells bad and all that.'

I glanced at Nicky and he squeezed my hand. He was smiling at me, and his teeth were so white they seemed to glow. *Teeth are bones*, I remember thinking. This made me smile.

'I promise,' I said.

'Good. Now here it is. Lean closer so I can whisper it.'

I leaned in. Nicky's breath was warm against my ear and cheek. He smelled like marijuana and cigarettes, but under that I detected a musky smell, like sweat only more pleasant.

'I'd like to kiss you. I'd like it an awful lot. And I think you'd like to kiss me, too.' The words were moist puffs that seemed to hit my skin and sink in, warming the flesh beneath.

'Would you?' he asked, his voice low and more gravelly than ever. 'Would you like to kiss me, too?'

I nodded. Closed my eyes like the girls in movies did. His lips came against mine softly, like a butterfly landing, but once there, pressed harder. He took my lips between his and sucked them, pried them open with his tongue. His tongue worked its way around my mouth like some kind of grub seeking the darkest, dampest corner of my mouth. His teeth hit mine, clacking so hard I thought we would both walk away with chips like the one Del had. I wondered if that's how she got hers: from kissing.

Kissing seemed like getting into a train

189

wreck. There was that much force. That much danger. As we kissed, I remembered the sound of that single shot fired right into the brain of the pig. My own head buzzed. My teeth ached. I thought I tasted blood.

We kissed until our lips were swollen and our mouths dry. Until I forgot all about what bad secrets Nicky might have. I learned to use my tongue the same way Nicky used his. He gripped my shoulders so tight that I had bruises the next morning. His breath was coming so hard and fast that I thought he would turn blue and pass out.

'Hang on,' I mumbled, or tried to mumble as he kept pressing his mouth against mine. It could have gone on forever. And may have. But Del's voice stopped everything.

'TRAITORS!' she screamed, her voice filling the cabin, a force all of its own, more powerful than the train wreck that was our kissing, more startling than the crack of her daddy's pistol. We jerked apart and looked down from the loft just in time to see Del bolt out through the open doorway. I turned to Nicky, but there was no question of whether we should go on kissing. What I saw in his eyes was not love or lust or even guilt, but pure, stark fear.

We scrambled down the ladder after Del, but she was long gone. Nicky told me to head home. He said he'd find Del back at their place and patch things up. She might need some time to cool down, but he promised she'd be fine by morning. I pulled the necklace I'd brought for her out of my pocket.

'Give this to her,' I told Nicky. 'And tell her I'm still her deputy.' Nicky nodded, and went down the hill after his sister.

★ ★ ★

When Del wouldn't look at me, refused to even look up from the ground the next morning at the bus stop, I realized that Nicky hadn't been able to keep his promise to make things right. And although I wanted nothing more than to get down on my knees and beg her forgiveness, I was afraid. Afraid she would just humiliate me further, make me feel worse than I did.

I wanted to ask if Nicky had given her the necklace, make some joke about Droopy Moose, say it was true that I was her deputy always. Her best friend forever.

But the only thing I could think of to say was about that crazy sow.

'I heard your daddy killed a pig yesterday.' This at least got her attention. She raised her head and I saw that her left eye was black and

191

blue, nearly swollen shut. She looked at me with such fierce hatred that I was relieved to hear the bus coming, to see the flashers go on as Ron slowed to a stop and swung open the doors.

★　★　★

All my life I have wished I could go back and live two moments differently. I do not long to travel back through time and change the fate that led me to drop out of med school and get married, or the choice I later made to abort the only child Jamie and I conceived. No, odd as it may seem, the two instants I wish I could do over both took place on June 16, 1971, when I was ten years old.

The first was that morning at the bus stop. I would get down on my knees and beg forgiveness. I would promise whatever Del asked, do whatever she wanted. I would demand to know who had given her the black eye, and swear vengeance upon him, upon anyone who would hurt her.

The second thing I would take back was what happened later that day. It was, I believe in my heart, even now, the worst thing I've ever done. Yes, I abandoned my mother; yes, I aborted a child that I truly wanted; yes, I have been unkind and uncharitable a thousand

192

times. But this is the one thing that comes back to me in endless bad dreams, keeping me awake at night as I replay the scene again and again, imagining that it turned out differently, but knowing it was too late.

And still, I'm left with that last image of Del running from me, frightened. For years, this is how she's haunted me. I should have known she wouldn't let it go at that.

10

The morning after Nicky returned my runaway mother and her dead cat, the phones were back up. I took out the list Raven had given me and made some appointments to visit nursing homes, and also phoned Meg Hammerstein — the memory specialist — who offered to see me that afternoon. I called over to the big barn and Gabriel agreed to come sit with my mother while I was out. Apprehensive as I was about putting my mother in a nursing home, it felt good to be making calls, crossing things off my list. Gabriel was overjoyed that I'd finally put things in motion.

I was jotting down some questions to ask Meg when the police knocked on the door. They were the same two men who'd been by to question me about the night of Tori's murder, then returned to ask about Del — they wore plainclothes and carried their badges in their pockets, their guns strapped into shoulder holsters. They reintroduced themselves — detectives Stone and Weingarten. I stood out on

194

the steps talking with them, leaving my mother inside, busy with her oatmeal at the kitchen table.

'We understand you've been out walking in the woods,' Stone began. He was always the one to do the talking; the other guy just seemed to take notes.

'Sure. And?'

'Were you out in the woods the night Tori Miller was killed?'

'No, I told you already. I was home all night with my mother.'

He nodded, then raised his eyebrows. 'With your mother who has a questionable memory.'

'She has Alzheimer's.' My voice shook a little. I strained to stay in control.

'Tell us about your mother's cat.'

'Magpie?' The absurdity of the question caught me off guard.

'The young lady . . . Raven, showed us the cat. She said you were in the woods a few hours before the cat was found.'

That's when I lost my temper.

'Just let me get this straight — Raven thinks I killed Magpie. That's great. Did she mention a *motive*? Do I make out like a bandit in Magpie's *will*?' They both stared at me, expressionless. 'Listen, I *liked* that cat,' I finished lamely.

'The night before last, we understand your

mother called nine-one-one and reported that you'd hurt her cat. She also said you knew the girl who was killed. Did you know Tori Miller?'

'No! I never even heard of her until a few days ago. My mother is sick and very confused. How many times do I have to explain that to you? Jesus, you met her. Didn't you pick up on the fact that she's suffering from dementia? She was talking about Del Griswold. She was saying I knew Del thirty years ago!'

'Why don't you tell us again about your relationship with Delores Griswold.'

Here we go again. It always came back to Del.

I took a breath. Regained my composure. 'There's nothing to tell. She lived at the bottom of the hill. We rode the bus together. That's all.'

'One more thing, Ms Cypher,' Stone said. 'Do you own a Swiss Army knife?'

I thought about lying, but it seemed silly. 'Yes, I do. It's in my pocketbook.'

'Would you mind getting it?' he said.

'Not at all.'

My pocketbook was on the table by the door and I opened it and began rummaging through it. Powder compact. Keys to the rental car. Key ring from home. Cell phone that was totally useless in the hills of Vermont. Pack of spearmint gum. Assorted pens.

'I'm sure it's here somewhere,' I said. 'Everything but the kitchen sink seems to be.'

I got no response. It was a pretty lousy joke anyway.

I unzipped the seldom-used side pocket, feeling something hard stuffed into it. Had to be the knife. But what I saw made me nearly cry out.

'Got it, Ms Cypher?' Stone asked.

'No, it doesn't seem to be here.'

My hands were trembling slightly now. My right hand was stuffed into the purse, touching what I prayed neither detective had caught sight of because if they did it was *Go to jail, go directly to jail* for me.

Tucked into the side pocket of my leather purse was Del's old silver sheriff's star.

I'm sheriff of this whole rotten town.

My upper lip and forehead were damp with perspiration.

Just breathe, I told myself. *Act natural.*

'Could this be your knife?' Weingarten asked, holding out a small plastic bag with a red knife inside.

I squinted at the bag.

'I don't know. It looks like that. Maybe. But I always keep my knife in my pocketbook.'

And now it's gone. Replaced by Del's star.

Did whoever took the knife give me the star? Was this some kind of setup? And how long, exactly, had my knife been missing? How long had I been carrying that star?

Breathe. Do *not* panic now.

'Well, we're running some tests on the knife.'

'Tests?'

'Blood tests. Just to make sure it's only cat blood on the knife. Ms Cypher, would you consent to being finger-printed?'

'What? No! I mean, it's a waste of time. The whole thing is absurd. I did not kill the cat, even if it turns out it was my knife that was used.'

But I am holding on to Del's old sheriff's star, right this moment as we speak.

'If we find anything to connect this weapon to Tori Miller's murder, I'm afraid we'll have to bring you in and get those prints,' Stone said.

I slowly pulled my hand out of the bag, making sure the star was tucked into the deepest, darkest corner of the pocket, then zipped it up tight.

Was I being framed? And if so, how far did the killer go? Was my little yuppie wine-and-cheese knife used to cut off a piece of Tori Miller's skin?

I gave an involuntary shiver.

'Is that all, gentlemen? I have to get back to my mother.'

'We'll be in touch,' said Stone.

★ ★ ★

I was in a low, brick, ivy-covered building of faculty offices looking for Meg Hammerstein and trying desperately not to think about my missing knife or the dead girl's star in my purse when I saw the name on one of the doors — Zachary Messier.

Find Zack, Deputy.

Well, here he was, only it felt more like he'd found me.

The door stood slightly ajar and when I peeked in, I saw a man with a receding hairline and a goatee sitting behind a desk. His hair, once a vivid auburn, was now dull and giving way to gray but still long, worn back in a ponytail. He'd filled out over the years and looked the part of the college professor: white shirt, open at the collar, tan corduroy jacket with elbow patches. The only out-of-character-for-a-professor thing was a large round silver pendant dangling from a strand of leather around his neck.

'Zack?' I called from the doorway.

'Hi!' he called back, smiling as he studied my face, struggling to put a name to it. He squinted over the top of the small rectangular glasses perched on the end of his nose.

'It's Kate, Jean Cypher's daughter.'

'Oh Jesus, sure. Of course. Raven said you were in town. Come in, please.' He gave a warm smile and gestured me in.

I made my way into the tiny office. The back wall was covered by shelves sagging with books. The ones that didn't fit on the shelves sat in piles all over the desk and floor — many of them seemed to be about the Revolutionary War. He had a couple of diplomas framed on the wall along with a picture of a group of people on a sailboat. It seemed he'd come a long way since his days at New Hope. Then I noticed the elaborate mandala painting and a guitar stashed in the corner, beside the desk. Maybe none of us really change, despite the diplomas, thinning hair, and spiffy wardrobe.

He stood up, the clunky silver pendant swinging out a little as he reached across the desk and took my hand, wrapping it securely in both of his.

'It's really good to see you, Kate.' His hands were as warm as his smile.

'I only have a minute. I'm actually here to see Meg Hammerstein.' I stood awkwardly, waiting for him to let go. When he did, he gestured toward the empty chair across the desk from him and I sat down.

'How's your mom, Kate?' I glanced down under the desk and was relieved to see he wore shoes. Black penny loafers polished to a shine.

'Um, not so good. I was hoping to get some advice from this woman Meg. Raven recommended her.'

'Meg's great. She'll be a wonderful resource.' He sighed, leaned across his desk, put one hand to his heart, and reached for mine with the other. He held my gaze, his blue eyes moist and sincere, the whites flecked with red. 'I'm so sorry about Jean. I get up there from time to time but work's been crazy the past few weeks so I haven't had a chance.'

I nodded understandingly.

On his desk was a plastic bag of cookies. He saw me eyeing them and offered me one. I declined. He helped himself.

'You sure?' he asked. 'Oatmeal carob chip. I'm addicted.'

I shook my head.

'I didn't even know you were in town. Last I heard you were in Canada.'

'I was. When I left Vermont I drifted around for a while and eventually ended up in Halifax, where I apprenticed as a boat builder. After a few years of that, I decided it was time to go back to school and ended up in Toronto. Once I got my Ph.D., I took a job teaching there. I stayed until just about two years ago, when I saw an ad in a journal for this position. It was like the job found me and told me it was time to come home.'

'New Canaan must seem pretty dull after Toronto,' I said.

'On the contrary. It's the best move I've ever made. My only regret is that I waited so long.'

I nodded, then my eyes went back to the sailboat photo on the wall.

'Is that my mother on the boat with you?'

He smiled and took the silver-framed picture off the wall and passed it to me for closer inspection. On the deck of the boat were Zack, Raven, Opal, and my mother, all with wind-tousled hair and sunburned cheeks.

'It was taken just last year. God, Jean loved the open water. She got such a kick out of the boat. She was a hell of a sailor, too. You should have seen her.'

'Is it your boat?'

He smiled proudly. 'She's moored up on Lake Champlain. Know what her name is? *Hope Floats*. An homage to New Hope. Gabriel was thrilled, but I haven't been able to get him out on the water. Too bourgeois, I guess.'

My mother had never mentioned these sailing trips to me. I didn't even know Zack was in town, never mind taking my mother out on Lake Champlain in his boat. How many little details of her life were there that I would never know now, gone for ever?

'So you and Raven have gotten to know each other?'

'Raven's wonderful. She's working on a psychology degree, you know. She's actually taking a class of mine now. She comes by to borrow books and bounce ideas off me. She's the one who baked the cookies. Sure you don't want one?'

I shook my head. Zack helped himself to a second cookie.

'And Opal,' he said. 'She's a hell of a kid. I've been so worried about her since her friend was killed. How's she doing?'

'Not great. Raven's made an appointment with a psychiatrist.'

'God, what a horrible thing to go through. I should call over there and see if there's anything I can do.' He brushed the crumbs out of his goatee.

I looked at his necklace, which I thought might be a small clock or pocket watch. It was thick enough to have tiny gears inside and looked like it had a catch on the top to open it up.

He saw me looking and held it out for closer inspection.

'Beautiful, isn't it? It represents the Wheel of Life. It's Tibetan.'

Engraved on the face were three concentric rings divided into spokes. The outer ring had twelve, the next six, and the final ring, two. In the center were a snake, a pig, and a rooster. Inside each spoke were other engraved pictures: a potter, a monkey picking fruit, a woman giving birth, and various gods and humans engaged in acts I couldn't identify from such a quick look.

'This outer ring represents the twelve links of causality,' Zack said.

I nodded as if I had the slightest clue what he was talking about.

'And here, in this ring, we have the six realms of existence: gods, titans, humans, animals, hungry ghosts, and hell.'

My eye was drawn to the image of the hungry ghosts: three ungainly creatures huddled together with long, thin necks and desperate eyes.

'Hungry ghosts?' I said.

'Those who, after death, are so attached by desire to this world that they remain ghosts, longing for food and drink but unable to partake.'

'That's rough,' I said.

He chuckled.

Then I noticed that above the wheel itself was a horrible face with fangs and furious eyes.

'And who's this fellow?' I asked, pointing.

'The God of Death. He turns the wheel.'

'So Death is turning the Wheel of Life? Isn't that sort of cruelly ironic?'

'It's really not as macabre as it seems,' he said.

You can give the hippie a Ph.D. and a membership at the local yacht club, but he was still a hippie deep down. I had to smile.

'Zack, can I ask you something that might seem kind of strange?'

'Sure. Not much is strange to me, though. Not for an old resident of New Hope.' He winked and settled back into his chair. Could this really be the nervous boy I remembered from my childhood, now so charming, so eager to please?

'I was wondering if you could tell me anything about Nicky Griswold. He did the oddest thing — left me this message that I should find you. Can you imagine why he might do that?'

Zack's jaw tightened a little and he drew in a breath. I'd hit a nerve. He stood up and walked behind me to close the door. I felt a little like the bad kid in the principal's office.

'What did this message say?' His head was cocked to one side, his eyebrows raised.

'Find Zack. That's all.'

He took a moment to gather his thoughts before continuing. He seemed to use the time to study the books on his shelves as if they held whatever answers he was looking for.

'Poor Nick,' he said at last, placing a hand on his chest again, but laying the other across his desk blotter this time. 'My heart goes out to him, it does. I just can't get involved anymore. The past is the past and he needs to let things go, walk his own path. Nicky comes around sometimes, wanting to go out for drinks. I've gone a few times, just for old times' sake, you know? I probably shouldn't have, but I did. But I may have sent the wrong message.'

'Message?'

'You know . . . ' There went the reddening ears I remembered so well. 'That I was, ah . . . interested again. Nicky's a great guy. I care about him, I do. And I'm not saying I have regrets about what happened back then, but we were kids, you know?'

I struggled to understand what he was getting at, not quite willing to jump to the conclusions he was leading me to.

'So, what, are you telling me you two had an affair?'

Zack studied me a moment, his whole face reddening this time. Then he laughed nervously, shook his head.

'Oops. I thought you knew. I don't mean to shock you. I guess you could say it was part of my free love period.' He grinned crookedly, then quickly looked away, eyes focused on his guitar. Was it the same instrument after all these years? The guitar he serenaded my mother with back in the tepee?

'God, Kate. I was sure he told you. You two were close for a while there. I was sure you knew.'

'I had no idea,' I admitted.

He plucked at his goatee.

'I was nineteen. I thought bisexuality was another road toward freeing the mind. Letting go of preconceived notions of gender and identity. Balancing the male and the female, the yin and the yang. God, it was 1971. It was *in* then.'

I nodded understandingly. I'm not a closed-minded person. It wasn't that I found the idea of Zack and Nicky sleeping together offensive, but it was quite a surprise. Nicky's determination to keep this a secret made sense to me, but I was a little hurt at the same time.

'Did Del know? I mean, about the two of you?' As I asked the question, I heard Del's voice in my head: *B-A-D spells bad*, she warned.

'Yeah,' Zack said. 'She walked in on us once. Poor kid. I think it scared the hell out of her. Then once it sank in, she held it over his head. Blackmail, really. She knew his big secret and she used it against him any way she could. She was really struggling to find her place in the world, wasn't she?'

I nodded, chewed my lip, wondered how far Nicky would go to keep Del from revealing his secret.

'Can I ask one more thing?' My voice came out small and timid. My ten-year-old voice.

'Why not? We've already dragged this many skeletons out of the closet — so to speak.'

'Did my mother know about you and Nicky?'

He hesitated, looking at me with what I imagined to be thorough consideration. I understood. I mean, this was my mother we were talking about. How in-depth do you want go when it comes to intimate secrets about someone's own mother?

For whatever reason, he decided to go for the full reveal.

'Sure she did. She thought it was sexy, I think. She said she didn't mind my being with a guy, but if I started sleeping with another woman, we were through. She didn't want any repeats of the Lazy Elk scene.' Here came his hand again, reaching for mine across the desk. 'Kate, your mom was an amazing woman. I was crazy for her back then. I know you weren't thrilled about it at the time, and I'm sorry. I never meant to ruffle anyone's feathers. I was just trying to follow my heart, you know?' He clutched at the Wheel of Life pendant again.

While I didn't think his heart was the only organ Zack was following back then, I accepted his apology. He wasn't such a bad guy after all. A little too touchy-feely for my liking, but I sensed he was being up front with me and this won him some points.

I looked at my watch and saw I was ten minutes late for my meeting with Meg. 'I should go,' I told him, getting up from the chair. 'Meg's probably waiting for me.'

'It's been a pleasure, Kate. Give your mom my love. I'll stop by to see her soon. Promise.' He moved from behind the desk to embrace me, smelling faintly of sandalwood and marijuana. It was one of those over-long, full-body hugs sensitive men are fond of. I couldn't help but squirm a little.

★ ★ ★

My meeting with Meg didn't go well — I'm sure she thought I was the one with the memory problem. I couldn't stay focused on our conversation. The entire time I sat in her office, I thought about who could have put Del's star in my purse and about Zack and Nicky's boyhood fling. I started to make a mental list of all the people who'd had access to my purse: my mother, Raven, Gabriel, Opal, Nicky. Someone could have dropped it in when I was shopping at Haskie's. But who? And why me?

Meg was saying something about 'a specialized facility,' which I took to mean nursing home, but I found myself remembering the day I met Zack coming out of the cabin — the day Nicky kissed me. Nicky, who had probably been making out with Zack just minutes before. Zack, who returned to the tepee to bed down with my mother. The whole thing made my head spin. And it continued to bring me back to my original question: Why did Nicky want me to know all this? Guilt? The need to reveal his long-kept secret in an effort to build my trust? And were there other secrets, darker secrets, waiting to rear their ugly little heads?

I thought of the God of Death, with his fangs and menacing eyes, turning us all around as if we were on some giant roulette wheel: gods and titans, mortals and hungry ghosts, Zack and Nicky, me and my mother, Opal and Raven.

Round and round and round it goes, where it stops, nobody knows . . .

When Meg suggested tentatively that we meet for lunch the following week, I agreed, relieved. I knew the situation with my mother was severe, but I just couldn't give it my full attention right then and there. I thanked her and headed for home.

★　★　★

Gabriel and my mother were making lasagna when I found them in the kitchen. My mother was at the table, beating eggs to mix in with the cheese Gabriel was grating. She was working in slow motion, studying the eggs as if there were something utterly perplexing about them. Perhaps she was pondering that famous old *which came first, the chicken or the egg* question. Or maybe she was remembering the walks we used to take down the hill to buy eggs from the Griswolds' leaning stand.

Lazy Elk says they're no good because they've got blood in them. That just means they're fertile.

Gabriel wore sweatpants with suspenders, a faded flannel shirt, and a misshapen green felt hat.

'Well, let's see, Jean. What do we do next?'

211

he asked, putting her in charge, or giving her that sense at least. When she didn't respond, he held the plate of grated mozzarella up, cocking an eyebrow.

'Cheese,' my mother said.

'You're still the best damn cook on the hill,' he told her, then leaned in to kiss her sallow cheek.

'You'll never guess who I ran into at the college,' I said.

'Could it be the infamous young Zachary Messier?' asked Gabriel.

'Is there anything you don't know?' I asked the old man.

'Plenty, my dear. Plenty. How is the professor these days?'

'Fine. It was good to see him.'

'I'm so glad he came back when he did. He's the reason Raven went back to school, you know. She needed the little extra push he gave her. And he's been a wonderful influence on Opal.'

'Zack,' my mother said, a dazed smile moving over her face. 'Zack was with me when that Griswold girl was killed. Poor little thing.'

Lucky you, I thought, remembering young Zack's dirty bare feet, wondering if he left her sheets filthy and smelling of sandalwood. I decided that, while I may have misjudged him back then, I still really wasn't comfortable with the image of Zack between my mother's sheets.

'You know,' I said, 'it's funny. Talking to Zack today was a little unsettling. It made me feel like I never really knew him at all.'

My mother laughed out loud and gave me a nod.

'You were ten or eleven last time you saw him, Kate,' Gabriel explained. 'You were a perceptive kid, but there's a lot you missed. Even now, there's a lot all of us miss. We think we know someone and then we learn something that just blows everything to hell. Keeps things nice and interesting, Katydid, don't you agree?' Gabriel asked, narrowing his eyes at me. It was a suspicious look and I imagined him wondering if I was the cat killer. I was sure Raven had gone to him with her concerns and wondered if he considered me a suspect in Magpie's death. Hell, maybe they both thought I killed Tori Miller, too.

If only they knew what I had in the pocket of my purse . . .

I had to get rid of that star one way or another. The sooner the better. *Tonight*, I thought. I'll take care of it tonight.

'I suppose so,' I said. 'I'm going to go change, then I'll come out and give you two a hand.'

'Hey, have a look at your mother's painting. She was in there most of the afternoon working on it. I finally had to stop her and give her some extra medication. Didn't I, Jean? I think you worked too hard and got yourself a little wound up. But you're feeling better now, aren't you?'

Sure she was. She was so doped up, she was practically drooling.

I walked into the studio and dropped my bag immediately. There was no mistake, even in the fading light of the room. The painting was more colorful now; there were pinks, purples, and blues that hadn't been there before. Also, in the top left corner was now a distinct pair of eyes. Blue-gray eyes. The kind that look straight ahead, but seem to follow you wherever you go. Eyes like Jesus's in those creepy velvet paintings of the Last Supper. All-seeing eyes. No face to go with them, just eyes staring out from the flames.

'Ma!' I called out. 'Ma, can you come in here a sec?'

My mother was soon in the doorway, followed by Gabriel.

'Ma, who is that?'

She only smiled at the painting.

'Who is that there in the painting?'

Her smile widened and she began to giggle. It was not the giggle of a seventy-two-year-old

214

woman. She raised her hands to her mouth to cover it, to stifle her laughter. But the sound that came out was the high-pitched giggle of a little girl. And once she started, it seemed she could not stop. Tears poured from her eyes and she tee-hee-hee'd until she became short of breath and Gabriel led her away, shooting me an irritated look before taking her into the kitchen and giving her yet another walloping dose of tranquilizers.

11

The body of twelve-year-old Delores Ann
Griswold was discovered by her brother
Nicholas at approximately 7:00 p.m. That is
what the eleven o'clock news out of
Burlington reported. We didn't have a
television in the tepee, but there was one in
the big barn and all of New Hope was
gathered around it. By then, the police had
already made their first of many trips up to
New Hope, asking if anyone had seen Del at
all that day and wanting to know where
everyone had been during the afternoon. I
said I'd only seen Del in school. I didn't tell
them what had really happened there. They
knew that Del had been picked on, but they
had no idea of the extent of it. Or that I was
the one who chased her back toward town,
right into the arms of her killer. The police
wouldn't tell us what had happened, but
when we walked down the road to see the
row of state police cars flashing in front of

216

the Griswolds' place, we knew whatever it was, it was bad.

As we watched the news and saw the school photo of Del fill up the screen, my mother put her arm around me.

'Were you two friends, Katydid?' she asked.

'Uh-uh.' I shook my head, denying her in death as automatically as I had in life. 'We just waited for the bus together.'

I knelt down right in front of the set, in the place my mother always forbade me to sit, saying it would ruin my eyes. This time, she gave no dire warnings. In the school picture, Del was wearing a large white puffy-sleeved blouse with a bow clumsily tied at the collar. It was clearly an old-lady shirt, something she probably found at the back of a closet that had once belonged to her mother or grandmother even. Up close, I saw that the photo of Del was made up of hundreds of tiny dots, black and white pixels that had made their way through the air right into our television. And I had the curious sensation that I was breaking apart like that, too; disintegrating into a million particles that no one would be able to put back together again in a way that might resemble a ten-year-old girl.

The anchorman said that Mr Ralph Griswold sent Nicky out to look for Del when she didn't show up for supper. The school had called earlier to report that Del had gone truant and had failed to pick up her diploma.

The news man didn't give many details about her death, except that it was a clear case of homicide. Later, it was reported that she had been found naked. The rumors in town started immediately, and they would continue for decades. Some people said Del was decapitated. Her body was cut into tiny pieces. She was found hanging upside down, her throat slit like a deer's. The killer had cut her open and placed a raw potato inside. It was her brother who did it. No, her father. Must have been one of the freaks at New Hope.

The truth was, no matter what the rumor of the week was, the underlying feeling in town was the same: What fate could you expect for a girl like Del — dirty, mouthy, running wild all the time, probably half-retarded?

The police had several suspects almost immediately. They brought Del's father in, because it was well known that he beat his kids (he'd admitted to giving her the shiner the day before she was killed) and the police found a pair of his overalls, soaked in blood, stuffed in the laundry basket. The detectives let him go when the lab tests showed it was only pig blood. They brought Nicky in because he seemed to be the one Del was closest to. They arrested him for the marijuana they found in his room and he was sent to juvenile detention after assaulting one of the state troopers who'd picked him up. They brought in Mike Shane after they found a stack of letters he'd written, confessing his love, but he was released shortly. They brought in Zack but let him go when my mother confirmed he'd been with her in the tepee all afternoon. Zack claimed one of the state troopers winked at him when his alibi was confirmed. Then they arrested a man who called himself Lazy Elk when a necklace found in Del's drawer turned out to be one of his creations. Eventually though, it wasn't enough to hold him — he'd been on his way to a craft fair in Middlebury when Del was killed, and a woman who worked at a gas station recognized his photo, confirming his alibi. So they let Mark Lubofski go. Del, they figured, must have stolen the necklace. She was that kind of kid.

Lazy Elk left town after that (unable to face the constant looks of suspicion — the people of New Canaan hadn't let him off the hook even if the police had) and was never heard from again. He called my mother just before leaving to apologize once more, say he loved her, and ask if she would go with him. She hung up, figuring that was all the answer he deserved. Years later, when Raven was older, she tried to find Lazy Elk, even hired a private detective. But there was no trace of either Lazy Elk or Mark Lubofski anywhere. My one act of theft had turned into something much bigger — it wasn't just a necklace I took; I stole Raven's father from her, sending him off into some anonymous life where no one had heard of New Hope, Lazy Elk, or the Potato Girl.

★ ★ ★

Two years after Del was killed, when he got back from the Brattleboro Detention Center for Boys, Nicky finally described to me what he'd seen in the loft the night he found Del. We met by chance in town one fall afternoon and sat on the steps of the general store drinking root beer. Nicky was sixteen then. He seemed more awkward. Taller. What I remember most is that he wouldn't look me in the eye.

Nicky and I would see each other from time to time over the next few years, but this was the last time we would speak before I moved away.

'She was just lying there, spread-eagled on

that old mattress. Naked. Wearing only this leather cord around her neck. Her face was sort of purplish, her tongue was sticking out a little. But then there were the cuts.'

'Cuts?' I asked.

'Yeah. The sick bastard cut a square of skin right off her chest, Like he was tryin' to cut a doorway to her heart or something. He took it with him like some kinda fucking trophy.'

Nicky, I realized then, hadn't known about the tattoo. No one, it seemed, knew but myself, Del, and her killer. The police, after interviewing the whole fifth grade, asked me about what I told Ellie and Sam about a tattoo. Frightened, I told the police I had made it up — that I had lied about everything I told the other girls. The truth was, I told the cops, I hardly knew Del at all. I had just wanted to impress Ellie and Samantha. I'd never seen a tattoo or even the edge of a tattoo. Del had mentioned it once, maybe, but no, I'd never seen it. And Del lied all the time anyway, so you never knew what to believe. If there had been a tattoo, I didn't know what of. At the time, I assumed they'd seen the tattoo themselves when they found her. What did they need me to tell them for?

After Nicky told me about the patch of missing skin, I thought of going to the police. I thought of it, but in my twelve-year-old mind I told myself I'd already broken enough promises to Del Griswold. Her secret would remain safe with me. I figured it was the least I owed her.

But at night, for years, when I closed my eyes to go to sleep, I was down in that root cellar again. And Del was peeling off her clothes. *Are you gonna look or what?* she wanted to know. And when I raised my eyes from the dirt floor, there it was: *M.*

A good kind of hurt.

12

All the kids told the police they'd seen the star pinned to Del's chest on the last day of school, but it wasn't with Del's clothes, which were found folded in a neat pile next to her body. And, of course, it wasn't in her room, tucked away in her drawer of treasures beside the dead dove, the letters from Mute Mike, the paint sample card, and the strange necklace made out of wood, aluminum pull tops, and shotgun shells — it was well established that Del had never made it home that day.

The theory was that the killer ran into Del shortly after she left school. Maybe they'd arranged to meet in the cabin. Maybe they met by accident along the way. Maybe he even saw her walking home that day and offered her a ride. Whatever happened, the silver star was gone, and the police suspected the killer may have taken it, along with a square of skin, cut neatly from her body with that old plastic-handled knife. Trophies, the police guessed. Something to remember her by.

But now, all these years later, *I* was the one with the star, wasn't I? Carrying this important piece of lost evidence in my pocketbook, reaching in to feel the sharp points, to run my fingers over the engraved word: SHERIFF.

I knew better than to hold on to it for long, though. It incriminated me. I had lied to the police, telling them I didn't know Del well at all. My Swiss Army knife was being held as evidence in the cat-killing, and might have been used on Tori Miller. How would it look if they found out I had the sheriff's star?

I decided to bury it.

I chose to lay it to rest in the place where Del had shared her first secret with me — the old root cellar. I went close to midnight, long after we'd eaten our lasagna, Gabriel had gone to the big barn, and I had locked my mother in her room for the night. I brought a flashlight and a trowel with me and picked my way down the path through the woods, across the old field and pasture to the heavy door in the hillside behind the old farmhouse. With hesitation, I reached for the worn metal handle and pulled. The door swung slowly on squeaky hinges, screeching as if I were opening some movie set crypt.

Cool, moist earth. Sagging shelves. Rotting baskets once full of root vegetables that had long ago withered to dust. Canning jars forgotten: tomatoes floating like tissue samples; pears like tiny fetuses. There, in a cracked jelly jar, was the stub of a candle Del once lit and held to her chest to show me her secret.

The air was stagnant, full of the smell of damp earth and rot. It was Del's smell. I held my breath, hurried down the worn wooden steps, picked a random spot in the dirt floor, and started to dig, with a terrible feeling that Del was right there with me the whole time. I could almost see her out of the corner of my eye.

I've got a secret to show you. Promise not to tell.

I buried it as deep as I could with shaking hands, stamped down the dirt, and used an old broom that hung on the wall to smooth away my tracks before leaving.

I ran back to New Hope, stumbling over tree roots and boulders, my heart pounding in my ears like someone else's footsteps.

Catch me if you can.

When I was just past the turnoff to the cabin, I saw a light dancing along the path in front of me. I stopped dead in my tracks and watched for a minute as the light bobbed along the ground, back and forth, back and forth, moving in my direction. I tried to still my wheezing breath.

Del?

No, it couldn't be. Del was long dead. And I didn't believe in ghosts.

I flicked my flashlight back on and raised the beam straight ahead, in the direction of the mystery light.

To my relief, I saw that it was no ghost, no spirit orb. It was a flesh and blood person with a flashlight of his or her own. Whoever it was wore jeans and a dark hooded sweatshirt. And once my light hit my fellow explorer, he or she turned to look at me, then took off running, up the hill toward New Hope.

'Shit,' I mumbled and began sprinting uphill, my light on the runner's back.

Now, running after some stranger in the woods where Tori Miller was killed just days ago didn't seem like the smartest idea I'd ever had, but like it or not, I knew I had to start putting some pieces together if I was going to save my own ass. Someone was framing me. Maybe the killer, maybe not. One thing I knew for sure — you had to have a damn good reason to be out in those woods at midnight. The garden trowel in my left hand reminded me what mine had been. I wanted to know what brought my friend out at this time of night.

Whoever it was, he or she was in good shape. I'm a pretty decent runner and I had trouble catching up, much less gaining ground. But my quarry stumbled, falling to the ground, giving me precious seconds to catch up. I got to the mystery person just as he or she was rising and grabbed the back of the sweatshirt, yanking the poor soul back down to the ground with a grunt.

Had I captured the killer? Or someone playing ghost?

I held my trowel like a dagger and pointed my light at the mystery runner.

The beam hit Opal's face and she let out a scream.

'Opal? Jesus! What are you doing out here? You scared the hell out of me.' I lowered the trowel to my side.

She started to cry. I leaned down to put my arm around her and she flung herself at me, clinging to me as hard as she could.

She's just a kid, I thought. *No older than Del was.*

And as she held tight to me, I thought of all the similarities between Opal and Del. They were both skinny girls with the bare beginnings of breasts hidden under boyish clothes. Their hair was the same washed-out dirty blond. And there was something else, something I couldn't quite put my finger on

— a sort of determined desperation each of them had, I guess; a desperation masquerading as charisma.

I wrapped my arms around her, desperate to protect her, and remembered the last time I'd held her like this, two years ago outside the big barn while she held her arm to her side like a bird with a broken wing.

There's someone up there.

Opal sobbed in my arms now. 'I . . . thought . . . you were the Potato Girl,' she gasped.

And I thought you were.

'Easy, Opal. It's just me. It's Kate, sweetie. You're safe.' I was rocking her now, back and forth, back and forth. 'What on earth are you doing out here at this hour?'

'Just walking,' she said.

No, I thought, remembering the way her light had moved across the path, *you were looking for something. But what?*

'What are *you* doing out here?' she asked, pulling away from me suddenly, as if she'd just realized good old Auntie Kate might not be what she seemed. 'And why do you have that?' She was pointing at the dirty garden trowel.

The last thing in the world I wanted was for Opal to be afraid of me. But I wasn't about to tell her my reason for the midnight trip to the root cellar, either. The kid was hiding something, and until she was upfront with me I sure as hell wasn't going to say anything to incriminate myself.

'Mushroom hunting,' I told her, realizing how totally absurd it sounded only after the words were out. A nature girl, I am not. I don't know the difference between a chanterelle and a toadstool, and I prayed Opal wouldn't give me a pop quiz on the fungi of New England.

By the light of my flashlight, we eyed each other skeptically, each of us fully aware that the other was lying.

'What do you say we head back?' I suggested, and she nodded, looking relieved. We began trudging uphill, side by side, both our flashlights illuminating the path. Every now and then, I had to turn and look at her, then remind myself it wasn't Del I was walking with.

'Kate?'

'Yeah?'

'Are you mad at me? About the watch, I mean.'

'No, I'm not mad,' I said. 'I was just surprised.'

'I would have given it back.'

'I know. And I would have let you borrow it if you'd asked. Do you do it a lot? Take things from people?'

She was quiet. 'Once in a while,' she said.

'Opal? Did you borrow anything else from me?'

Like a red Swiss Army knife, for instance.

'No. Just the watch.'

'Promise?'

'I swear,' she said. And her next words made me turn and shine my light on her face like some dime-store novel interrogator. *Is your name really Opal? Or are you, in fact, Delores Ann Griswold, back from the dead?*

'Cross my heart and hope to die,' she said.

★ ★ ★

'Ma, your painting kinda creeps me out,' I confessed. It was late evening, after supper, and she was in front of her easel, adding more layers by lamplight. We had spent the day together at home — no appointments, no discussion of nursing homes.

The only interruption had come earlier that afternoon when I answered a knock at the door and found Zack standing on the front steps with a bunch of flowers. He was wearing jeans, Birkenstocks, and a loose cotton shirt embroidered with mythical-looking birds under the same corduroy blazer I'd seen him in the other day.

'I brought these for Jean,' he said, leaning

230

in to give me a hello hug around the bouquet. This time I nearly got high from the amount of pot smoke that clung to his clothes. He must have toked up in the car on the way over.

'Thanks. Come on in. She's in the studio. I'm sure she'd love it if you popped your head in to say hi.' Zack followed me inside and made his way to the studio while I took the flowers to the kitchen and found an old canning jar to put them in. I was arranging them on the table when I heard a crash from the studio and went running.

I got there in time to see Zack, ashen-faced, shut the door tight behind him.

'What happened?' I asked.

'I guess she wasn't in the mood for company,' he said. Then I noticed the left sleeve of his blazer was covered in bright red paint. He started to dab at it with a handkerchief.

'Go on in the kitchen. There's soap, water, and a brush at the sink. I'll be right there.'

Zack headed for the kitchen and I knocked on, then carefully opened, the door to the studio, to see my mother hard at work in front of the canvas.

'You okay, Ma?'

'Fine, Katydid.'

I shut the door quietly behind me and went

into the kitchen, where Zack was scrubbing at the sleeve of his corduroy jacket.

'I'm so sorry,' I told him. 'She's not herself. There's just no way to predict how she'll be from minute to minute.'

I went for the lockbox and made a mental note to call Dr Crawford in the morning. It seemed we were upping her meds every day now with little effect. She was building a tolerance awfully fast. Or was her illness worsening in some profound way?

I put a couple of pills in my pocket, planning to take them in to her as soon as Zack left.

'It's not a problem, Kate. I shouldn't have surprised her like that.' He smiled. 'Next time, I'll wear coveralls. And a big old bell, maybe.'

'Jeez. Why don't you take your jacket off and we can soak it? Or I can have it dry-cleaned.'

'No need. I have to get going in a minute anyway.' He was dabbing at the stain with paper towels now. 'Kate, the main reason I stopped by was to talk to you about Opal.'

'Opal?'

'Gosh. This is a little awkward. Raven came to see me in my office this morning. She was beside herself.'

'Look, Zack, if this is about the cat . . . '

'Cat? No. She's having a hard time with some of Opal's recent behavior. She's very concerned and thinks that maybe your spending time with Opal isn't such a good idea.'

I scowled. 'Raven asked you to come here to tell me this?'

'I offered. I was afraid that if she tried to talk to you in the state she was in . . . '

'I get the picture,' I said.

'Look, Kate, I think Raven will come around; she's just a little crazy right now, which is to be expected. She's a stressed-out mom just trying to do what's right. She's worried about Opal's obsession with those silly Potato Girl stories and the way Opal seems to have latched on to you because of your connection with Del.'

'Opal and I had a relationship before all this interest in the Potato Girl,' I said defensively. 'She latched on to me during my last visit and it had nothing whatsoever to do with Del.'

'I know, Kate,' Zack said. He put his hands up in surrender. 'Don't shoot the messenger. I understand that your connection with Opal isn't just about Del. In fact, I imagine the truth is that you're a positive influence on Opal. But that's not the way Raven sees it right now.'

'Opal needs someone to talk to,' I said.

'I know she does. I'll try to be there for her as much as I can. And Raven's taking her to a psychiatrist next week — the grief counselor the school brought in referred her to him. He's supposed to be the best in the area.'

'A psychiatrist is just going to spend an hour with her, if that, and introduce her to the wonderful world of psychotropic medication. She needs someone to really talk all this through with. Someone who isn't being paid to listen. Has she told you what she's seen? That she believes Del is out to get her?'

He took in a breath. 'I know. She told me. I know she's hurting and trying to make sense of what happened to Tori any way she can. I also think Raven's being unreasonable by saying she doesn't want you spending any time with Opal, and I'll do my best to get her to come around, but it seems like, for now at least, the best thing to do is honor her wishes. I'm sorry.'

'It's okay,' I told him with a dramatic sigh. 'I should be used to being seen as the bad guy by now.'

Zack smiled, touched his Wheel of Life pendant. 'We're all just working through our karma, doing the best we can.'

'Isn't that the truth,' I said, looking back at the pendant, at the God of Death perched on top who returned my stare with a menacing grimace.

★   ★   ★

The eyes in the corner of my mother's painting were starting to develop a body — just the shadow of a form, really. Nothing identifiable.

'I almost feel like those eyes are watching me,' I told her.

'She sees you,' my mother confirmed, dabbing at the painting with her brush.

'Who?'

I was getting tired of this game.

'She's watching. You have something that's hers. She wants it back.'

A strange new fear awoke inside me, speaking of impossible things.

'I don't know what you mean, Ma.'

My mother continued to stand with her back to me, facing the painting. She hunched her shoulders forward, then pulled them back, standing tall — erect as a soldier standing at attention.

'GIVE IT BACK!' she shouted.

The voice, like the giggling the day before, did not sound like my mother's. It was a child's voice. A girl's firm demand. The voice that came from my mother's mouth sounded like Del's.

But that, of course, was quite impossible. Was I losing my sanity? Had the stress of the past week worn me down that much?

'What?' I stepped away from her, terrified, in spite of all my rationalizations, that she would turn to face me and it would be Del's pale eyes staring out from my mother's wrinkled face.

'I said you better give it back, Katydid.' Her voice was her own again. Her shoulders slumped forward, relaxed. She went on painting. Her body was positioned directly in front of the canvas so I couldn't see just what she was working on.

'What did you just say, Ma?'

'Don't know. Stroke took my memory. Fire stroke.'

'What is it I'm supposed to give back?' I did my best to conceal the panicked frustration in my voice. I must have misheard her, that's all.

My mother giggled, set down her brush, and stepped away from the canvas. An oil lamp hung above the easel, and a candle burned on the table next to her wooden palette. The flickering light illuminated the painting, dancing over it, making it seem more alive. My eye caught something light and shiny in the left corner. I stepped up to the easel to get a closer look.

My throat opened and I could feel a guttural cry rising up. I clapped my hand over my mouth. I blinked hard, sure I was hallucinating. It *couldn't* be. But it was.

There, on the torso of the shadow figure with the pale roaming eyes, my mother had painted a five-pointed silver star, the word SHERIFF spelled out in tiny, dark letters.

★   ★   ★

My hands shook as I dialed the phone.

'Hello?'

'Nicky, it's Kate. Something crazy's going on. Can you come over?'

He was silent for a moment.

'Is that an apology, then?' he asked.

'Yeah, I'm sorry I was such a shit. I'm going nuts here. I need to talk to you.'

'I'll be there in fifteen minutes.'

'Bring some Wild Turkey.'

'Gobble, gobble,' he said, and hung up.

I checked on my mother — sound asleep. I fastened the lock and closed her in securely for the night. I went into the kitchen and lit some candles, threw another log in the stove. Back in my mother's studio, I changed clothes and started to brush my hair. I caught a glimpse of myself in the mirror above the bureau and stopped short. My image was not alone. In the upper right-hand corner, I could just make out the figure in my mother's painting — its eyes watching me watch myself. At that instant, there was an insistent *rap-rap-rap* at the front door. I damn near jumped out of my skin. Just Nicky, of course. I swallowed hard, grabbed the lamp, and went to let him in.

★   ★   ★

We settled at the kitchen table. I put out some cheese and crackers and Nicky poured us two good-sized glasses of bourbon.

Nicky had shaved, combed his hair, and put on a clean, recently ironed white shirt that made him look downright civilized. To prove he was still a country boy, he had on a denim jacket, nearly worn through at the elbows and fraying at the collar.

'Why didn't you tell me?' I asked, not wanting to waste time with small talk.

'Tell you what?' He eyed me cautiously.

'About you and Zack. I talked to him yesterday and he told me everything.'

'Just what did he say?' Nicky asked.

'Enough. God, I feel like you had this

whole other life back then that I didn't have a clue about. I mean, I had no idea. I thought he was your drug dealer.'

'He was,' Nicky said, looking down into his glass.

'But he was more than that, wasn't he?'

'In a way,' Nicky admitted, still staring into the amber liquid.

'Look, Nicky, there's been a lot of weird shit happening here and I'd sure appreciate it if you'd just be honest with me for once. I mean, how can you expect me to take anything you've said about the ghost stuff seriously when you've been lying to me all along?' My voice started to crack. 'I just need one person to be straight with me here. Everyone in this town has secrets piled on like those Russian nesting dolls. So please, I'm begging you, no more lies.'

'I never lied.' He continued to stare down into his glass, then lifted it to his lips and drained it quickly.

'I'd say the omission of the little detail about you and Zack counts as being lied to. Now come on, Nicky. Tell me about it. You owe me that much.'

Nicky chewed on his lip a minute. He raised his eyes to meet mine, then looked away guiltily. He reached for the bottle and poured himself another drink, downed it, then lit a cigarette.

'I'm not queer, you know.'

'Nicky, it doesn't matter.' I placed my hand on his.

'No more so than anyone else. I've had some lady friends over the years. Never went and got married like you did, but I came close once. This thing with Zack, it was crazy. I mean, when I think about it now, it feels like some far-off dream. Like it was a movie I was watching. Does that make sense?'

I nodded. So many parts of my life felt the same way. All the affairs Jamie had had, the years I played the helpless martyr.

'The guy was nuts about me,' Nicky told me as he exhaled a cloud of smoke. 'And I got swept away in it. I believed whatever he told me. He said sexuality was fluid and being with him didn't make me, you know, gay. He read me. Walt Whitman. Pretty deep shit for a kid whose biggest excitement had been shooting crows and squirrels. Looking back, I think it was the danger, the *wrongness* of it, that made it so powerful. It happened only a few times, and each time, I told myself it wasn't gonna happen again, but then he'd show up and put his hands on me, and I couldn't refuse. It was the fear of getting caught that added so much fuel to it, ya know? Does that make sense?' He looked up at me, his eyes boozy and moist. I nodded.

'Why didn't you ever tell me?' I asked.

'I tried. I planned to dozens of times. But I didn't want to risk scaring you off. I was a little in love with you back then.' Nicky's cheeks colored and he gave me a self-conscious smile. 'I didn't understand it myself, much less know how to explain it to some girl I was sick over.'

Now my face reddened. I squeezed Nicky's hand, then let go.

'And Del knew,' I said, pouring myself another drink.

'Yeah, Del caught us all right.' He let out a regretful, smoke-filled sigh. 'Little shit snuck right up the ladder and watched. Didn't even know she was there till we were, you know . . . through.'

'What did she do then?'

'Hell, you remember how she was. She threatened to tell. She used it whenever she needed to get her way with me. Worked damn near every time, too.'

'But did she ever tell?'

'Uh-uh. Not that I know of. I thought maybe she'd told you, but I guess not.'

'Nicky, is there anything else you're not telling me? Anything about Del?'

'Like what?' Nicky's voice had an angry, defensive edge. 'Like did I kill her? Jesus, Kate!'

'That's not what I meant.'

'Now it's your turn,' Nicky said. 'How about you tell me something I don't know.'

I had a bite of cracker and a sip of bourbon. I decided it was time to fess up — to tell Nicky how I betrayed his sister. Nicky had told me his secret at last; now it was time for me to tell mine. I began with the tattoo.

'Jesus, an *M*?' Nicky asked, sitting up straight. 'Are you sure it was an *M*? Do you know what this means? It's a fucking clue. It's probably the initial of the killer. The police suspected it was someone she knew, someone she felt comfortable with.'

I nodded, agreeing. Then I continued. I told Nicky about my plan with Ellie, about the double-agent scheme, about how it went so wrong. I tried not to make excuses for myself. I described Del's last afternoon at school. Nicky's eyes brimmed with tears, then seemed to darken with rage. I let myself go on, fearful that maybe I had gone too far, that I was at risk of alienating him, being seen as the enemy, but it was too late. And as much as I was ashamed of what I had done, it was a relief to finally be telling my story.

I described how in my last moments with Del, I was chasing her, a rock in my hand. Then I jumped forward in time, telling him everything that had happened since I had come back to New Canaan: the cat's disappearing and then turning up dead next to my missing knife, the footprints in the snow, the matchstick message, my mother's painting, Del's sheriff's star mysteriously showing up in my purse. I told him all about Opal: that she said she'd seen the Potato Girl, that she was sure it was she herself who was the killer's intended target, that I'd caught her twice searching the woods for something. I described the scene earlier that evening, when my mother demanded her star back. I told him I thought I was going crazy, that I didn't believe in ghosts and the supernatural but was running out of rational explanations. Either I was completely losing my mind, or my tangible, scientific, orderly way of looking at the world was just shit. Lousy choices.

When I was finished, I poured two fingers of Wild Turkey into my empty glass and sucked it down fast. My hand shook. Nicky didn't look me in the eye. I wanted to take his face in my hands, turn him gently toward me so I could read some response in his eyes.

Nicky poured himself another drink and studied the flame of the lantern.

When he finally spoke, his voice was hoarse, like he was on the verge of either crying or screaming. I felt a little afraid.

'Do you know where Del got that star, Kate? Did she ever tell you?'

'No. She never told me.'

'That mute kid, Mike Shane, gave it to her. That's what I finally figured anyway. She said the boy who gave it to her loved her. She told me that it was supposed to remind her that she was his guiding star or some shit like that. Puppy love, ya know? He gave her notes, too. Poor bastard couldn't talk, but he sure could write. Poured his mute little heart out. God, how Del loved that damn star. Thought she was really the sheriff, like it gave her some kind of power or something.'

Her talisman.

He fiddled with his lighter, turning it around and around in his fingers. He had mechanic's hands: blunt fingers, dirt under the nails, grease deep in the lines of his skin. Like it or not, I found myself longing to be touched by those fingers. To be taken back in time.

'I remember.' I nodded, taking my eyes off his hands. 'I remember Mike Shane, too. Do you know what ever happened to him?'

'I hear he's up in Burlington. A buddy of mine at the garage knows his family. Real trailer trash, the whole lot. Sammy, the guy I work with, says Mike's dad used to burn the kids with cigarettes and shit. Sad story.'

'Yeah, I'll say. He got about as much crap at school as Del did. It's no wonder they were drawn to each other.'

Nicky nodded. 'Kate, I'd like to see your mother's painting.'

I grabbed a candle and led him back to the studio. He walked right up to the canvas, still clutching the bottle of Wild Turkey, and squinted at the shadowy form in the flames. I stood behind him, holding up the candle.

'Spooky,' he whispered, taking a step back and bumping into me. We stood like that a moment, his back pressed into my front, me breathing on his neck. I knew I should step away, retreat while I could, but it was too late. I leaned forward, pressing into him, bringing my left hand up to his shoulder, tracing the outline of his arm, reaching around to his chest, where I felt his heart racing through the soft cotton folds. But as I slid my hand inside his jacket, that wasn't the only thing I felt.

Suspenders? I thought at first when I felt the webbed nylon strap, but when I followed it to the bulge on his left side, I knew just what it was.

'What is this?'

'Protection,' he said, reaching in and removing the small automatic pistol, then laying it down on the cot.

Like it or not, seeing the gun gave me a little shiver of excitement. What can I say? I guess I have a secret thing for gun-toting bad boys. Give me an outlaw over a cardiologist any day.

'From little old me?' I whispered into the back of his neck, my hands feeling the straps of the nylon holster.

'You can never be too careful,' he said.

My fingers found the top button of his shirt and undid it, then the second. I let my hand slide beneath his shirt, brushing gently against his right nipple.

'That's so true,' I said. 'Maybe you shouldn't have been so quick to give up your weapon.'

At last, he turned.

Our second kiss, some thirty years after the first, was no less violent, and fueled by a raw desperation unknown to us as children.

★ ★ ★

'Kate, what happened to the star? What'd you do with it?'

Nicky was facing me, leaning on his elbow, holding the bottle of Wild Turkey between us. The candle flickered on the table beside the cot, the light playing in his hair and over his skin. He looked lovely.

'Buried it in the root cellar,' I answered drowsily. 'I did it just last night.' My fingers traced their way from his throat to his sternum. I didn't want to think about the star. It felt good to be with a man again. Too good. Now here he was, about to ruin it.

'You know what we have to do, don't you?'

I didn't respond. I was pretty sure I wasn't going to like the answer. Sure enough:

'We have to go get it. We have to give the star back to her.'

I jerked my hand from his chest and sat up, irritated.

'Jesus, Nicky. We're talking about a girl who's been dead more than thirty years. How are we supposed to give her an actual, tangible thing? You want to dig up her grave and throw it in?'

He shook his head. 'I think we have to give it to your mother. I think she'll know what to do.'

This was great. My sexy hero and his brilliant suggestions.

'My mother! Oh Christ, this is perfect.' My words came out with a slight bourbon slur. 'My mother — in case you don't recall — is just a step away from being stuck in a nursing home. I'm taking her to visit one in the morning, as a matter of fact. You've seen her. Her mind is mush. She's not going to know what the hell is going on if we go handing her some rusted-up old star. It'll just confuse her even more.'

'Maybe so. But she seems to be communicating with Del in some way. The painting sure shows that. And what about the way she talked to you in Del's voice, asking for the star back?'

'I imagined that. It was a voice that didn't sound like hers — that's all. It wasn't Del's. She doesn't know what she's saying, Nicky. She's sick.'

Now he sat up.

'Whatever, Kate. You can backpedal all you want. I'm just saying I think we should go get the star. You don't have to give it to Jean tonight, or ever even. Let's just go find it. What harm can that do?'

I didn't answer. I didn't remind him that I'd ditched the star in a desperate attempt to keep myself out of jail. That Del's old badge was what the police would consider crucial evidence and whoever was caught with it would have an awful lot of explaining to do.

'No harm, that's what,' he said, giving me his sly, flirtatious grin as he leaped up from the cot and began dressing. 'It can't do no harm at all. Now come on, Desert Rose, put on some clothes and let's go.'

Reluctantly, I obeyed. As I was buttoning

my blouse, my gaze fell upon the painting and the figure within it. The eyes — *her* eyes — seemed to bore into mine.

Caught again.

★　★　★

I ran the beam of the flashlight over the shelves, then down to the dirt floor. There was no trace that I could see of last night's activity — I had done a good job covering my tracks. And in my drunken state, I didn't have the faintest notion where I'd buried the star. Nothing to do but start digging. Just pick a place and begin. *Heigh-ho, heigh-ho.*

Nicky took a swig from the bottle he'd carried with him, then set it on a shelf. I picked a spot toward the back — I had been near that candle in the jelly jar, right? — stepped back, then stomped the metal spade into the ground, nearly tumbling over.

I was good and drunk. This had sunk in on the walk through the woods and down the path on the hill. By the time we got to the old pea field, I was clinging to Nicky, asking him questions that all started with the word *remember.*

Remember when you were Billy the Kid?
Remember when you taught me to shoot

249

that old BB gun?
Remember the way our teeth banged together
  when we kissed?
Such force. Like an accident.

Nicky helped steady me as we walked, though he stumbled now and then over a tree root or a clump of weeds. Yes, he told me. *I remember.* I leaned into him, felt his heat, yearned to be back on the cot.

Then we were at the root cellar and he was pulling the door open and I was feeling my way down the steps, smelling Del all around me. I missed the last step, twisted my ankle, landed on my knees in the dirt. I looked around with the flashlight. Nicky put the shovel in my hands. He held the small trowel in his own.

'Let's do it,' he told me. 'Dig it up.' Only it sounded almost like he said *her.* Dig *her* up.

Digging. Digging. Digging to China. Grave digging. Digging potatoes. One potato, two potato. I started to hum it, then felt bile rising in my throat.

'Gonna be sick,' I said.

'Keep digging,' he told me. 'It'll pass.'

This too shall pass. I dug like an old dog trying to find the tasty bone she'd just buried. Teeth are bones, I remembered. What are Del's bones like now, deep inside their metal coffin? I wondered. Metal. Metal shovel. Metal star. My mouth tasted like tin.

The star wasn't in the place I thought it should be. The place I'd just buried it.

'We need a metal detector,' I complained.

'We'll find it,' he promised. 'You just have to remember.'

He stabbed the trowel into the earth floor.

Remember. Yes, I remembered. Remembered the way that letter *M* looked on Del's chest. Puffy. Infected. Her secret. A good kind of hurt. I stopped digging and reached for the bottle, polished it off, rinsing the metallic taste from my mouth. Said, 'Gobble, gobble,' then went back to work. A dwarf in a mine. *Heigh-ho, heigh-ho.*

'What were the seven dwarves digging for anyway?' I asked Nicky, laughing, nearly falling over. 'Fucking dwarves,' I said. 'Made it look so easy.'

I forced my spade into the earth once more, a foot over to the right, knowing the star had to be there. Star of wonder. Star of light. Star with royal beauty bright.

'Remember,' I started to ask, 'that first day? How you threw open the cellar door and there was Del with her shirt off and there I was looking and none of us knew what was coming. None of us knew it was all an accident we were getting on board, a fucking

251

derailing train. Remember how none of us knew?'

There was the click of my shovel hitting something metal. I bent down and felt around in the dirt. There it was once again. Rusty and pointed. Heavy in my hand. More like a burden than a wish come true.

'Christ,' I said. 'The deputy found it.'

Then I leaned over and threw up.

PART 2

The Last Days

NOVEMBER 17, 2002
JUNE 16, 1971

One potato, two potato, three potato, four
She's coming after you now,
better lock the door

13

'I'm not staying here!'

'No one said you had to, Ma. We're just here to look.'

My mother's eyes were blank and wild, focused on a spot above my right shoulder.

'I'm not staying here!'

I turned to give an apologetic look to the woman giving us the tour — a Mrs Shrewsbury, who did, in sad fact, resemble a small, beady-eyed rodent.

'Perhaps,' said the shrew, as she peered over the top of her glasses, 'your mother would be more comfortable sitting in on an art class while we finish the tour.'

I nodded and we sat my mother down at a long table where several old people were set up with fat brushes, huge sheets of newsprint, and cups of tempera paint in primary colors. I helped my mother into a plastic smock and watched the art teacher get her started.

'I'm not staying here,' she repeated, but some of the intensity had gone out of her voice. Once she had the brush held clumsily in her bandaged hand, she settled right down, forgetting her surroundings.

Mrs Shrewsbury showed me the residents' rooms, dining hall, visiting lounge, and a calendar of events. I nodded vaguely at everything, too hung over to do much else. My ankle throbbed and I walked with a slight limp. I was eager to end the tour and escape the terrible smell of the place — a sickening combination of antiseptic and boiled peas.

The events of the night before were a blur. I knew Nicky and I had gone to the root cellar to dig up the star and that we'd been successful — the rusted sheriff's badge was under my pillow in the morning, dirt from the root cellar floor still clinging to it. I didn't remember getting home, or into bed. I didn't remember Nicky leaving, but knew it must have been near dawn. When Raven stopped by on her way to work to drop off some bran muffins, she commented on it. *I see you had an overnight guest*, she said. When I explained that we'd just been talking she only raised her eyebrows and said, *Mmm*. It was clear that Raven didn't believe a word I said anymore. And I didn't exactly have warm and fuzzy feelings toward her after my visit from Zack. If she didn't want me to see her daughter, so be it, but come on — she should have at least had the guts to come and tell me herself. Was she really that afraid of me?

★ ★ ★

'I know how hard this can be,' Mrs Shrewsbury was saying. 'It's a big decision and your mother may seem . . . resistant. As a nurse though, you know the level of care a person in your mother's condition requires. It's just too much for one person, twenty-four hours a day.' I nodded, thinking of my mother's painting, her new habit of speaking in Del's voice. *You don't know the half of it, Shrew.*

'There's always a lot of guilt involved,' Mrs Shrewsbury continued. 'But in time, you'll see you did the right thing. She'll settle in. Honestly, people in your mother's condition don't hold grudges. After a few weeks, it will be like she was always here.'

And that's supposed to be a comfort?

Then I thought of how easily distracted my mother had been by the paints in the art room. Maybe it wouldn't be that hard for her to settle in after all.

'She'll be safe here. Well taken care of. As I said on the phone, we have two vacant rooms. She could move in this week if you wanted.'

I nodded, said it wasn't a decision I wanted to rush into. Though in truth, I was more than a little eager to be done with the whole mess and get on a plane back to Seattle. Safely ensconced in a nursing home, my mother could paint whatever she wanted, speak in Del's voice to her heart's content. But as I thought of leaving, I felt a little tap on my shoulder: *The killer's still out there. And what if Opal really is in danger?*

Mrs Shrewsbury patted me on the arm and said again that she knew how hard it was.

Then she led me into the dayroom where a television blared. Three old women with their walkers parked nearby stared at a game show. An old man sat on an orange plastic chair in the corner, smacking his gums and singing a song. The tune was familiar to me, but I couldn't make it out — something childish, singsong. I got a little closer so I could hear him over the applause on the television.

'*Potato Girl, Potato Girl, smells so rotten she'll make your nose curl,*' he sang.

Jesus. My mouth went dry. I wondered if I had misheard him.

'What did you say?' I asked, leaning down so that I was at eye level with this toothless old man in stained pajamas. His blue eyes were watery and pale. He smelled like spoiled milk.

'Oh that's just Mr Mackenzie,' said Mrs Shrewsbury. 'He's quite the singer, aren't you, Ron?'

'One potato, two potato, three potato, four — she's coming after you now, better lock your door.' He was chanting now, not singing, his cloudy wet eyes fixed on mine.

'Ron Mackenzie? Did you used to drive a school bus?' I asked.

The old man only grinned, smacked his lips. A little drool trickled down his stubbled chin.

'Sure you drove the bus, didn't you, Ron?' asked Mrs Shrewsbury. 'Drove until you retired. You were a mechanic, too, down at the town garage, weren't you?'

'She's coming after *you* now, better lock your door,' Ron repeated, his eyes on me, his gummy smile wide.

'Do you remember Del Griswold?' My voice was squeaky and desperate. 'The Potato Girl? She used to ride your bus.' I had my hand on his sleeve and was holding back the impulse to shake the answer out of him.

He grinned. Drooled a little more.

'She was a monkey,' he finally said. 'Dirty little monkey. Her brother, too.'

'Which brother? You mean Nicky?'

'Potato Girl, Potato Girl, she smells so rotten she'll make your nose curl.' He was muttering now.

I stared down at the old man, leaning in so that his hot, sour breath was on my face.

'She was a m-monkey,' he whispered.

A terrible possibility dawned on me then under the fluorescent lights of the day room, some studio audience laughing behind me, the shrew by my side, her head cocked with mild curiosity. It was there in the sour milky heat of this old man's breath — a possibility equally as rancid.

'Did you give her the *M*, Mr Mackenzie? Did you give Del her *M*?' I forced the words from my mouth, dreading to know what his answer might be. Was it possible that I was face-to-face with Del's killer, a senile old man in soiled pajamas?

Ron Mackenzie smiled, began to rock back and forth in his chair, humming. The hum turned into a low moaning howl. My old bus driver was howling like a coyote, getting louder and louder each time he drew a breath. Mrs Shrewsbury clutched my arm to lead me away, saying we should go before he got much more wound up. We turned to leave the room, but then his howling stopped and he gently called out to me, his voice shaky now, worn out.

'Hey, girlie!' he said. I stopped in my tracks. Cold crept up my spine. 'You better give that monkey what she wants. Better look out for the Potato Girl!'

I turned back to look at the old man who once had worked for NASA in time to see a dark stain spreading across his lap. He looked at me and laughed as the urine trickled over the edge of the plastic chair, pooling on the checkered floor.

★　★　★

'I want to go home,' my mother said when we joined her at the art table. 'You can't leave me here.'

Believe me, we're getting the hell out of here as fast as our little legs will carry us . . .

I turned and glanced back down the hall, sure I'd see that old Ron Mackenzie had followed me. There was only an aide in a pink uniform pushing a mop and bucket.

'I'm not leaving you, Ma. We're going now.' My voice was as shaky as my hands as I fumbled to get the smock off her. It took all the control I had not to grab her hand and run screaming from the place, dragging her behind me.

'I made a painting,' my mother said. 'It's for Opal.'

'That's nice, Ma.'

One potato, two potato, three potato, four

She's coming after you now, better lock the door.

Was someone else singing the words now, or were they only in my head?

'I'd hoped you'd stay for lunch,' Mrs Shrewsbury said. 'We could look over some of the paperwork.'

'I want to go home,' my mother repeated.

'I know, Ma. Me, too. Come on, put your coat on.'

I apologized to the shrew, saying we had to leave but that I would call her as soon as we made a decision.

I turned back to help my mother get her coat around her shoulders and glanced down at her painting. Once again, I found myself having to stifle a scream.

There, on the large sheet of newsprint, was a giant sheriff's star carefully painted in shades of gray.

'Ma? Why's this for Opal?'

'What, Katydid?'

'The painting. You said it was for Opal.'

'Did I say that?' She mused for a moment, cocked her head. 'Poor little Opal. Do you think she knows?'

'Knows what, Ma?'

'Who her father is?'

'What are you talking about? Who is he?' I was sure she was going to say Lazy Elk — she had Opal confused with Raven, of course, who she confused with Doe half the time. God, it was hard to keep up with her.

'Why, it's Ralph Griswold, silly! The man

with the eggs and pigs who lives down the hill. You knew that didn't you, Katydid?' She eyed me quizzically, as if to say, *Is something wrong with your memory?*

★ ★ ★

'Listen Kate, I talked to Jim today and asked him about Mike Shane. Can you guess what the fucker does up in Burlington?'

Nicky and I were sitting at the kitchen table eating tuna sandwiches. My mother was working on her painting. I'd called Nicky to invite him to lunch as soon as we got back from The Hollows Care Center. I wanted desperately to tell him what my mother had said about his dad being Opal's father as well, but I decided to bite my tongue for the time being. It could have been some figment of her imagination.

But what if it wasn't? What if Opal was really Del's half sister? I knew if I wanted the truth, I'd have to go to the one person who was least likely to share it with me: Raven.

Nicky didn't wait for me to guess about Mike. 'You're not gonna believe this. It's perfect. Mike Shane is a fucking tattoo artist. He owns Dragon Mike's Tattoo Emporium up in Burlington.'

I let this sink in, considering the possibilities this bit of news brought with it. Maybe

Del's tattoo was one of Mike's first attempts. A more permanent gift than the silver star. Maybe I was on the wrong track with my hunch about old Ron Mackenzie.

'That's quite a coincidence,' I admitted.

'A coincidence — hell, I'd say it's evidence. Didn't you say it was a letter *M* on Del's chest? *M* for Mike. I bet it was him. He tattooed her, then killed her and had to cut off the tattoo so he couldn't be linked to her.'

'It's definitely worth checking into. But I can't really see Mike Shane killing Del. He was like eleven or twelve years old. And he was in pretty bad shape that last day of school — I think he wound up in the hospital.'

'But Kate, the guy's a fucking tattoo artist!'

'I know. It's a hell of a coincidence. Like I said, we should check into it. But let me tell you what I found out today. What do you remember about Ron Mackenzie — the school bus driver?'

'Not much. The guy had a temper, but he kept it hidden. He called us monkeys. I remember that.'

I told him about my morning at The Hollows and what Ron had said.

'Jesus, the tattoo could have been a way of branding her,' Nicky said. '*M* is for monkey. Like the scarlet letter or some such shit. Dirty fucker.' Nicky's face twitched.

'I don't know . . . it was such a delicate and pretty *M*,' I said. 'If it had been done in hatred by a guy like Ron, you'd think it would be crude, hurried. I've always had this idea that whoever did the *M* cared for Del.'

'Cared enough to choke the life out of her and carve her up like some piece of meat. I think we should talk to both Mackenzie and Shane. Hell, maybe we should go to the police,' Nicky suggested.

I shook my head.

'With what? On the basis of something a senile old man mumbled just before he wet himself? If he is Del's killer, he got what he deserved. He's in a prison of his own. I almost pity him. And we sure as hell know he didn't sneak out and kill Tori. The only proof we have about Mike is the letter *M* I saw that no one else seems to know about. Hell, they'd probably make me their number-one suspect, if I'm not already. Especially if they found out I had that damn star.'

'What? The police never thought you were a suspect,' Nicky said.

'Not then, but now. Judging by the way they've been acting, I think I'm at the top of their list.'

'That's just crazy! You had nothing to do with any of it.'

'Yeah, neither did you, but you're a

suspect, too, aren't you? Weren't you the first one they went looking for when Tori Miller was killed? It's just shit luck, Nicky.'

He took this in a moment. I cleared the plates from the table.

'And what about the star?' Nicky asked. 'Don't you think you better do something with it? If, like I've been telling you, it is Del we're dealing with, she knows you've got it.'

'Listen to yourself, will you? You sound almost as crazy as old Mr *I used to work for NASA and now I just sit around wetting myself.* Yeah, I've got the star, but there's nothing to do with it. We'd be better off if we'd left the damn thing in the ground. I never should have let you talk me into digging it up.'

'Maybe you're right,' he admitted. 'You were pretty drunk. I kinda took advantage.'

I laughed at this. 'I'm not sure who took advantage of whom.'

He gave me a shy little smile. Blushing, I studied the lines around his eyes. Crow's-feet. Like that bird he'd killed got him back somehow. There was something wounded, boyish, about him.

'Nicky, I've gotta be honest. I'm not too good at the relationship thing. My marriage fell to shit pretty early. I'm kind of an emotional basket case.'

I looked at the man before me and saw once again the fourteen-year-old boy, his skin dark brown from working in the fields, his eyes moist with need. He smelled of cigarette smoke and gasoline. He took off his John Deere cap and set it on the table.

'Last night meant a lot to me,' he began. 'And I sure hope that wasn't the end of it. It's not like I'm asking for some big commitment. I know you've got your life and I've got mine. I can't make any promises about what this might or might not lead to, but shit, we're all grown up now. We can't go back, but we can move ahead, know what I'm saying? So take a chance on me, huh? Let's just see where it goes.'

His voice was smooth as whiskey, and when he whispered there was that raspy edge to it that made the back of my neck warm. I leaned in and put my lips against his.

There was no clashing of teeth this time, no terrible force as there had been the night before. It was gentle and sweet. There was no desperation, only a hint of restrained longing. Longing, perhaps, not just for each other, but to go back. To go back and live things over again — to have our second chance. I put my hand on the back of his head, pulling him closer, trying to hold on. And just for one moment, we were kids up in the loft again, needing to come up for air, but loving the feeling of breathlessness.

'Kate and Nicky sitting in a tree, K-I-S-S-I-N-G!'

My mother's singsongy voice jolted us back to the present, jerked Nicky and me away from each other. It was a child's voice, and, glancing over at Nicky's frightened face, I saw I was not the only one who thought so.

Perhaps it was having a witness, perhaps it was the emotional exhaustion, or the hangover, or even the hormones, but it was in that moment that my subconscious fears came crashing forward into my conscious mind. Del was speaking through my mother, using her like one of those talking dolls, pulling some invisible cosmic string. That was simply the fact of the matter. She had found a way back, and, just as Nicky had warned, she was royally pissed.

'When's the wedding?' she asked. Hearing the voice of a vengeful child coming from my poor old mother's mouth was obscene. She turned away, cackling all the way back to her studio, where she slammed the door. This was followed by crashing sounds, as if she were tearing the room apart.

'You should go,' I whispered. 'I'll call you later.'

'Kate, I . . . '

'Just go. It's okay. We'll talk later.'
So much for second chances.
He picked up his greasy cap and put it on.
'I'm sorry,' he said.
'Me too,' I answered, then he was gone.

14

An hour later, I was sweeping up broken glass in the studio when Opal arrived.

'Holy shit!' she said. 'What happened in here?'

'My mother decided to do a little redecorating.'

The room had been torn apart. It was mostly my things she'd tried to destroy. She pulled all the clothing out of my suitcases and ripped what she could. The cot I slept on was turned over and the covers scattered.

'I came over to tell you I finished the Jenny. I just now glued the wing walker on and hung it up.'

'She must be happy up there, especially when you consider that all her other plastic brethren are going to be stuck waving at toy trains going around in circles.'

Opal nodded. She took a seat on the floor. 'I'm supposed to stay away from you, you know.'

'Yeah, I know.'

'My mother says you could be dangerous,' Opal said.

'Does she?'

'And I bet you don't know a thing about wild mushrooms.'

'And I bet you still haven't found whatever it is you were looking for in those woods. What is it, Opal? Is it something connected to Tori's murder? It isn't my knife, is it? Did you take my Swiss Army knife?'

The color drained from her face, and she resembled the ghost she was so afraid of.

Could she be Del's half sister? The resemblance at that moment was staggering. And the overriding feeling I had was one of fierce protection. I wanted to protect Opal in the way I'd never been able to protect Del.

'I can help you,' I said. 'You just have to be honest with me. Please, Opal. You can trust me. What were you looking for in the woods? What is it you're not telling me?'

She opened her mouth to speak, to tell the truth at last, then something stopped her. I followed her gaze to the easel in the corner, where my mother's painting stood, the only thing in the room that hadn't been disturbed during her latest rampage.

'What is this?' Opal asked, her face going whiter still as she walked up to my mother's painting.

'My mom's latest work. It's supposed to be the tepee fire.'

Take no notice of the pair of roaming gray eyes in the corner.

'But there's someone in there,' Opal said as she reached out to touch the figure in the painting. 'Someone with a sheriff's star. Who is it?'

'I don't know, Opal,' I said.

'It's her, isn't it? It's Del. Did she have a star like this?' Opal's voice was wavering now.

'Opal . . .'

'Tell me! Tell me the truth about this one thing and I'll never ask any more about her. I'll leave you alone just like everyone wants.'

It wasn't like Del's star was some big secret. All Opal needed to do was talk to anyone who was around back then or go down to the library and look through old newspaper articles.

'Okay, okay. Yes, Del had a silver sheriff's star. Just some junky tin thing. A kid's toy. She wore it all the time. She had it on the day she was killed, only it was never found.'

'So the killer took it?' Her face twisted into a grimace of concentration.

'That was the theory.' I waited for the barrage of follow-up questions, but there weren't any. Opal just stood staring at the painting.

'So now what, Opal? Does this really mean we're all done talking about Del?' I asked.

'Cross my heart,' she said as she turned from the painting and hurried from the room.

I was grateful she'd left off the *and hope to die*.

★　★　★

I dialed the number to the big barn and Raven answered on the second ring. I only hoped she hadn't seen Opal coming or going.

'Hi, Raven. I have to go out for a while. Up to Burlington. Would you stay with my mother until I get back? I'd ask Gabriel, only he was just with her yesterday. I should be back around suppertime. I'll phone from Burlington to check in, just to make sure you're okay.'

Raven hesitated before answering, making it clear she didn't want to do me any favors. She wasn't going out of her way for this cat killer.

'What's in Burlington?' she asked suspiciously.

'I want to look up an old friend.'

She sighed. 'I don't mind helping Jean out. Before you got here I was with her every free minute. She never got lost on my watch.'

I ignored the jab.

'I appreciate it,' I told her. 'Listen, my mom had kind of a bad spell a little while ago. I gave her a Haldol and put her to bed. She'll probably sleep the whole time you're here.'

'I'll be over in ten minutes,' she said.

* * *

'I thought we could have a cup of tea before I go,' I said to Raven when she arrived, gesturing toward the kitchen, where I'd laid out the teapot and cups. Raven looked suspicious.

'There's something I want to talk to you about.'

Raven took a seat at the table and poured a cup of green tea, carefully spooning in honey from the pot in the center of the table. I half thought she was going to ask me to take a sip first to make sure I hadn't poisoned it.

'If it's about Opal, I'm afraid the subject isn't up for discussion. I think you're an unhealthy influence on her at this point.'

'As a matter of fact, it *is* about Opal, but it's got nothing to do with me.'

'What then? Do you have some terrific parenting advice? If that's the case, I think it's safe to say you can skip it.'

'I want to know who Opal's father is.'

Raven looked truly blindsided.

'*What?*'

'You heard me.'

Her face twisted into a disgusted scowl. 'That is *none* of your business! Who do you think you are?'

'Was it Ralph Griswold?'

Her dark eyes turned a murky black.

'Who told you that?' she demanded.

'A reliable source,' I lied.

'Was it Nicky?' She ran her hands through her hair. 'I am going to kill that drunken jackass.'

So it was the truth after all. And another secret Nicky had been keeping.

'Opal doesn't know, does she?'

'Jesus. Of course not. Didn't your 'source' tell you I was raped? I'm not going to lay that on her: your biological father was a disgusting redneck rapist, and probably a pedophile to boot, Opal. How is she supposed to take that?'

'I really didn't know how it happened. I'm so sorry.'

Raven snorted. 'I don't need your sympathy. It was a long time ago and the son of a bitch did us all a favor and dropped dead soon after. I got a beautiful daughter who means the world to me. If you even *think* of telling her, I'll make you more sorry than you could possibly imagine.'

I suddenly understood why she'd been so adamant about not wanting to indulge Opal in stories about Del and the Griswolds.

'Of course not,' I said carefully. 'That's your place, not mine. But I wonder if on some level she suspects. I mean, that would explain a lot about her obsession with Del, wouldn't it?'

She shot me an exasperated look.

'Don't you have somewhere you have to be, Kate? You'd better get going. The weather's not supposed to be too great later on.'

I took the hint and grabbed my coat and keys, leaving Raven sitting at the table.

Who else, I wondered, knew the truth about Opal's father?

★ ★ ★

Before getting on 1-89 up to Burlington, I stopped in town at Haskie's for a cup of coffee and a bottle of aspirin. My ankle still throbbed and my head wasn't doing much better. I had resolved to steer clear of Wild Turkey for the rest of my visit.

'Heard about your mother's cat,' Jim Haskaway said as he rang up my purchases. 'Damn strange thing — its throat being cut like that.'

Oh, come on. Not this. I was in a hurry and not in the mood for anymore small-town gossip.

I nodded.

'Another funny thing,' Jim continued, 'about that old murder — Del Griswold. When I saw Ellie Miller at Tori's funeral, I mentioned you were back in town helping your mother out. We got to talking and Ellie said you and little Delores were the best of friends back then. Now I figure Ellie's all shook up with her daughter being killed and all, and must be confused. 'Cause the way I remember it, you told me you hardly knew that Griswold girl.'

He eyed me with practiced suspicion. Great, a small town amateur detective — look out, Angela Lansbury. I wanted to suggest he stick to his role as fire chief, but was interrupted by a chime coming out of Jim's scanner that seemed to get his full attention. It was followed by the staticky voice of a dispatcher saying that there was a car accident in town near the waterfall, then another series of electronic beeps.

'Ellie must be mistaken — it was a long time ago,' I confirmed, laying my money on the counter and hurrying away before he gave me back my change. He was too focused on the scanner to call after me. Saved by the bell.

I had parked the rental car in front of the Millers' antiques shop and when I looked in through the filmed-over window, past the CLOSED FOR THE SEASON sign, I saw a woman I immediately recognized as Ellie sitting at a table thumbing through a stack of cards. She looked much the same as she had when I'd last seen her at high school graduation. She still had perfect posture and was dressed in a fashionable yet tidy way. Her hair was lighter than ever and she wore it in a neat bun. When she looked up and saw me, I felt compelled to say hello and made my way to the shop door, which was unlocked despite the CLOSED sign.

'I heard you were in town,' she said flatly.

Good to see you, too, Ellie.

The store smelled like old leather and furniture polish. A string of sleigh bells that were hung on the door jingled as it swung closed.

'Word gets around,' I told her, forcing a kind smile. Ellie turned her attention to the pile of old postcards she was sorting on the desk. Old sepia-colored images of a Vermont long gone. In front of the piles of yellowed postcards was a silver letter opener, a pad, and a pen. The desk was small, almost child-size, and Ellie sat with her knees pressed beneath it, looking terribly uncomfortable.

The shop itself was in a state of disarray and looked to be in the middle of a major off-season reorganizing project. At the back of the store stood a ladder resting against a set of floor-to-ceiling shelves that had been stripped bare. Carefully labeled boxes were stacked around the shop along with clip-boards, price stickers, and reference books on antiques and collectibles.

'I'm sorry for your loss,' I said. The words sounded hollow. She didn't look up, and continued working through the postcards like they were a tarot deck, dealing them out to tell an uncertain future.

'People are talking,' Ellie said at last, her voice quavering. 'People are saying you might have had something to do with what happened to Tori.'

Her face twitched as she spoke her daughter's name. She fingered a stained postcard showing a picture of the old waterwheel that once ran the mill in town. Long gone. Wood rotted. Metal turned to dust.

'Me?'

'You and Nicky Griswold.'

Perfect. The dynamic duo of crime.

I laughed, unable to stop myself.

'Me and Nicky Griswold,' I repeated. 'Is that what you think, Ellie?'

She pursed her lips, squinted down at a picture of a man with a team of horses hauling buckets of maple sap. Quintessential Vermont.

'I don't think anymore. When you lose a child, you stop thinking.' Her words were sharp and her eyes never left the postcard. I nodded down at her sympathetically, knowing she didn't see.

'I heard what *Nicky* thinks,' Ellie said. 'He's been going around town saying the Potato Girl did it.' She snorted derisively. 'The Potato Girl's the one who gets blamed for everything around here. If there's a drought, it's her doing. A car wreck, she's responsible. But it makes me sick to hear people blame her for this. Just to hear her name and Tori's in the same sentence makes me sick.' Her fingers trembled as she raced through the cards, seeming to put them into random piles.

'I understand,' I said.

'No!' Her tone was sharp. Angry. 'No, you don't. What'd you come here for, anyway, Kate? To reminisce about old times? To say how sorry you are about my daughter?' She looked up at me for the first time, her eyes burning into mine. She sat up even straighter, banging her knees into the bottom of the tiny wooden desk.

'I *am* sorry.' My voice was nearly a whine. 'I just wanted to offer my condolences. I'll go now and leave you to your work.'

'Good idea,' she said. 'Why don't you get in your little car and get out of New Canaan, Kate. No one wants you here. You showed up and the trouble began.'

She was right about that. Had my arrival triggered something? Put forces in motion? Or was it all just an unhappy coincidence?

'Just *go*!' Ellie barked. She stood up fast and flung an arm toward the door. As she rose, her legs caught the edge of the desk and it overturned, spilling postcards everywhere. The letter opener skittered across the floor to my feet. Ellie crouched, snatching up postcards, and began to cry. I picked up the letter opener and took a step toward her, thinking to help her collect the cards. Ellie jumped back, putting a hand to her throat.

'Are you going to hurt me now? You think I haven't been through enough? You think there's anything you could do to me that would hurt worse than the pain I already feel?' She was sobbing now. I dropped the letter opener to the floor.

'God, no. I'm so sorry. I was just trying . . . I'm sorry.'

She kept her hand protectively over her throat.

'You know, the truth is, I don't think you killed my daughter,' Ellie said through her tears.

Before I could think how to respond she went on.

'But I think you know who did. I can see that in your eyes. I see it just as I saw that you really were friends with Del back then and that everything you told Sam and me about her was bullshit. Am I right, Kate?'

I opened my mouth to say something, anything — *none of your business, we were in fifth grade for God's sake, what difference does it make* — but instead I snapped my jaws shut, turned on my heel, and slipped out the door. She had made me feel like a criminal after all.

'Am I right?' Ellie called after me, her voice raised in desperation. I shut the door hard, hopped into my car, and drove away without glancing back.

★ ★ ★

Dragon Mike's Tattoo Emporium was on Pearl Street, tucked between a cosmetology school and a Chinese take-out. The front room was poorly lit and the walls were plastered with tattoo designs. There was a large metal desk set up in the corner with an upholstered chair behind it and a metal folding chair in front. Behind the desk hung a red curtain and I could hear voices — a man and a woman, and a steady mechanical humming. In a minute, a woman with spiked magenta hair emerged from behind the curtain. She was dressed in tight jeans, biker boots, a white T-shirt, and a leather vest.

'Howya doin'?' she asked.

'Okay.'

'Yeah? Good. Take your time. Check out all the flash. We got books to look through, too. Ask if you need a price on anything. You ever had a tattoo before?'

'No.'

'A virgin, huh? Well, it's true what they say. You can't stop at just one. There's just somethin' about it. You can't get enough. An addiction, I guess.' She held her arms out for my inspection. They were encircled with dozens of red roses. Woven into the flowers were several hearts, a black panther, and a few brightly colored butterflies.

'This is just the tip of the iceberg,' she said with a wink. 'The real beauties are hidden.'

I prayed she wouldn't offer to show me.

It's a good kind of hurt.

'Actually,' I confessed, 'I didn't really come for a tattoo. I was hoping to talk to Mike.'

She eyed me skeptically.

'You know Mike?'

'Yeah, we went to school together.'

'Then you know he won't be doing a whole lot of talkin'.'

I nodded. She continued on, a wistful look in her eyes.

'Some of my girlfriends wonder what I'm doin' with a guy that can't talk, but the way I figure it, God took away one thing and gave him another. The man's an artist. He's got a gift. You know what I'm saying? We gotta be thankful for what we got, not bitter about what we don't. Right?'

I nodded again.

She smiled widely, showing several gold-capped teeth.

'He's just doing a touch-up job. I'll let him know he's got someone waiting. What'd you say your name was?'

'Kate. Kate Cypher. I don't know if he'll remember me.'

'I'll let him know.' She disappeared behind the curtain again, leaving me to study the walls. I found myself face-to-face with skulls that had snakes crawling out of the eyes and skulls with roses surrounding them.

Bones, I thought. *Del's just bones now.* Or is she? I shivered.

The woman emerged from behind the curtain.

'He'll be out in a minute. I'm headed home. Make yourself comfortable.' She gestured toward an old vinyl recliner in the corner. Next to it was a coffee table piled high with tattoo magazines. She grabbed a leather jacket from under the desk and walked out. 'See ya,' she called to me.

In a few minutes, an enormous man with a shaved head came through the curtain, followed by a tall wispy man who wore his hair in a ponytail. I remembered how tall and thin Mike had been and it seemed like not much had changed, until I heard the skinny guy speak.

'Thanks, Mike,' he said, passing the hulking giant a wad of bills. The giant nodded and smiled. The skinny guy left the shop.

'Mike? Mike Shane?'

I was nearly struck mute. My old classmate now resembled a biker version of Mr Clean, complete with gold hoop earring. He wore ripped jeans and a black leather vest with nothing beneath it. His exposed flesh literally rippled with muscles. His biceps were nearly as big around as my waist.

He nodded at me, his face expressionless.

'I'm Kate Cypher. We went to school together. Remember?'

This got me another nod.

'The thing is, I'm here for a reason. A kind

of strange reason. I'm here about Del Griswold.'

No nod this time. He took a breath and seemed to hold it, his impossibly large chest looking larger still. He gestured me over to the desk and I sat down in the metal folding chair across from him. He pulled out a pad of paper and a pen and wrote a sentence, then turned the paper toward me.

What do you want?

'I want to know about Del's tattoo.'
He narrowed his eyes.

What tattoo?

'The letter *M* on her chest. You gave it to her, didn't you?'
He studied me a minute, didn't write anything down. I realized he wasn't going to give me anything if I didn't give him something first.
'No one knows about the tattoo, Mike. I think I was the only one Del showed it to. She was really proud of that tattoo. She told me someone very special had given it to her.'
He scribbled violently on the pad.

I didn't kill Del.

'I believe you. I just want to know about the tattoo.'

He wrote rapidly for a moment, then shoved the pad toward me defiantly. It was covered with neat, slanting block letters, amazingly legible for the speed with which he wrote them.

I was in the ER when Del was killed. I was there 5 hours. They took X-rays. Set my arm and nose. You saw the beating I took that day. Police knew I couldn't have killed Del. All it took was a phone call to the ER and one look at my busted arm.

'The police never knew about the tattoo, Mike. The killer cut it off her.' His face went slack and he looked down at the desktop, his eyes glassy as marbles. I continued. 'I'll make a deal with you. If you tell me the truth about the tattoo, I won't go to the police about it. I believe you didn't kill her. Like you said, you couldn't have. But I think you may have given her that letter *M*. And I also think the police would be mighty interested in that part of the story.'

He looked me in the eye, scribbled on his paper.

It was 30 years ago.

'Yeah, I know. But in case you hadn't heard, there's been another murder. A copycat killing. Ellie Bushey's daughter. So the police are all of sudden interested in the unsolved case of Del Griswold. Now am I going to go to them with what I know, or are you going to help me out? I'm not interested in getting you in trouble, Mike. I just want to know what happened. I want to understand everything I can about Del's last months alive.'

I wasn't good at giving hard-boiled detective ultimatums, but I needed to get somewhere. I felt I was getting close to finding out what had happened to Del, and Mike was an important piece of the puzzle.

He looked at me a moment, then down at his yellow pad. He picked up the pen and started writing. His brow furrowed and his eyes squinted. He held the pen so tight that I was sure it would crack in two. The writing came slow at first, then faster, the letters scrawled quickly, like he was running a race. He filled three pages — as he finished a page he would tear it off and push it toward me, already starting on the next. When he was finished, he wiped sweat off his wide brow and set down the pen.

Most people didn't know Del like I knew Del. They thought she was just some dumb retard, which I guess is the same way they thought of me. 'Two peas in a pod,' that's what I used to write in my notes to Del. Del said we were more like onions than peas, each of us with all these layers. When people looked, they saw our dirty outsides, that was all. That's how Del used to say it.

I gave myself my first tattoo when I was 12. Tiny heart with the initials DG inside it. It's on my right thigh. Dear God. That's what I tell Lucy those initials stand for, but she must know I'm lying. Never mentioned Del to her. Not now, not ever. I don't think she'd send me packing, but it would wreck her. To know I'd cared for some other girl so much. Even if I was only a kid. And if she found out that girl was dead, there'd be no contest. You can't compete with a 1st love — especially not one who's dead. You'll always feel 2nd best.

I sure did love Del. All her layers. Even when peeling them back made me cry. Seems like that girl was always finding some new way to make me cry. She said there were other boys. Described what she did with them to me sometimes, like it was supposed to get me all hot or jealous or something, but really it just made me cry. But she said I was her only one. I was special. And to prove it, she asked me to tattoo my name across her chest. That way we'd be bound together . . . for ever. Yeah, for ever.

Well, like you know, there's no such thing as for ever. I only got as far as the M. Then some fucker, one of the other guys, I guess, killed her. Maybe he saw the tattoo and freaked out in some jealous rage. Maybe that's why he cut her like that. To make her all his. I could almost understand that in some fucked up kind of way. I had no idea the tattoo was cut off. I always expected the police would connect me to the M, but they never did. Anyway, like I said, I didn't kill her and I don't know who did. The girl was a fucking mystery. I loved her yeah, but I never got anywhere close to the center, if you know what I mean. The heart of the onion. I just scratched the surface. Left my M there as a mark.

I finished reading the pages and pushed them back to Dragon Mike. 'Thank you,' I mumbled. I felt a combination of things. Jealousy, humility, sorrow. Had I ever let myself love anyone as Mike had loved Del? Loved someone enough to carve their initials in my skin, to carve mine in theirs? I was jealous that he had known such love. And that he had had that chance to know Del in that way. I realized that I hadn't had the courage to peel back those layers, not just with Del, but with anyone. Not even with my husband. Ex-husband.

One thing was clear — I hadn't known Del at all. She'd had a whole other life I knew nothing about. A life of boys who loved her, tattooed her, messed around with her. And one of them had killed her. My gut told me it wasn't the huge man across the desk from me. He'd loved Del, he'd given her the *M*, but I didn't think he'd killed her, nor did he know who did.

'I think I'd like a tattoo, Dragon Mike,' I told him, feeling suddenly spontaneous and brave. The big man smiled at me.

'I'd like a name,' I told him. 'Desert Rose.'

Mike nodded, turning to a clean page in his pad. He wrote down the name in scripted letters, not unlike the letter *M* he'd done on Del's chest.

You want any flowers around it? A red rose maybe?

'Uh-uh. Just the name.'

Where do you want it?

'On my chest, the same place you did Del's M.'

Mike nodded and took me behind the curtain. As he was setting up, I asked him about the star.

'Mike, do you remember that sheriff's star you gave Del?'

Mike looked puzzled, reached for his pad of paper, scribbled his answer, and passed it to me.

I didn't give Del that star.

'Well, who did?'

Not sure. I think maybe she said she got it from her brother or someone her brother knew, maybe. Yeah, I think that's it. Some friend of her brother's.

'Which brother?'

The youngest one, maybe. The one she was close to. Can't think of his name.

'Nicky?'

Yeah, Nicky. Some friend of Nicky's.

Didn't he have some friend Del was close to? An older guy? Lived up at that commune. He's the one who gave her the star.

15

JUNE 16, 1971

The last day of school was a field day — kickball, a watermelon seed-spitting contest, a three-legged race. The recorder band played a concert they'd been practicing for all year. And all the graduating fifth graders would get a diploma — even Artie Paris would be handed a paper and pushed on to junior high at last.

The back soccer field was a wide-open space behind the playground, and it was here that all the kids from Number 5 Elementary were gathered. We spent the morning playing games, and around eleven, the principal started grilling the hamburgers and hot dogs.

After a long and chaotic lunch, Miss Johnstone announced that it was time for the fifth grade scavenger hunt. We were each given a list of things to find and clues telling where we might find some of the more obscure items. Some of the objects were simple: *a dime-sized stone, a buttercup.* Others were things that had been planted by the teachers: *Find and write down the poem in the trees. Somewhere around the storage shed there is a picture of a famous man. Tell us who he is and what he did.*

I was looking at the picture, writing *President Abraham Lincoln*, telling how he freed the slaves then got shot in a theater by a man called John Wilkes Booth, when Ellie came up behind me, breathless from running.

'They've got the Potato Girl and Mute Mike down by the river. Come on,' she said, taking my hand and pulling me along behind her.

To the teachers, we must have looked like two playful, innocent girls on a scavenger hunt, running happily across the soccer field. We were moving fast and Ellie was laughing, her white-blond hair streaming behind her, her pretty yellow dress flapping around her unscathed knees. *Isn't it nice that weird Kate has finally made some friends,* the teachers might have said to one another. *Isn't it nice how well she's fitting in?*

Beyond the soccer field lay a swath of tall grass, which gave way to bamboo-like reeds a little way in. I had heard that if you knew where to look in the shoulder-high grass, you could find the hidden opening that was the beginning of a path. This path would lead you through the grass, reeds, and wildflowers down to the river. It was here that kids snuck away during recess to shoot off caps or even make out (so the rumors went). Ellie seemed to know the way and did not hesitate before diving into a slight parting of the reeds, dragging me in tow. The damp grass soaked my jeans and Ellie's fingers dug into my palm as she pulled me toward the sound of running water and teasing voices.

Bloodroot River was not much of a river at all. About the only fish in it were minnows, and during the spring floods you could walk across it and get wet only up to your knees.

When we came into the clearing on the bank of the river, I saw that about a dozen kids were gathered there, standing in a rough semi-circle, looking down and singing Potato Girl rhymes.

When Ellie and I moved into the circle, she still held my hand. I imagine this is what Del first noticed when she looked up at me.

Del was lying on her back in the sand, propped up on her elbows. Artie Paris stood at her feet and had Mute Mike's arms pinned. Artie held the taller boy as if he were some gangly puppet.

> One potato, two potato, three potato, four!
> We don't want this rotten potato 'round us anymore!

The kids were chanting, shouting each word down at Del. A few boys spat on her, and Fat Tommy kicked Del in the ribs.

One potato, two potato, three potato, four!
Del Griswold is a trashy, potato-eating bore!

Del looked relieved to see me.

'Desert Rose,' she mumbled. Her lip was bleeding. I thought maybe she bit it in the fall. Or maybe someone clocked her one. It was hard to say. The one thing that was clear was that Del was in trouble and it looked like I might be her only chance. Her deputy had arrived.

The dozen or so kids gathered around began throwing pebbles down at her; tiny stones they'd stuffed in their pockets. The stones pinged off her, made her twitch like she was being stung.

★ ★ ★

I know that I should have gone to Del's side, hoisted her up from the dirt, snarled a warning to Artie. I should have done what a good deputy would have: backed my sheriff up, right up until the end.

In college, I read in a sociology textbook about a sort of mob mentality. I guess that is the closest I have to an excuse for myself. I got swept away with the feeling that I was part of the group, and in those few confused moments, that felt more real, more exciting to me than my friendship with Del.

I was ten, for Christ's sake. Doesn't everyone make mistakes like that back then? Have moments of weakness, cruelty born of fear?

Most people, probably. But I suspect most people don't spend the rest of their lives reliving those moments, playing the if-only game: *if only I had picked Del up out of the dirt that day, if only I'd been brave and true, as she would have been for me, then she might not have been killed.*

But that's not what happened.

*   *   *

One potato, two potato, three potato, four!

Your daddy is your brother and your mother is a whore!

It was a rhyme I knew well, had heard hundreds of times, but had never joined in on. That day, with Del in the dirt at my feet and Ellie's hand in mine, part of the pack, I sang along.

Del continued to study me, her pleading face cracking into a twisted, jack-o'-lantern smile, showing her chipped tooth. Then, down in the dirt, pelted by stones, she began to laugh. She laughed as if she could not stop, and her laughter made the crowd around her all the more angry. I was enraged.

'Shut up!' I yelled. 'Just shut the hell up!'

The rocks were getting bigger. She flinched each time one hit her, but made no move to escape. She rolled back and forth in the dirt, cackling. Ellie leaned down to get a rock and I did, too. The stone I held was smooth and dark, the size and shape of an egg. It fit perfectly in my palm.

'I got somethin' for you, Del,' Artie sang, as he shoved Mute Mike away with disgust. The kids stopped throwing rocks and waited to see what would happen next. We all watched in silence as Artie walked over to the edge of the river, where he picked up what looked like a large brown stone. He pulled a jackknife out of his pocket and cut into the object, which I quickly realized was a potato, slicing the end off and carrying the piece over to Del.

'Open up wide, Potato Girl.'

Del kept her jaw clamped shut, but Artie pried her teeth apart and shoved the piece in.

'Have some more, Delores,' he said, straddling her. He pushed another hunk of raw potato into her mouth and she gagged, started to choke.

'Hey, Mute Mike, did you know your wife

has a secret?' asked Artie, as he tossed the rest of the potato away and wiped his hands on his thighs. He remained in position, straddling Del, pinning her under his weight. Mike was kneeling in the dirt beside them, holding the same position he'd been in since Artie let him go. Del twisted her head, spat out bits of potato. Then she began her mad, grinning laughter again.

'Why don't you show us your tattoo, Del?' Artie asked.

The smile disappeared from Del's face and she fell silent. She turned her gaze to me again, but now her eyes glared.

'Traitors get shot in the back,' she hissed.

'What?' Artie asked. 'What the hell is that supposed to mean? Who said you could talk, Potato Bitch?'

Del began to fight then, tried to wrestle Artie off, twisting and bucking, but he held fast. I saw that she was wearing the silver star pinned to her chest, but it would take more than that to protect her. So much for talismans.

'Who wants to see the Potato Girl's tattoo?' Artie called out. 'A quarter a look. Come on. Step right up. Where's that tattoo at, anyway, Delores? Is it on your butt?' At this, he lifted off her, flipped her body over, and jerked down her pants. Her underwear was covered with faded flowers. The elastic had sprung and the panties were loose and clown-like. Artie jerked them down, exposing her bare ass.

'Nothing here,' he bellowed.

But there *was* something there: both buttocks were bruised brown and yellow, roughly in the shape of hand prints. Ellie let out a little gasp and let go of my hand.

'Jesus, who's been at you, girl?' Artie asked.

Seeing Del like that was more injustice than Mute Mike could bear. He was skinny, but tall, and when he dove at Artie, no one expected it.

Mike and Artie rolled around on the riverbank that afternoon, stirring up sand, gasping and grunting like neither one of them knew how to speak. Artie proceeded to beat the shit out of Mute Mike. It was the worst fight I've ever seen — worse than any of the scuffles in the state hospital years later, or the boxing matches my husband dragged me to when we were dating. I watched that day as Mike's nose was broken and his left arm was pulled from its socket, where it hung like a loose and useless wing. But Mike fought on, no doubt fueled by his love for the Potato Girl, his need to honor her in some public way. Mike was too busy getting whipped to notice Del as she rose from her place on the ground and backed away, slowly at first, then turned and ran. The other kids, distracted by the fight, yelling, 'Kick his ass, Artie,' and 'Mutilate Mute Mike!' didn't seem to notice Del leaving. She ran not back toward the safety of the soccer field and teachers, but along the river, toward town. And without much thought, I took off running right behind her, carrying my stone. In the commotion of the boys' fight, no one seemed to notice us. On we ran.

Del was always faster than me and although I tried, I could not gain any ground, and, in truth, I'm not sure what I would've done if I'd caught up. The rock in my hand said that I wasn't chasing her to apologize.

There was no playful *Catch me if you can* called back to me. There was only the sound of our footsteps pounding over dirt and rocks, our own heartbeats deafening in our ears. I followed her nearly a mile to the bridge on Railroad Street, then I watched her turn into Mr Deluca's hayfield and run faster still, heading home.

In my last picture of Del alive, she's running through that field, her yellow cowgirl shirt billowing behind her, in some ways a ghost already.

16

I stopped at a pay phone off the highway to call home at just after six. The name on my bandaged chest burned like a hundred bee stings. I had been hurrying back to New Canaan, hoping to beat the snow that the deejays kept warning about on the radio. They reported that it had started to snow in southern Vermont and the storm was working its way up. It was going to be a messy night. The forecasts reminded me of what Ellie had said about people blaming bad weather on the Potato Girl. Maybe this was Del's storm coming.

'Hi, Raven. Just me checking in. I'm on my way back.'

'Kate! It's good you called. There's been an accident.'

'Mom?'

'No, no, not Jean. She woke up just after you left and has been in her studio painting all afternoon. No more redecorating. She's been very calm. It's Nicky. He wrecked his

303

truck earlier this afternoon. It happened just after you left. Right by the waterfall.'

I remembered the chimes on Jim's scanner.

'Jesus, is he all right?' I held my breath, fearing the worst.

'It was a bad accident, but I guess he's going to be okay. He has a broken ankle. Some cuts and bruises. They're releasing him from the hospital. He's been calling every twenty minutes to see if you're back yet. The phone's been driving me crazy, ringing off the hook. He was hoping you would pick him up. He said he *needs* to see you.' Her voice was childishly sarcastic as she spoke this last line.

'Well, if you're still okay with my mother I'll swing by the hospital and pick him up.'

'I'm fine, Kate. I'm still waiting for Opal. She took off on her bike just before I came to sit with Jean. She's supposed to meet me here for supper. I made ratatouille. We'll save some for you and Nicky.'

★ ★ ★

The ER nurse went over Nicky's condition with me, telling me they hadn't ruled out a concussion and giving me a list of warning signs. When I told her I was an RN, she seemed relieved.

304

'Then you know he needs to be watched overnight.'

'He can come stay with my mother and me. We'll take care of him.'

She led me into Trauma Room 3, where Nicky was resting on a gurney. There was a cast on his left foot. His face was cut and swollen. He had seven stitches over his left eye and two in his left earlobe. He smiled when he saw me.

'Hiya, Desert Rose. Looks worse than it is. I really don't feel all that bad.'

'No, I don't imagine you would, with all the pain meds you're on. What happened, Nicky?'

'Tell you what, you take me outta here and we'll talk in the car. My place isn't all that far if we take the back roads.'

'Uh-uh.' I shook my head. 'You're coming to my mother's. You're in no shape to be by yourself. In the morning, we'll swing by your place and pick up a few things. You'll stay with us as long as you need to.'

'Well, Nurse Kate, I guess I'm in good hands. I woulda had the accident sooner if I'd known it meant I got to shack up with you.'

He grinned up at me from the gurney he was stretched out on.

The nurse came back in and had Nicky sign his release forms. His gun was being held by one of the cops on duty at the ER, and she told us how to get it back from him. An aide wheeled Nicky out to the car while I carried his crutches and pain medication. I also took charge of the gun, telling him it was out of the question with his pain meds.

'As I recall, you're a hell of shot,' he said. 'I could be in danger.'

I tucked the gun into the pocket of my parka after Nicky showed me that the safety was on.

Nicky managed to maneuver himself into the front seat and get his seatbelt on. The first thing he asked me for when we pulled out was a cigarette.

'I don't have any. We can stop on the way and pick some up.'

'A bottle of booze, too, maybe. I could use a drink.'

'Not with the narcotics, Nicky. No booze. You're loopy enough. Now are you going to tell me what happened?'

He was quiet a second.

'Well?' I asked, impatient.

'All right. I'll tell you. You're probably about the only one who might believe me, what with all the weird shit you've been through lately. I told the cops I swerved to avoid a dog in the road, but that wasn't how it was, Kate. I was driving home from your place this afternoon, right? And I was thinking things over, kinda lost in my own thoughts. Thinking about you mostly. About last night.' He reached out, put a hand on my thigh, and squeezed. Then he began running his fingers slowly up my leg until I clamped down with my own hand, stopping him.

'So what happened next?' I asked.

He took his hand away, looked out the windshield into the black night.

'Then I got to the turn by the river, right where the waterfall is, you know?'

I nodded, thinking of the postcard of the old waterwheel Ellie had had in her hands earlier. The place Nicky described was the spot in the photograph.

'And damned if this little girl doesn't run out into the road. She ran right in front of the truck, Kate. Fast as a fucking coyote. I jerked the wheel hard to the right. Just instinct. The next thing I know, the truck's headed down the embankment and I'm rolling. I guess I blacked out or something. When I came to, the truck was right side up in the middle of the river beside the waterfall. Thank God it's not much of a river, the water only came up to the top of the wheels. The windshield was shattered, it seemed like there was glass and blood everywhere. I wiped the blood out of my eyes and looked out the side window and there she was, just standing there at the top of the bank, laughing. It was Del. It was my fucking little sister. I blacked out again and the next thing I knew, Jim Haskaway and a couple of other firefighters were pulling me out, strapping me down on a board.'

I didn't say anything, just gripped the wheel tighter and stared out into the dark road ahead of us. It began to snow.

'I know what you're thinking,' Nicky continued. 'You're thinking I imagined it. Hallucinated. But damn it, Kate, it was Del standing there looking down at me just as sure as you're beside me right now. It was Del.'

The truth was, I almost believed him, but found it more comfortable to stay in the well-rehearsed role of skeptic. It made the whole thing a little less terrifying.

'And you hadn't been drinking?'

'Christ, Kate! I'd just left your house. I was stone-cold sober! All I had in my belly was the tuna sandwich and glass of milk you'd given me.'

It was snowing harder and driving was like captaining a spaceship moving at warp speed through the stars. I slowed down to a crawl, afraid I'd lose sense of where the road was.

'I have one more question,' I told him.

'Fire away.'

'Do you know who Opal's father is?'

I took my eyes off the snowy landscape in front of me and focused on Nicky for a few seconds. He began moving around like he was trying to get comfortable, but wasn't having much success.

'I know. Raven told me. She told me at Daddy's viewing, of all places. I think she came to the funeral home just to see for herself — to make sure he was really gone. Hell, probably half the people in that room came for the very same reason. My father was no saint. He hurt a lot of people in his day — me and Del included. He used to treat us worse than dogs when he'd been drinking. And sometimes at night, I'd hear him go into Del's room. I knew what he was up to. But Del never said a word, and neither did I. So when Raven told me what he'd done to her, I wasn't all that surprised.

'I don't know what it was Raven expected from me but whatever it was, I couldn't give it to her. I couldn't apologize for him, or explain why he was the way he was. Then, when she told me she was pregnant and that she was going to keep the baby, I about shit. I offered to help, you know, give her whatever money I could, but she refused. Guess she didn't want anything to tie an innocent baby to our fucked-up family. I don't blame her. I just wished there was more I could do for her.'

Nicky and I were silent the rest of the way home. I left the car running while I went in to buy a pack of cigarettes at Haskie's. I was relieved to see a teenage girl behind the counter, no sign of Jim. The lights in the antique shop were off. Ellie had gone home, too.

When we got to the bottom of Bullrush Hill, I looked past the destroyed mailbox and the swinging sign at the Griswolds' place and saw movement in the yard. It was dark and the snow was heavy, but I was sure I caught a glimpse of a fair-haired child disappearing behind the back of the house.

'Did you see that?' I asked, hitting the brakes. The car skidded about two feet.

'What?' Nicky followed my gaze over to the ruin of his old house.

Del. It was Del.

'Nothing, I guess. Must have been an animal.' I decided Nicky was agitated enough without me telling him what I thought I had seen. Maybe it had been an animal after all and my eyes were just playing tricks on me. The driving snow made it difficult to make things out, gave everything an ethereal, dreamlike quality. Del's storm.

I stepped on the gas and continued up the

hill, the rental car's tires slipping and spinning in the snow.

* * *

Raven was frantic when we got back to my mother's. Gabriel was with her in the kitchen.

'Opal is missing,' she said. 'She's just gone. I've called all her friends. No one's seen her. She's been gone four hours now and she wouldn't be out on her bike in this weather. Something's happened.'

Nicky sat down awkwardly at the table, resting his crutches against his chair.

As much as I wanted to tell Raven to relax and that Opal was going to turn up fine any minute, I knew immediately that it wasn't true.

'Have you called the police?' I asked.

'Of course,' Raven said. 'The detectives said not to be concerned yet, but they're planning to stop by in an hour or so anyway to take a look at the knife I found.'

'Knife?'

'I found this in your mother's locked drawer when I was cooking this afternoon. It's not hers. I've never seen it before.' Raven held out a sealed plastic bag with a small paring knife in it. I recognized it as the one my mother was using to slice strawberries on

311

my first morning home. The morning after the murder. My mind flashed to how disheveled my mother had looked with leaves, dirt, and what appeared to be dried blood on her bandages. Had my mother gone into the woods and found the knife there?

Another, more horrifying thought surfaced: one that I'd been pushing back for days. Had my mother used the knife? Was it possible that this frail, sick old woman could be the one who killed Tori Miller? She was clearly out of her head most of the time, but capable of murder? I doubted it.

But if, somehow, Del had gotten inside her . . .

'There's a small piece of blond hair caught under the handle,' Raven said. 'If you look carefully, you can see it.'

I held the bag in my hand and searched until I saw that Raven was right, there was a fine strand of hair there. Pale blond.

'I don't suppose you know where the knife came from?' Raven said, and I shook my head.

'It's been here since I have,' I told her. 'We used it to make strawberry pancakes my first morning home.'

Raven squinted at me, took the knife back, and tucked it carefully into her purse.

'We're going to go take a drive around in

the Blazer,' Gabriel said. 'See if we can find any sign of Opal.'

'Do you want me to come with you?' I asked.

'No,' Gabriel said. 'You stay here and look after your mother. We'll let you know if we find anything.'

'Be careful out there,' I said. 'The roads are getting pretty slick.'

'I'll go warm up the car,' Gabriel said, leaving us.

Raven hurried into the front hall for her coat and boots. I followed at her heels. 'There's ratatouille on the stove — your mother wouldn't eat. She worked on her painting till about six thirty or so, then went to her room to lie down. She said the painting was done.

'Kate, one more thing.' Raven was doing up the top button of her coat. 'I'm curious. Where'd your mother find that old badge?'

'Badge?'

'Yeah, she's got some rusted sheriff's star pinned to her shirt. Looks like a kid's toy. I thought maybe it was some old thing of yours.'

I stared dumbly at her, as if she had been speaking some strange tongue.

I wondered if Raven had ever heard about the little detail of the missing star in the unsolved Griswold murder case. If she had, then surely she would have had the police waiting for me with handcuffs and leg irons.

'I'm just worried she'll hurt herself with it,' Raven explained. 'The points look pretty sharp. You might want to try to take it away.'

'Yeah,' I agreed. 'I'll get it away from her.' *Damn right I will. Especially with the police on their way.*

When Raven left, I went into the kitchen, hurriedly scooped some ratatouille into a bowl for Nicky, and told him I was going to go change my clothes. I needed to be alone with my thoughts for a minute.

Opal was missing. I knew the killer had her. I had a lot of jumbled pieces of the puzzle spinning around in my head, but some of them were beginning to fit. I knew the next step was to talk to my mother. But first, I wanted to take a look at her finished painting.

The thought of going into the studio alone frightened me, but I wouldn't drag Nicky along. This was something I had to do on my own. Besides, I told myself, it was only a painting.

'Aren't you having anything to eat?' Nicky asked as I put the bowl down in front of him.

'No. I ate up in Burlington,' I lied.

'What'd you do up there anyway? Raven told me you went to see an old friend. Was it Mike? Did you find him?'

'No. I went to his shop, but he wasn't there.' The second lie came easier than the first. It seemed easier and safer than to go ahead and tell him everything I'd learned and all the things I was beginning to suspect.

'Be right back. I'm just going to change.'

'Into something more comfortable?' he asked, grinning slyly.

I combed my fingers through his hair and he leaned in, resting his head against my belly. He pulled up my shirt and began kissing me, gently at first, then running his tongue along the top of my jeans until I shivered, pulling away.

'I think you're a little stoned on pain meds,' I told him. He reached out to pull me to him again, but I danced away, promising to be right back.

I carried a candle into the studio, shutting the door behind me. My mother had draped an old white sheet over the painting on the easel.

I moved closer, holding the candle out in front of me, hands trembling. When I pulled back that sheet, it would be like disrobing a child in her Halloween costume. I worried that it would be Del herself I'd find underneath. I looked at the sheet and swore I saw it move, rippling slightly in some breeze I didn't feel.

It's only a painting. Only a painting.

I reached forward, grabbed the sheet, and threw it back.

The flames were almost three-dimensional, hypnotic in shades of red, orange, yellow, blue, and purple. The shadowy figure in the corner was now a fully fleshed-out person who seemed at home in the flames. Like she was born of them. The girl my mother had painted in the corner was the exact likeness of Del.

She wore her yellow cowgirl shirt and blue corduroy pants with a thick leather belt — the outfit she had on the day she was murdered. Her gray-blue eyes stared out at me and she had a half smile on her face as the flames shot out around her, licking at her feet like hungry dogs. The sheriff's star was pinned to her chest, just above her hidden letter *M*. *M* for Mike. My own tattoo burned in response. I could almost hear Del saying the name out loud: *Desert Rose*. A pretty name for a pretty color. *Hello, Desert Rose.*

'Hello, Del,' I said to the painting, thinking if I could hear myself speak, the fear would lessen.

The flame of the candle I carried leaped up, illuminating the painting. Del's face glowed, surrounded by the colorful, lively sea of flames my mother had painted. Then I

316

heard a sound, something like quiet laughter. It did not seem to come from the painting exactly, but from all around me — the walls, the windows, under the bed. The candle flame jumped back down, flickered, then was out, leaving me in complete darkness.

I knew I was no longer alone.

17

Over the years, I've thought a lot about Patsy Marinelli — remembering her words on the night I told her about Del: *The dead can blame*. But mostly, what I've thought about is what finally became of the huge woman we all called Tiny.

I wasn't there when it happened, but I arrived for my shift in time to see them taking her body out. The swing shift nurses told me their version of what had happened, and I filled in the details with what I read later in the log.

After dinner, Patsy went around saying good-bye to people. One of the nurses, humoring her, asked her where she was headed. *My husband's coming for me*, Tiny said. *I'll be gone soon*. And then she went into her room, closing the door behind her.

Poor Tiny, the nurses said to one another. *Now she's forgotten her husband is dead*.

During bed check at ten, they found Patsy Marinelli, blue-faced, eyes wide open. She'd choked to death on her own tongue.

The dead can blame.

★　★　★

I froze in the darkness, waiting for my eyes to adjust. There was a faint glow coming from the window, but other than that small square, I was surrounded by utter blackness. The giggling got louder, more shrill. I thought of crying out for Nicky, but knew he'd have a difficult time getting to me, if he even heard me at all. Ron Mackenzie's warning raced through my mind: *One potato, two potato, three potato, four / She's coming after you now, better lock the door.*

I took a step back, then another, and slowly turned toward the door, my arms in front of me, fingers groping out into nothingness. The air in the room was cool and getting cooler. It felt damp. The floor beneath me seemed to give, like I was walking on dirt. Like I was back in the root cellar. Del's smell was all around me — damp, rotting potatoes and dirt. It filled my nose and throat until I imagined I could feel actual soil packed in there, stopping my breath.

I shuffled quickly to where I thought the door should be, but my hands found only the wall. I felt my way along it, to the left first, five paces, then back to the right. The wall felt like cold cement, not the smooth shiplapped pine I knew should be there. I remembered my first visit to the Griswolds' root cellar — how when Del closed the door, I was sure she'd locked me in. I felt that same blind panic setting in.

When my hand found the brass doorknob at last, it was so cold it burned my palm. I pulled my shirtsleeve down and managed to turn it. I twisted the knob to the left and pulled, but the door would not open, as if it had been locked from the outside, but I knew the door had no lock.

Was someone holding it shut? My mother getting back at me for locking her in her room each night, or Nicky maybe, in an effort to prove that his sister's ghost existed? But the laughter . . .

I pounded on the door while my mind struggled to give a plausible explanation for what was happening, but all I came up with were wild excuses.

'Nicky! Mom!' I screamed. 'Let me out! Open the door! Jesus Christ, open the door!'

I put my ear against the door, listening for the sound of someone coming to my rescue, but there was only that laugh. It seemed to be coming from everywhere. It was the laugh of a trickster. An *I'm gonna get you* laugh. The laugh I'd heard as Del rolled on the ground the last day of school.

The dead can blame.

I rattled the door handle, collapsed against the wood, sobbing, quietly begging now.

'Please,' I whispered. 'Please let me out.'

I wasn't making excuses or inventing plausible scenarios now. Del had me. She had come back just as Nicky tried to warn me she would. Just as Opal had been insisting all along. I leaned against the jammed door feeling that old familiar feeling that whatever happened next would be up to Del. She was making the rules. There was no use fighting the inevitable. My shoulders sagged.

'Okay, Del,' I said. 'You've got me. What now?'

The laughter stopped abruptly, like a switch had been thrown, but the thick smell of soil and rot intensified.

The door swung inward with great force, sending me toppling to the floor. I slid and hit the legs of the easel, and the painting crashed down on top of me — I shoved it away, a bit desperately, squeamishly. Light spilled into the room. Beside me lay the painting of Del, her eyes on me still. I scrambled away from her, butt sliding across the floor, when I realized I was in the shadow of whoever — or whatever — had opened the door.

It took a lot of willpower to turn my head

to face the doorway.

When I looked up, it was not Del's ghost I saw hovering over me. It was my mother who stood in the doorway, grinning. She had on a calico housedress and rubber galoshes. Her hands wore their gauze bandages, thickly padded, like two bright white boxing gloves. Pinned to her chest was Del's old sheriff's star.

I stood up to face her, but took a step back when I realized the rotten potato smell was now coming from her.

'I know you!' my mother exclaimed in Del's voice. She rocked back on her heels. 'You ain't seen nothin' yet, Deputy. You ain't seen nothin' yet.' She turned, marched to the front door, and swung it open. I stepped through the living room, following her at a safe distance. A flurry of spinning snow let itself in through the open door, her own private storm. She walked out into the dark.

'Ma! Ma, where are you going? Get back in here. You'll freeze to death!'

'Catch me if you can, Desert Rose. Catch me if you can!'

'Ma! Wait!'

I hurried to the front door and pulled my boots on. I snatched my parka from the coat peg and the flashlight from its hook on the wall.

'What's going on, Kate?'

Nicky had hobbled in from the kitchen and stood awkwardly balanced on his good foot and the two crutches.

'My mom just took off. Only I don't think it's her, exactly. I think she's Del.'

Nicky squinted at me — now the great believer wore a look of doubt on his face.

I didn't have time to explain.

'Nicky, just stay here, okay? And lock the door. If she comes back alone, don't let her in. Wait for me.'

'Don't let your mom in?'

'It's not *her*, Nicky.'

I zipped up my parka and stepped out into the snow, clicking the flashlight on.

'Lock the door behind me.'

The snowflakes stung my face. I swung the beam of light around the cabin and along the tree line but saw no trace of my mother. There were only her footprints, leading exactly the way I knew they would.

I felt for Nicky's gun in my pocket, praying I wouldn't have to use it, but feeling reassured by its presence. Would I shoot my own mother if I had to? Did it still count as matricide if I was actually gunning for a little girl ghost? And how could you kill someone who was already dead?

I started off toward the path, and when I got to the boulder at the head of it, I turned right and began my journey down the old trail once more. Surrounded by the forest, the darkness deepened. My feet slipped, and the snowy night just seemed to absorb the flashlight's beam. I could see about two feet in front of me.

'Ma?' I called out into the dark. But no, that wasn't who I chasing, was it? 'Del? Del, wait up! Wait up, Del!'

My feet shuffled into a slow snow jog, doing more sliding than running. I fell once, then twice. The third time the flashlight flew away from me and I had to crawl on my hands and knees into prickers to get it back. As I rose to my feet the wind kicked up and blew the light powdery snow in gusts. Trees groaned. I kept my eyes on the tracks in front of me, illuminated by the flashlight's beam.

Was she taking me to my death? Had Del waited all these years, plotting and planning her revenge? Were Opal and Nicky right all along? Was Del Tori Miller's killer? Del in the form of my vacant, heavily medicated mother? My mother, who just happened to have bloody, leaf-littered bandages and to be wielding a paring knife the morning after the murder.

We were close now. So close. I hurried along through the woods, keeping my light on the footprints in front of me, sure I would lose my way without them. The snow was falling hard and fast, and the wind was blowing it right into my face. I had to keep stopping to wipe the snow out of my eyes. It froze on my lashes, blurring the already dim view I had.

My mother's tracks turned right at the fork and went in a straight line toward the old leaning cabin. But as I squinted down at the snowy forest floor, I saw that her tracks joined two other sets of footprints that had come from the other direction, from the Griswolds' field: one smallish set, one very large. They were filling in quickly, and crisscrossed each other, turning here and there from individual prints into dragging streaks.

'Hurry, Desert Rose!' my mother's voice came floating back out of the darkness, muffled by the snow. 'There isn't much time!'

I looked down at the footprints in the snow and suddenly understood.

Del wasn't taking me to my death.

She was taking me to save Opal.

I made out the shadow of the cabin just ahead of me. Its lean seemed dangerous. I stopped and ran my flashlight beam along the front of it. There was a soft glow from inside and the windows and open door formed a frightening, crooked face. I saw no movement, but heard voices inside. Then a muffled scream.

I sprinted up to the open doorway — or was it a mouth? — and stepped inside.

My mother was beside the old potbellied stove, looking up at the loft where an old oil lamp swung from a hook on the ceiling. On the floor of the loft, Opal was laid out on her back, her hands bound by thick cord; another length of rope was looped around her pale neck. She had a handkerchief stuffed into her mouth. Her eyes were bulging with terror. And straddling her, holding the two ends of loose cord in his hands, was Zack.

18

'Oh, look! Company!' Zack said, turning away from Opal to study us, but still gripping the ends of the cord like a Boy Scout ready to show off his knot-tying skills.

'Jean, Jean, Jean. What on *earth* are you doing out in this weather?' He loosened his grip on the rope, giving it more slack. 'And Kate, shame on you for letting your mother run around on a night like this in just a night-gown. The poor dear will catch her death.'

But she's not my mother. She's Del.

Little by little, I was putting things together, stringing clues like bits of junk on one of Lazy Elk's old necklaces. Like the one I stole and gave to Del. The only gift I ever gave her.

A friend of Nicky's gave Del the star. Someone special.

Zack was looking down at us ruefully, shaking his head like a disappointed — but not altogether surprised — mother. Opal

327

seized the opportunity in his moment of inattention — she thrashed her legs fiercely, bucked with her whole body, trying to dislodge him. For an instant I thought she would free herself, roll off the edge of the loft, and fall the eight or ten feet to the floor below. *We forgot the mattresses*, I thought crazily. But Zack barely budged and simply readjusted himself, setting his knee down in the center of her chest to keep her still. She let out a quiet *ooof* on impact.

All that practice flying and falling; the jumps from the hayloft, the way she and her bike were airborne going over the ramps she built. Her obsession with stunts that defied gravity and the wing-walking women who hung from rope ladders and did target practice in the sky. And now there Opal was, pinned flat on her back with no tricks up her sleeve, no one to save her but me.

I'd never had the chance to save Del. Thirty years later, she was giving me the chance to save Opal from the same fate.

'Tell me one thing, Zack,' I said. 'Why Opal?'

I thought maybe if I could get him talking, he'd let down his guard and I could make my move, though I wasn't sure just what that move might be.

Zack gave me a greasy little smile and

paused for a minute. Just when I was sure he wasn't going to answer, he spoke.

'Little Miss Light-fingers here borrowed the wrong thing.'

Ah, it all made sense now. Here was the final missing piece. It had nothing to do with Opal's being related to Del. It was all about Opal's borrowing.

'Del's star,' I guessed.

'Ding, ding, ding! Give that lady a prize,' Zack called down, looking truly gleeful. 'Opal found it in my desk drawer the day she was waiting for me with the cookies. Not only did she take it, but she actually pinned it to her mother's jacket and walked around wearing it! The little bitch was taunting me, playing games. It was just like Del all over again.'

'So you decided to kill her and get the star back before someone recognized it,' I said, filling in the rest of the all-too-familiar story. 'But Tori was wearing the jacket and you got her by mistake. But at least you got the star.'

And poor Opal kept going back to the woods to search for it, never realizing it was such a crucial piece of the puzzle. She just wanted to get it back to your drawer before you noticed it was missing.

'They really did look alike, don't you think?' Zack sighed a bit. 'And that dreadful jacket; yes, I admit I was misled by it. But

now there's a little piece of Tori keeping Del's
M company. I've kept that little piece of Del
next to my heart all these years.'

'Inside the Wheel of Life,' I said, sick at
the thought of that tiny square of skin held
prisoner inside the silver wheel by the God of
Death himself.

I remembered the huge-eyed faces with
long necks in the lower right quadrant of the
Wheel of Life — the hungry ghosts. What
could make you hungrier than to have some
crucial piece of yourself missing, held hostage
by the man who killed you? Then to have that
same man threaten the life of your sister, who
you've been watching over for twelve years.
Del was hungry all right. Hungry enough to
find a way back.

I looked over at my mother, her white
bandages like boxing gloves at her sides, Del's
star gleaming in the lamplight. The talisman
that I now understood helped bring her back
and keep her here, in my mother's borrowed
body. It was an anchor to her old life, to the
physical world.

The increasing amounts of medication
we'd been giving my mother had been working all along. My mother *had* been tranquilized.
It was just that the deeper she went, the more
room she made for Del — the medication left
her body flashing a bright red *vacancy* sign.

'How did you get my mother to cover for you?' I asked. 'She told the police she was with you the afternoon Del was killed. Surely she didn't know the truth.'

Zack smiled down at my mother. 'I told her I'd been with Nicky. She knew enough about my relationship with him to understand why I would want to lie.'

Just then, as if on cue, Nicky tottered in on his crutches. He took in the scene with a narcotic haze in his eyes and said, 'What is this? Zack? Kate? Would somebody please tell me what the hell is going on?'

'Hello, loverboy. We were just talking about you,' Zack called down.

'The professor here was just telling us how he used your relationship with him to convince my mother to give him an alibi,' I said.

'Alibi?' Nicky asked.

'He was also telling us how he's kept a scrap of Del's skin inside his Wheel of Life,' I said. 'That *M*'s been right there around his neck the whole time. Now he's got a piece of Tori, too.'

Nicky squinted up at Zack. 'You? *You* killed Del? But me and you, we . . . I thought . . . *Jesus* . . . ' His voice trailed off into a soft hiss, like the last air out of a deflating balloon.

'Poor Nick. You were just part of the

package. The red ribbon on top. Your sister was the box of cherries.'

He tightened his grip on the cord in his hands and looked down at Opal the way he must have looked at Del. Maybe he *was* seeing Del.

'She was too good for you all,' Zack said. 'I was going to take her away from her squalid little life: day after day of digging in those godforsaken fields, her fingers always cut open and bruised; listening to those stupid schoolyard Potato Girl rhymes; going to sleep at night only to wake up and find her daddy beside her with his pants down. I was going to save her. But she ruined it.'

'I understand, Zack,' I said. 'You loved her. What you had was special — that's why you gave her the star. But then she got that tattoo . . . ' I shrugged. 'You really had no choice. But Zack, that was *Del*. There's no need to punish Opal. Drop the rope and let her go.'

'Oh, I'm afraid I can't do that,' he said. 'This little bitch is going to join her sister.'

Opal's eyes widened as the truth was revealed at last. But she didn't have much time for processing.

'No!' Nicky screamed and began crutching his way to the ladder as fast as he could.

Zack yanked on the cord, lifting Opal's

head off the floor. She kicked and thrashed as she struggled for air and I finally got a horrifying glimpse at what Del's final moments were like.

The sound of the gunshot filled the cabin, echoing in my ears, ripping through the thin fabric of time. Zack slumped down over Opal (or was it Del?). The cord around her neck fell limp.

It was terribly quiet and still for what seemed like a long moment.

Nicky said, 'Uh, Kate?'

I glanced down — Nicky's gun was in my hand, my palm wrapped around unyielding metal, my finger still on the trigger.

At last, I had saved the girl.

★　★　★

I climbed up into the loft in what felt like slow motion, thinking of all the times I'd gone up as a child, hurrying behind Del and Nicky. I thought I could still smell our cigarette smoke, hear the *thunk* of the knife hitting the target on the wall. The knife Del used to cut into our fingers, mixing our blood, making us bound not just in life, but even in death. Blood sisters.

I stepped around Zack, kneeled down, took the now slack cord from around Opal's neck, and then untied her hands and feet. She let out several wracking gasps when I pulled the wadded-up handkerchief from her mouth.

'You're okay,' I told her. 'You're going to be okay. I'm going to get you out of here in just a minute.'

Then I turned to Zack, whose body was curled in the rough shape of a question mark. I didn't need to check for a pulse to know he was gone, but my fingers felt for the carotid artery just the same and found only cool, damp skin. There was surprisingly little blood and the hole in his chest looked small, reminding me of the dove Del had shot all those years ago and the way she pulled back the feathers, covering the entrance wound with her finger.

This man was my mother's lover, I thought. He used to make her laugh. Back in the tepee. Back when we all believed that Utopia was something you could create.

I put my hand on the Wheel of Life pendant and coaxed it gently over the dead professor's head. It was surprisingly light, considering its size and what it held. The God of Death grimaced; the hungry ghosts seemed to breathe a collective sigh of relief.

I helped Opal down the ladder, holding the Wheel of Life in my right hand. I sat the trembling girl down on one of the moth-eaten cots and carried the pendant to my mother, who accepted it with a grin and pressed it to her chest, just over her heart.

There was so much I wanted to ask, so much I wanted to say, but it was Del who spoke.

'I reckon we're even now,' Del's voice said. I caught the moldering scent of damp places and rotting potatoes on her breath. 'You're still my deputy.'

'Always,' I promised. 'Cross my heart.'

And to prove it, I unbuttoned my blouse and tore the gauze off. There it was: my own secret in black ink, red and puffy at the edges, right above my heart.

My mother smiled then closed her eyes, as Del whispered my name one final time: 'Desert Rose.'

The Wheel of Life slipped from my mother's fingers, hitting the old pine floor with a dull *clunk*.

A familiar look of confusion swept across my mother's strangely placid face.

'Katydid?' she said, her eyes wide open.

And just like that, Del was gone.

PART 3

NOVEMBER 24, 2002

19

Opal tugged at the turtleneck she wore to cover her colorful necklace of bruises — a literal choker — coming out in splotches of purple, yellow, and brown. Sometimes, since that night in the cabin, she felt panicked and short of breath, like an asthmatic, and the trick, her shrink had told her, was to count slowly in her head: breathe in, one, two, three, four; breathe out, one, two, three, four.

This is what she was doing as she sat across the table from Kate in the airport coffee shop. She picked at the cherry pie on her plate, the berries looking strangely limp and pale in their bright red syrup. Kate's plane was boarding in twenty minutes and there was still so much Opal wanted to say, there were so many questions she thought Kate might know how to answer. Raven and Nicky had gone downstairs to the gift shop to get some maple syrup for Kate to bring home.

'I always wanted a sister,' Opal said.

'So did Del,' Kate told her.

339

Del's sister. It was going to take Opal a while to get used to the idea, though in her heart, she knew it was true the second Zack said it. *This little bitch is going to join her sister . . .*

Opal went back to counting breaths, picking at the overly sweet cherry pie. She moved her right hand off the table, reached into the pocket of her coat, and felt for her latest prize: a small bottle of tea tree oil shampoo. Something Kate probably wouldn't even miss, and if she did, she'd figure she just forgot it in the shower in the big barn.

The borrowing would stop. She knew she *had* to stop. Look at the trouble it had caused. If she hadn't taken the star from the cigar box in Zack's desk the day she dropped off the cookies, then Tori would still be alive.

There was the constricting feeling again. Coarse rope pressing into her neck. She tugged at the turtleneck, rubbed the painful bruises. *Breathe in, one, two, three, four. Breathe out, one, two, three, four.*

She thought about what they'd learned just that morning: there was a third piece of skin inside Zack's necklace and the police were looking into unsolved murders of young girls in the Toronto area. It still didn't seem real to her that her beloved uncle Zack was capable of such monstrosities. She couldn't imagine the cold-hearted calculation; the planning and foresight; the skill involved in not leaving a trace of evidence behind.

She had been so sure there had to be some mistake when Kate first told her about Del's star. She had gotten on her bike and ridden out to the college to ask Zack where he'd gotten it, positive there was a reasonable explanation. And he had seemed so genuinely surprised when she told him that the star she'd found in his drawer may have been Del's. In fact, he had suggested that they go straight to the police that very minute. He'd said he'd tell her the whole story of where the star had come from on the way. They'd thrown her bike into the back of his Subaru, and he'd driven, waxen-faced, not to the state police barracks, but to the Griswolds' old place, where he'd steered the car across the snow-covered fields and parked it in the woods. By the time she knew she was in trouble, it was too late.

Breathe in, one, two, three, four. Breathe out, one, two, three, four.

'I still don't understand how your mother — Del, I mean — ended up with the star,' Opal said.

'She found it in my room. Zack took it from Tori and planted it in my purse. I don't know if it was part of some strange, psychotic game or if he was hoping the police would find it on me. After all the trouble he went to to get the star back, you'd think he'd want to keep it. But maybe some tiny, still-rational part of his brain knew it wasn't safe to hold on to something so incriminating. I'm guessing he took my Swiss Army knife at the same time.'

'So he was . . . what? Trying to frame you or something?'

'Yeah,' Kate said. 'It was perfect, really — my showing up in town right when I did, with everyone knowing my connection to Del. I was a likely suspect. He went to a lot of trouble to set me up, even leaving the knife he used the night he . . . hurt Tori . . . on my mother's kitchen table. I found my mother with it the next morning. Christ, he even had me suspecting her! She was out in the woods the night Tori was killed. I don't suppose we'll ever know what she did or didn't see. I'm guessing it was really Del using my mother to try to save you.'

'The ghost I saw when I went back for the jacket was really your mother?' Opal asked.

Kate nodded. 'I think it must have been.'

'What about that night you and I met in the woods?' Opal asked.

'It's funny,' Kate said. 'I was trying to get rid of the very thing you were out looking for.

I buried the star in the Griswolds' old root cellar. Nicky convinced me to dig it up the next night — I stuck it under my pillow and my mother found it. I think finding the star was what gave Del the strength to come back all the way.'

Opal let out a long sigh. 'I was so wrong about her,' she said quietly.

'We all were.' Kate said. 'It's sad really. She was as misunderstood in death as she was in life.'

'All those times I saw her, she was watching out for me, right? Checking on me, trying to warn me?'

'Yeah,' Kate said, staring down into the dregs of her coffee, turning the cup in her hands. 'I think so, Opal, I really do.'

Raven and Nicky came up to the table, wielding a bag full of syrup, maple sugar candy, a moose T-shirt, and a copy of *Vermont Life* magazine.

'This should hold you over until you come back for Christmas,' Raven said.

'I feel like a true tourist now,' Kate told them, accepting the bag of treats.

Kate looked over the coffee shop bill and laid some money down on the table, then began gathering up her things.

'I can't believe I'm leaving,' she said. 'That tonight I'll have dinner in my very own kitchen. God, I've missed my microwave — and my dishwasher! But it's strange, after everything . . . '

'Kate,' Raven said. 'Don't worry about your mother. Meg says Spruce View is the best. And we'll visit her all the time, won't we, Opal?'

Opal nodded vigorously. They'd left Jean earlier that morning, sitting down to tea in a small dining room with cloth napkins. She'd picked up the jar of jam on the table, winked at Kate, and said, 'Strawberry, Katydid. Our favorite. Mimi and I put up extra jars of preserves this year. It was a good crop.'

'It sure was, Ma,' Kate had said. 'The best season ever.'

★ ★ ★

After hugs and kisses and promises to call, they watched Kate pass through the security gate and down the ramp to her flight. Opal touched the shampoo bottle as she watched Kate go. When she turned back, she saw that Nicky had tears in his eyes, which was a little weird, but then again, he'd been through a lot in the past few days.

'She'll be back for Christmas,' Opal said to the man she'd just learned was her half brother. He smiled weakly, like a little boy who's been promised dessert if he can just get his spinach down.

'Can we go up to the observation tower?' Opal asked.

'If you're up for it,' Raven said.

'I'll wait here,' Nicky said, easing himself into a seat.

Opal led the way down the gray-carpeted hallway, around the bend, and up the winding narrow metal steps to the top of the tower, which had always been her favorite part of the airport. It was the size of a small bedroom, with huge windows covering each wall. An old man who sometimes gave tours said it had once been the control tower, before they built the new one. There were some ugly orange seats facing the windows, and a crackling speaker in the ceiling playing all the radio contact from the control tower. Opal and Raven were the only two visitors.

Opal went to the west window and spotted the small DC-9 that would take Kate to Boston, where she'd catch a bigger plane for Seattle. Opal watched as the last of the passengers climbed up the metal boarding stairs. In a few minutes, the stairs were retracted, the door closed, and the plane was taxiing to the runway, the pilot jabbering radio-speak with the guy in the control tower.

'Come on, sweetie, let's go,' Raven said as

she made her way to the stairs and started down, the heels of her boots echoing on the metal steps. 'Nicky's waiting.'

'Coming,' Opal called after her mother. But then, out on the tarmac, something caught her eye just as Kate's plane was taking off. A little glint of light coming from the wing, like someone was using a mirror to send a signal. It hit her face, bounced off the window behind her, and was gone. The plane lifted off the ground and banked to the left, climbing steadily.

If Opal squinted hard enough, she could just make out Del — a ripple of movement on the right wing. And even through the thick glass of the observation tower, Opal was sure she could hear laughter in the wind followed by a playful taunt: *Catch me if you can.*

ACKNOWLEDGMENTS

I would like to thank my agent, Dan Lazar, and my editor, Jeanette Perez, along with all the folks at HarperCollins who had a hand in bringing this book to life. Also Juliet Ewers and everyone at Orion.

Many thanks to Michael Hatch, Coleen Kearon, Donna Thomas, Paul Garstki, and my parents, Donald and Dorothy McMahon. And finally, Drea Thew, who is behind every success I have, both in writing and in life. *You think it is a secret, but it has never been one.*

We do hope that you have enjoyed reading this large print book.

Did you know that all of our titles are available for purchase?

We publish a wide range of high quality large print books including:
Romances, Mysteries, Classics
General Fiction
Non Fiction and Westerns

Special interest titles available in large print are:
The Little Oxford Dictionary
Music Book
Song Book
Hymn Book
Service Book

Also available from us courtesy of Oxford University Press:
Young Readers' Dictionary
(large print edition)
Young Readers' Thesaurus
(large print edition)

For further information or a free brochure, please contact us at:
Ulverscroft Large Print Books Ltd.,
The Green, Bradgate Road, Anstey,
Leicester, LE7 7FU, England.
Tel: (00 44) 0116 236 4325
Fax: (00 44) 0116 234 0205

Other titles published by
The House of Ulverscroft:

PICK UP

J. A. O'Brien

Jack Carver is experiencing the most horrible of all nightmares: being an innocent man who is the prime suspect in the brutal murder of two women. Forensic evidence is found at both crime scenes, which implicates Carver. And when the police request that he should come forward, he goes on the run instead. He is finally apprehended, but an incident from Carver's past shakes his absolute certainty that he is not the killer. Then he is charged with murder. Can DS Andy Lukeson prove his innocence when a chance incident prompts him to reassess the case?

BROKEN SURFACE

Seth Garner

Fifteen years ago two teenagers killed a mentally handicapped boy called Doofy. It was an accident, but things had got out of hand. They never reported it and they hid the body. But as Duncan and Richard grow up, the secret continues to haunt them both. While Richard has become a psychopath, Duncan achieves a life as a respectable and successful businessman with a lot to lose if the truth ever comes to light. Now the secret, like Doofy's body, is about to be revealed with dire consequences.

LOCKED IN

Peter Conway

Is Father Carey a saint or sinner? Comforter of the sick — or a heavy drinker not to be trusted with secrets, confessional or otherwise? Opinion at St Cuthbert's Hospital is divided. Michael Donovan, paralysed after a rugby accident, views him as the only person to give him support. But when Father Carey is poisoned, Donovan loses the will to live. On a respirator and locked inside his paralysed body there is nothing he can do about it. Or is there? Though unable to speak or move, there is nothing inactive about his mind. Can he find a way to track down the killer?

A BLOW TO THE HEART

Marcel Theroux

The violent death of Daisy's husband leaves her a widow in her early thirties. As she struggles to build a new life, a chance encounter with her husband's killer leads her on a journey into obsessive hatred. Daisy stalks the man, a small-time criminal and boxer called Joel Heath, and secretly pursues him into the twilight world of professional boxing. She befriends Tate, a boxing has-been, and his deaf protégé Isaac, in order to strike back at Heath. But Isaac's disability and his once-in-a-lifetime talent present Daisy with harder choices and more dangerous opponents than she could ever have imagined.